THE X

A NOVEL

DEREK WALKER

THE X by Derek Walker
www.phantomfevers.com

© 2020 Derek Walker

ISBN: 9798631495081

For Amanda
Quinn, 5
Maple, 2

The last man on Earth sat alone in a room.
There was a knock on the door...
Fredric Brown

Is this the way a toy feels when its batteries run dry?
Brand New

Some of us think holding on makes us strong,
but sometimes it is letting go.
Herman Hesse

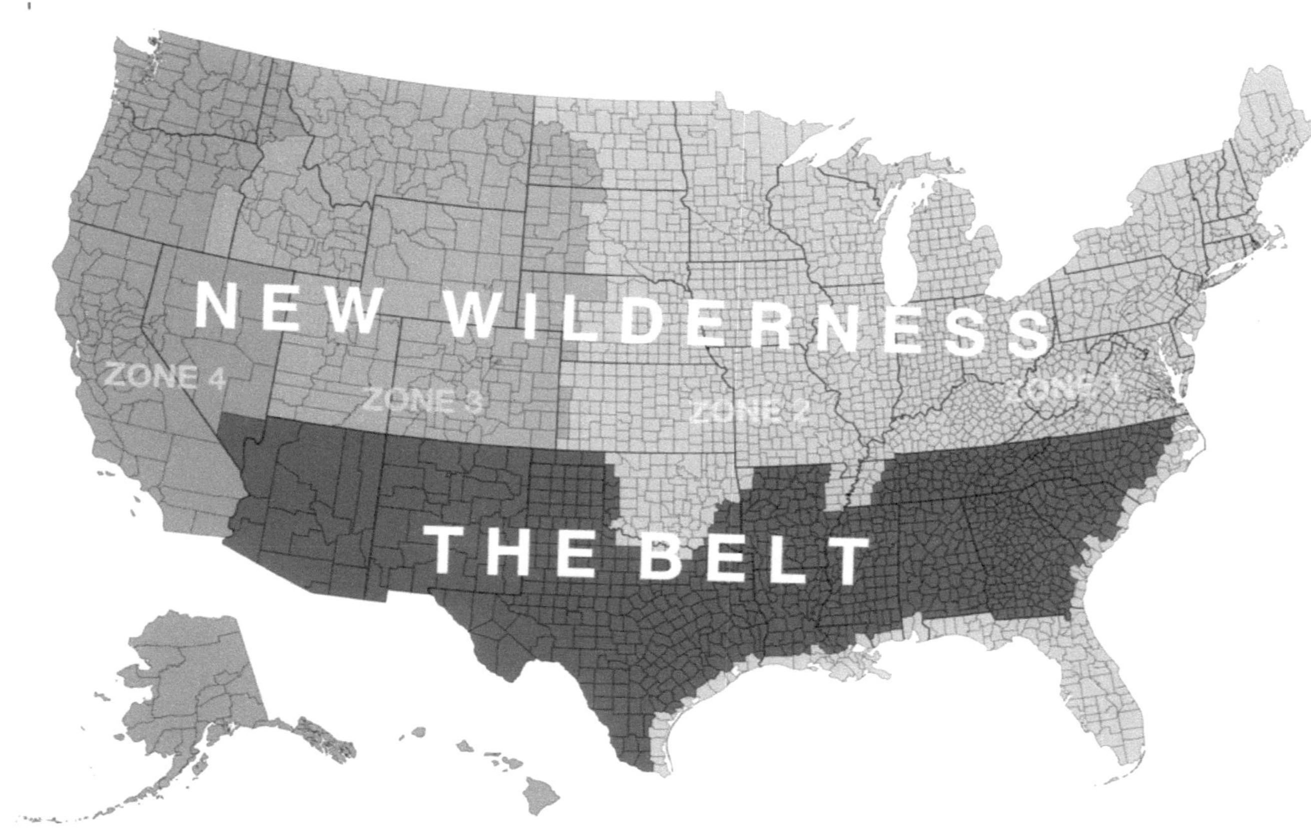
NEW WILDERNESS
ZONE 4
ZONE 3
ZONE 2
ZONE 1
THE BELT

PART ONE
THE BELT

01

NEW RATON MEETS OLD RATON, the headline says, followed by an oversized picture of five teenagers posed awkwardly around an old man in front of city hall. It's yet another miserable front page which further confirms my belief that the Belt's tagline should be *The Land of Forced Smiles.*

On second thought, the picture is a perfect representation of the sentiment surrounding the Move. Half of America fake-happily leaving their homes behind, half of America fake-happily welcoming them.

I find the political cartoons on the second to last page and flatten the paper. One cartoon depicts a government worker sifting through a ring of color palettes at a paint store. *Do you have anything a little more, uh, bland?* the caption reads.

"Leo Kline," the receptionist announces. "Room eighteen."

I nod to the two other people I had been sharing the waiting room with and walk through the automatic doors, following signs to the *Session Rooms.*

A plump woman with tight curls is seated at the small laminate wood table of room eighteen. She clicks absently on her tablet while I take a seat.

"It looks like you worked in finance before the Move?" she says without looking up.

"Well, yes, until about four years before the Move."

"What did you do during those four years?"

"Ski operations in Breckenridge," I say. "Colorado."

"Why the change?" she says. "From finance to resort operations, I mean."

"The Big One, the first Big One."

"Salt Lake?"

"Yeah."

"Hm," she says, then coughs into a closed fist. "Did someone die?"

I purse my lips. "Um, yeah, like a million people."

"I mean, did you know someone who died in the first Big One?"

"Ah, of course," I say. "Yes, my parents. My brother, Tripp. Countless friends. I grew up there but was living in Denver at the time."

"I'm so sorry," she says, the furious taps continuing.

"Thanks."

She looks up at me with a forced smile.

I force-smile back, hoping that will somehow move the conversation forward.

She leans back. "And then what?"

"Well, the Big One made me realize life was too short. I hated my job in Denver, so I decided to propose to my girlfriend—"

"Nova?" she says, referencing her tablet.

"Yeah—I proposed to Nova, she said yes, and we packed up and moved to Breckenridge."

"That's where you had Xandra?"

"Bingo."

"I'm sorry, what?"

"Um yeah, we had Xandra about a year later," I say.

"That makes her four now?"

"Yep. Four and a half."

More tapping. "Leo, how have you processed all this? I mean the Move, the loss of your family, moving to the Belt, all of it?"

Do you really want to know?

"To be honest, most days I'm numb. It's been that way since the Big One."

"Were your family's bodies ever recovered?"

"No."

"Hm," she says, taking a sip of her blank white coffee mug. "Well, Leo, I'm going to recommend you try some self-healing before we get you in the job cycle, okay?"

"What does that mean?"

She looks at me with a stern face. "At least once a week, I want you to sit down somewhere quiet and do nothing but reflect on these things. Confront them. All of them. Don't block them out, don't distract yourself. Let the thoughts and feelings enter and exit as they please. Like clouds passing by," she says and takes another sip of coffee.

Isn't it a little late for coffee?

"It won't be easy, but over time, your relationship with these events—these tragedies—will begin to take on meaning," she says.

I lean back in my chair and exhale. "I haven't been able to work in over a year. I get what you're saying but I'm bored out of my mind."

"Do you have any hobbies?"

"Not aside from obsessing over the Move."

"Try something else. Something that can't be monetized or that won't drive you insane. Like birdwatching," she says and stands up, motioning me out of the room.

—

I walk the sterile, freshly constructed commercial corridor toward home. Of course, Raton already has a Main Street— one that I'm sure supported its pre-Move population of 10,000 quite well. Now that its population has grown by more than fifty times since the Move, let's just say you can see traces of pre-Move Raton only if you look *really* closely.

Streetlights click on as the evening twilight fades to dark. The dry desert air quickly turns cold. A woman with a yellow reflective vest jogs past me, breathing hard.

As I turn the corner onto Chestnut, I hear the muffled crooning of a saxophone coming down the street. I check my watch. It's still happy hour at The Move Blues, the demon on my shoulder whispers to me. As I get closer to the bar, I decide against it. As much as I might be in the mood for a drink, the alcohol is likely getting in the way of me confronting my problems—something that I'm supposed to be doing, according to the government lady. And my wife. And strangers on the internet. And basically everyone I've talked to since the Big One.

I fix my gaze ahead and move past the single door entrance, the blue neon lights and secondhand smoke beckoning me in.

"Leo? Hey, it's Leo!" A familiar voice comes from the open doorway.

I glance between my watch and the lonely sidewalk ahead of me, then turn around.

—

"They want you to take *more* time off?" Alec says.

"They want me to focus on self-healing," I say.

"Hey, enjoy it man. Work sucks," Chris says, tipping his bottle back.

"Yeah, but I'm bored as hell."

"Spend time with Xandra. Be a kid, you know?"

"Xandra's in Pre-K and Nova works all day," I say.

"Get a hobby, man," Alec says, eyebrows raised.

"Hey, you could—" Chris starts then gets distracted by the pretty bartender walking by. "You could watch birds. Be a bird watcher."

"Birdwatching?" I glance between him and Alec. "What is the deal with birdwatching? The government lady told me to try birdwatching."

Alec chuckles and calls for the bartender.

"Or…" Chris says, leaning in. "You could go exploring."

"Now *that* sounds fun," I say. "Imagine all the cookie-cutter subdivisions and chain restaurants I could find."

"No no no. *Explore*-explore. I'm talking about the Wild, man."

"What—" Alec says.

I furrow my brow. "The Wild? How might I do that? And why would I want to do that?"

"The fact that you'd even suggest that it *wouldn't* be the most fascinating venture ever, tells me that the Feds have gotten to you with their Pro-Move propaganda," Chris says.

"He's got a point there," Alec says.

"Ok, elaborate," I say.

"The Upper States—the top two-thirds of mainland United States—abandoned. Deserted. Your playground to explore."

"Well, I thought the roads were destroyed leading into the Wild."

"I know of a clean crossing. It's close to here. Twenty miles west."

I look between the two of them. "Clean?"

Nova's probably expecting me home any minute, but the prospect of spending the next few months until my next job cycle readiness assessment watching birds sounds blander than the Belt itself.

"Clean as in no roadblocks," Chris says.

"No checkpoint?"

"I don't believe so."

"So, you haven't been there yourself?"

"I'm chipped, man. I'm in the job cycle. I can't go near there. But you—"

"Another good point," Alec says. "I'm chipped too. What about Nova?"

"No chip for Nova, she's privately employed," I say.

"Private employment, a relic of the old economy," Chris says and tips his drink back.

As the night progresses, the bar grows louder with animated conversations, occasional outbursts, and the clanking of glasses. The jazz band hums in the background.

"Do it, man! Just go for the day. Drive up to Denver, break into a high-rise or something. Snap some pictures, then come back. Bada bing bada boom."

"Isn't it dangerous up there?"

"The Feds said the Move was 100% successful, didn't they?" Alec says.

"Yeah, but you really believe that? You really believe that not a *single person* stayed behind?"

Both Alec and Chris take sips of their beers. I swirl my Rye Whisky on the rocks and take a drink.

"I don't know. Why would the Feds lie about that?" Alec poses.

Although trust in the government has never been higher, the 100% claim never sat right with me. I mean, I know why they'd peddle a lie like that. I can't imagine it'd sit well with the public if the Feds came out and said that the Move—their precious Move—was only 95% successful, or even 99%

successful. One percent is still millions of people.

I turn and face the jazz band shuffling around the stage. The crowd sways in all directions to the music.

The bartender approaches us again. "You guys need anything else?"

I glance at Chris then to the bartender. "You wouldn't happen to have a roadmap, would you?"

—

The pitter patter of little footsteps echoes down the hallway. I rotate my chair towards the door, smiling in anticipation.

"Rarrrrrrr!" Xandra screams bursting into the study with her arms high above her head.

"Ahhhh!" I say, pretending to bite my nails.

She drops her arms and smiles, taking a minute to catch her breath. "Hello daddy," she says in a fake British accent that comes out *huhlo diaddy.*

"Hey, bugaboo. What's goin on?"

"Daddy, I found a dinosaur. Come on," she says, pointing down the hall, eyebrows raised.

Xandra is smaller than the average four-year-old. Her long, light brown hair swoops across her comically cute, oversized forehead. She twists back and forth, watching the lace hem of her nightgown brush past her shins as she awaits my answer.

"Can you bring the dinosaur to me, sweetheart?"

"Ummmmm, okay," she says and skips out of the room.

I smile and stand up, leaning forward to get a better look at the collage of framed pictures above my desk.

Confront them. All of them. Don't block them out, don't distract yourself. Let the thoughts and feelings enter and exit as they please. Like clouds passing by.

My tired gaze finds the picture of my parents, Tripp, and me on a Caribbean cruise—our last trip together before Salt Lake City was destroyed in an earthquake known affectionately as the Big One. Well, the *first* Big One. Now everyone in that picture, except me, is presumed dead. I feel a deep sinking in my chest.

Next is a photo of Nova, Xandra, and me in ugly Christmas sweaters from the year before in Breckenridge. Now abandoned.

My childhood home in suburban Salt Lake. Now in ruins.

A picture of Nova and I on our honeymoon in New York City. Now deserted.

It's been nine years since the first Big One, six years since the Move was announced, three years since the Move began, and one year since Nova, Xandra, and I moved from our forever-home in Breckenridge, CO to Raton, NM—the Belt's northernmost town.

I sit down, eyes moving carefully from picture to picture, and doodle blindly in my notebook.

In a lot of ways, the Move was happening on its own. I mean, when SURA—the Sunbelt Relocation Act—passed, it didn't exactly feel out of the blue. The common line of consent heard around the country was *desperate times call for desperate measures*. The country *was* divided about the Move, but in general, people understood that things couldn't be brushed under the rug anymore. Congress could no longer snap their fingers, pass a disaster relief bill or whatever, and make life go back to normal.

Everyone knew that *going back to normal* was unrealistic. The US population was shrinking. The world population was shrinking. City budgets were shrinking. It turns out the whole economic model built on forever-growth doesn't work so well when growth stops. Some parts of the world have done better than the US, others worse. I'd say we're middle of the pack.

Then the slew of natural disasters began plaguing the country. The first one was a 7.9 earthquake that struck Salt Lake City. It was the first major natural disaster that did not get relief funding from Congress. A couple years later, a similar earthquake struck the Seattle area—the Second Big One. A year after that, San Francisco. The polar vortex in the Midwest increased in intensity every couple years, killing thousands of people, and causing billions of dollars' worth of damage. Hurricanes pummeled the East and Gulf coasts. Sea level rise all but drowned Florida. Oklahoma was hounded with Tornados.

To the Feds, the massive geography of the United States had become a colossal liability. The Feds figured that if they could relocate everyone to a more controlled area—one that has a higher potential for energy independence and a lower risk of natural disasters—many of the country's problems could be drastically mitigated. Hence, the Move—a consolidation of the entire US population into the southern 1/3 of the mainland, an area that somewhat resembles what was previously known as the Sunbelt.

Xandra rushes back into the room. "Look, daddy! A dinosaur!" She holds a toy horse high above her head. "Rarrrrrrr!"

Her recent dinosaur obsession means that all of her existing toys—horses, rubber ducks, trains—have become dinosaurs.

"Awww help!" I slide off my chair and roll into a ball on the floor.

Nova enters. "Oh no, a dinosaur! I'll help you," she says, kneeling next to me. "Go away, dinosaur!" She squeezes

Xandra's side.

Xandra's *rarrrr* turns into a staccato laugh as she tries to push Nova's hand away.

Nova and I smile at each other for a moment before returning to Xandra's fantasy world.

"I'm gonna get you, dinosaur!" Nova says, jumping onto her feet in a crouched stance.

"Run away!" Xandra screams and runs out of the room.

Nova turns to me before chasing Xandra, smiling. "T-minus five minutes on the pizza."

"I'm on my way," I say, looking down at my notebook through drunken eyes.

100%...

My mind wanders to my childhood home.

My childhood lives in those walls, now rotting piles of rubble. I think about our home in Breckenridge, the home we brought newborn baby Xandra to.

Confront them. All of them.

I think about sitting across from Nova at Publik Roasters in downtown Denver. The snow falling outside, muting the lights of the early-evening streetscape. Nova's bright smile contrasted against her green sweater and olive skin. Her dark hair spilled out of her gray beanie in a single braid on the left side of her face. Her thin nose ring—the one she was terrified of getting—glistened in the coffee shop's studio lighting.

I look back to the cruise picture and zero in on Tripp's face. He was two years younger than me, had his whole life ahead of him. Now he's gone. If he would've known—if he could've predicted the earthquake—what would he have done differently? He spent the last two years of his life in medical school, a venture I know he regretted.

For as calculated as I've lived my life, I don't want to end up like Tripp. Of course, he was young. Far too young to die. But those two years he spent burning the midnight oil are gone forever.

But their bodies were never found…

"Leo!" Nova calls from the kitchen downstairs.

"Leeeeeooooooooo!" Xandra follows.

I set the pen down and go downstairs to find Nova, Xandra, and my mother-in-law, Megan, sitting at the table, the pizza neatly divided into squares before them.

"Grace?" Megan asks in her Brazilian accent, her palms turned upward.

"Sure," I say, forcing a smile.

—

That night, I dreamt Tripp and I had broken into the abandoned Royale Center Mall—a once-thriving regional shopping center just a ten-minute bike ride from home. The mall was demolished two or three years before the Move was announced but had been vacant twenty years before that.

In my dream, Tripp and I were in the prime of our childhood. Me 12, Tripp 10. We rode our ten speeds to the side entrance of the Royale Center and laid our bikes down on the cracked, weed-infested sidewalk in front of the boarded-up theater. Broken glass crunched beneath our feet.

We walked through the food court and into the atrium. The formerly-glass ceiling had fallen victim to a thousand kids—including myself and Tripp—armed with BB guns and rocks. We waded through the sea of blue and green pebbles of glass to the old koi pond, a spectacle of mold and dried chlorine.

"Look at this," Tripp said, jumping into the empty pond. He bent over and picked up a quarter. "Guess the year," he said, extending it toward me.

That's when I realized I was lucid dreaming.

"Tripp, are you dead?" I asked.

"Leo, guess the year, dude."

"2012," I said.

"2000 right on the dot. Have you ever seen that?"

"Tripp, look at me. Are you dead?"

Tripp flipped the coin in the air and caught it, pocketing it in his dirty denim shorts. He climbed out of the pond, his brown curly hair bounced with his head movement. "Yes, I'm dead, Leo."

"You died in the earthquake?"

"Yeah."

"Mom and dad too?"

"Yeah."

I looked around. The decayed retail storefronts turned a tinge of purple like it was under ultraviolet light.

"Tripp, am I gonna die?"

Tripp's face darkened. The rings under his eyes grew increasingly deeper. His face matured as he morphed into adult Tripp. Adult *dead* Tripp, decaying like the walls around us. "Everyone dies, Leo. Some before others. Some die while they're still alive, Leo. Think about that."

"But isn't that how it works?"

Tripp's cheeks and lips tightened, revealing missing teeth. His fingernails grew long and yellow. Something crawled out of his mouth and scurried across his face. "Some live dead, Leo. Do you understand?"

I forced myself awake, ending the disturbingly lucid

conversation with Tripp. My stomach turned thinking about what I saw, even though it was purely a product of my imagination.

But was it?

Either way, I sat up in bed with an odd sense of clarity. I checked my watch, it was 2:02 AM.

Some live dead.

02

"But what about Xan?" Nova says, rolling over in bed.

"Meg's good to watch her. Two days, one night. That's it. We'll be back late tomorrow."

"You're kidding. All the way to Breckenridge?"

"Does this face look like I'm kidding?" I say, pursing my lips. She doesn't even open her eyes to get my joke.

"What time is it?"

"Three."

"Oh God," she says and sits up. "How would we even get there?"

"Chris told me about a clean crossing about twenty miles west."

"There's no way. It's dangerous out there."

"My therapist told me I need to confront the things of my past," I say.

"Therapist?"

"The government lady I met with. You know what I mean."

"For the job cycle thing? Ya know, she probably didn't mean like literally forage into the Wild to confront things of your past."

I brush her hair behind her ear. "Come on, we'll be back tomorrow."

Dead-Tripp's parting wisdom has been bouncing around my head since the dream woke me up an hour ago. *Some live dead.* Once I woke up, I sat down at my desk and mulled over a US road map I keep in my files. Somehow, I convinced myself that Chris and Alec were right. I need a little adventure in my life. Especially before I get put in the job cycle, if that day ever comes.

I packed clothes, ski equipment, road lunches, and all the tools we have—which wasn't much—into our hatchback. After some internal debate, I packed our never-used Victory .22. *If I'm nervous enough to bring a gun, maybe this* is *a bad idea.*

"There's no way you got everything," Nova says, now alert and rummaging through the bag I packed for her.

The plan is simple: drive to Breckenridge by way of Denver, explore a bit, ski a bit, break into Chrystal Peak Lodge—Nova's former place of work—stay the night, and drive back the next day.

After a few more qualifying questions, Nova agrees.

While she gets dressed, I nudge Megan awake to let her know we're leaving. Nova and I stop in Xandra's room on our way out and kiss her goodbye. She doesn't budge.

It's only two days, I remind myself.

As we pull out of the driveway of our generic three-bedroom two-bathroom townhome, my mind runs amok.

What if one of us gets hurt? What if there are others out there? What if they're dangerous? What if our car breaks down? What if we get lost? What about rabid animals?

I push the thoughts away—*a billion years of evolution and you just push us away?*— and remind myself why we're doing this. Confront it. All of it.

Nova lays her seat down and turns onto her side. Within two minutes, her deep, rhythmic breathing begins, signaling slumber.

We drive to the Colorado border and take a county road directly west for about thirty minutes before arriving to the crossing. Chris wasn't kidding, the crossing is clean—intact and unobstructed. The frontier of the New Wilderness.

A single brown sign stands crooked on the side of the road,

chilling me to my bone. I slow the car down and nudge Nova awake.

ZONE 3 IS PERMANENTLY CLOSED
THE AREA BEYOND IS WILDERNESS
NO SERVICES AVAILABLE
ENTER AT YOUR OWN RISK

"Are you sure we should be doing this?" Nova says, interrupting the silence. "What if something happens?"

I try to mask my own hesitation. "I've got jerry cans secured to the rack. We've got a spare tire."

"Like, what if something happens to us—like we break a leg skiing?" Nova sits up.

"I've got a first aid kit?"

"Very funny."

"Hey, it's a risk. But 'no-risk, no reward,' right?"

Nova exhales and looks at the metal sign again. "You're crazy, Mr. Kline."

No, I'm that fun-loving, spontaneous husband you've always dreamed about.

I slowly press on the gas pedal and we officially enter the New Wilderness.

—

After a couple hours of navigating the profoundly vacant highways to Denver, morning twilight creeps in, reminding us that the Move happened. Boy, did it happen. The roads are mostly clear of snow, revealing layers of dead weeds splayed through splintered cracks in the asphalt. As we get closer to the city, the wide-open spaces fill up with single-family homes and nondescript apartment buildings.

Nova sits up and looks out the window. "Oh my God."

I feel a pit in my stomach as the rapidly-decaying Denver suburbs pass by. Just two years ago, these buildings were full of life, cared for, enjoyed. Now they are nothing but distant memories, lifeless collections of brick and mortar.

We pass Moochie's Subs, one of our regular stops on the way to Colorado Springs. Dark. Dusty, broken windows. Channel letters missing. Frosty, dead, moldy leaves and garbage piled in and around the building—every building for that matter.

The State Capitol looks even more haunted now than it did occupied. Its dark grey façade serves as a visual representation of the cold and empty city. I fantasize about a madman who made the Capitol his home after the masses left.

We stop the car outside the 16th Street Mall. Nova has a blanket wrapped around her. After the thud of our closing doors reverberates down the empty streets, the unnerving silence creeps in. For the first time since Breckenridge, I can hear myself think. I close my eyes and inhale deeply. I think about the irony of finding this level of clarity and peace in the middle of a major US city.

The wind blows, bringing with it a smattering of dust and snow. Without all the people and cars and doors being opened and shut to absorb and divert the air, the wind feels stronger.

Nova and I take in our surroundings in silence, each drumming up memories of what these spaces looked like with people in them just a year ago. I think about the time our intoxicated friend, Donny Matthews, stumbled over to a public piano in the plaza and sang 'yoooo hoooo yoooo hoouu a pirate's life for meeeeeeeee!' at the top of his lungs.

I smile at the blue and green striped life-size bull sculpture that Xan loved to ride. It's also the same bull that Donny tried to climb up on that drunken night. It was now somewhat appropriately tagged EAT MOR CHIKIN in black spray paint.

We continue down the street in silence.

"Publik Roasters," Nova announces, pointing to what's left of our favorite downtown coffee shop. The once-vast glass storefront is now in pieces at our feet. Nova gasps and leans her head against my shoulder. Her trembling breath tells me she's crying. Publik Roasters also happens to be the place where I, with the generous assistance of the baristas, proposed to Nova almost ten years ago.

Nova's breathing picks up and she stands erect. Her clenched jaw shifts back and forth. "What a joke," she says and scoffs. "We gave up everything. Do you realize that? *Everyone* gave up *everything* and no one bats an eye. We just put our heads down and follow blindly like good Americans. I'm sick of it." She kicks a pile of glass, the pebbles dancing into the street. "I am sick of it." She picks up a metal chair resting against a street tree and tosses it aside.

"Nova?"

"Do the Feds know what it's like to have a home—to have a lifetime of memories torn from you? Do they even *feel at all?*"

"at all… at all… at all…" Echoes down the street.

"Now we live in Raton, New Mexico. A perfect little cookie cutter town manufactured in the middle of the desert by our oh holy federal government. That's supposed to be our home now."

"Listen, Nova—"

She exhales deeply, her breath quivering.

I step back to give her space. A minute passes in silence.

"I'm sorry," she says. "It's just a little overwhelming being back here. Back in the *New Wilderness*," she says accompanied by sarcastic air quotes.

"I know," I say and walk her back to the car.

The drive from Denver to Breckenridge usually takes no more than two hours, but without snow plows clearing the way, we're pushing three. At the mouth of the canyon, I stopped the car in the middle of the highway and put chains on our tires.

For the first time in a long time, Nova and I genuinely connected. The Move had put a weird tension on our relationship. Not that either of us did anything wrong—we were both in our own heads throughout the whole process. Megan moving in with us didn't help.

"You think you can still rig your way into Chrystal Peak?" I ask.

"In my sleep," Nova replies. "Pun intended."

"Ah, because it's a hotel," I say.

"You got it."

"That you sleep in."

"Shut up."

During late nights, when the skeleton crew was running Chrystal Peak, Nova would break us into the secret hallway that ran through the ground floor of the hotel, connecting the restaurants, spa, and uppity conference rooms. We felt like teenagers sneaking through that hallway, no destination or end goal in mind. Voyeurs of the upper class.

"Any chance room service left any wine behind?"

"Well, I doubt Breckenridge *ski resort* reopened in the Belt. There's bound to be something," Nova says.

The snow is blanketed evenly across the roads and sidewalks, making the buildings appear smaller than they are. We swim through Main Street, passing Gnarly Shawarma and

Dancing Moose School—the one that Xan went to before the Move. We pass the fire station, a cluster of luxury hotels, and the collection of hole-in-the-wall pizza and Mexican places.

"It's so peaceful," Nova says, her tone surprising me.

"I thought you'd be sad being here."

"I don't know—I think I got it out of my system in Denver," she says, letting out a long exhale.

We turn the corner on Washington and follow it two blocks to High Street. Our High Street.

The neighbors' houses are hardly recognizable with the snow piled up like this. Nearly every other house has snow spilling in through shattered windows. Normally, windows are boarded up when they're winterized, but the Move was a bit more permanent than leaving a vacation home behind for the season. The Feds actively discouraged winterization to make staying behind—or coming back—less appealing.

We stop the car in front of our little red house, fourth in from Washington.

"There she blows," I say.

"Looks so lonely. The snow, the unplowed roads, the broken windows. No lights. No people. The whole place is like, void of existence."

"If a tree falls in the woods and no one is around to hear it, did it make a sound?" I say.

"Exactly. It's like, the structures are still here, obviously—until there's another earthquake or something—but, without people actively experiencing it, I guess, does it *really* exist?"

"That's deep, Nov."

"This isn't our home anymore." Her voice drifts. "This isn't our home anymore."

—

It starts snowing as we pull up to the maintenance warehouse on the southern end of the ski resort's base. Getting from the car to the warehouse proves to be a task, trudging through waist-deep powder. I clear enough snow to try the man door, but it's locked. I walk up the side of the warehouse, hugging the building as tightly as I can to take advantage of the 18-inch roof overhang. I find an intact window five feet off the ground and shatter it with a swift punch of my gloved fist. I look back at Nova, still waiting in the car, and give her a thumbs up. I climb inside, breathing the cold, stale air, and turn on my flashlight. The warehouse is in almost the exact same condition as it was when I was last here a year ago. Of the four snowcat bays, three are occupied. Three snowcats mean three runs for Nova and me.

With how long I worked at the resort, I had a go at just about every job the resort had to offer, which included a brief stint operating a snowcat. The resort guests—generally old wealthy guys—were not the strongest candidates for theft or vandalism, so we didn't lock up too often. I climb inside the first snowcat and feel around the right side of the steering wheel until I meet the clank of the keys dangling from the ignition. With a silent and mostly sarcastic prayer, I turn the ignition and bring the engine rumbling to life. The dial of the gas gauge slides upwards, signaling half a tank of gas. Beautiful.

If it wasn't for the generous cash offers given to seasonal businesses affected by the Move, I'd feel somewhat bad about leaving half a million dollars' worth of snowcats on top of the mountain.

I climb out of the snowcat and open the garage door with the manual pull. Nova takes the skis off the rack, her ski goggles fixed on top of her white beanie.

"All aboard!" I shout, returning to the snowcat's cabin. I ease out of the garage and pull next to the car, marveling at how small it seems in comparison.

"Anyone around here need a ride?" I say, leaning out of the window.

"Dang, this thing is badass," Nova says and loads the skis in the back seat of the cabin. She climbs into the front seat and we take off.

"Haven't driven one in a couple years."

"Is it weird that I think it's sexy that you can drive this thing?"

"It's not weird at all—just don't make any 'big truck, tiny penis' jokes please."

"Big snowcat, bigger penis?"

I shake my head, smiling. Nova nudges my arm.

We climb the terrain with ease, arriving to the top of Mercury in twenty minutes. I feel the flutter of anticipatory butterflies as I pull the brake and kill the engine.

At an elevation of almost 13,000 feet, we are far above the clouds and snowstorm below. We sit in silence and take in the view of the endless blue sky in front of us. Nova reaches for my hand.

"We are the only people in the whole world," I say.

"We almost literally are," she says.

Another minute passes by.

"You think Xan is ok with my mom?" Nova says.

We pop our doors open and unload.

"Of course she is," I reply. "Meg only raised like fifteen kids of her own."

"Four. Four kids, Leo."

"Oh, that's right."

Nova smirks and rolls her eyes. She clicks into her bindings and takes one more deep breath. She looks back at me. "Oh crap, is that a—"

I whip my head around. About 100 feet behind us on the other side of a cluster of pine trees is another snowcat. Presumably the missing snowcat from the garage. Snow is piled on top and around it, the windows dusty but undamaged.

"You think someone else had our idea?" I ask.

"I don't know."

I pull myself through the snow to get a closer look.

"Leo, don't go closer. Please," she says, panic in her voice.

I stop. "I don't see any tracks around it. Do you?"

"No, but—what if someone is in there?"

Don't feed the suspicion, I think, as tempting as it might be. I pretend to inspect the situation from afar for another minute.

"Forget it, it's probably nothing," Nova concedes.

"You sure?"

"Ha—famous last words," she says and pushes off down the mountain.

—

We float down the hill taking long, deep turns through the untracked powder. The snow glistens in the sunlight while we ski above the sea of clouds. As we descend into the storm, the temperature drops, the wind picks up, and it gets darker. For the next run, we take the snowcat to the top of Peak 8 in an effort to diversify terrain, but mostly to avoid the mystery snowcat at the top of Mercury. Despite skiing *very* carefully, not wanting to create an emergency in the middle of nowhere, we have the time of our lives.

We repeat the routine of skiing to the warehouse, Nova waiting outside, me climbing back into the warehouse and firing up the final snowcat. With only a quarter tank in the final machine, we decide to make Sunshiner—one of the lower elevation peaks—our last run. Nova and I share bottled lattes on the drive up.

"I really don't want this to end," Nova says.

"It does not get anymore untracked than this."

"I mean, I don't want to go back to the Belt," she says.

"I know."

"It's so horribly bland. No mountains, no snow, no rivers. Just flat, bland, and brown."

"There is a lot of brown in the Belt, huh?"

"Brown everywhere."

I kill the rumbling engine at the top of Sunshiner and we begin our final descent. I soak in the utter silence of the deserted mountain, the slicing of my skis into the fresh powder, the cold dry air against my face.

By the time we make it back to the warehouse after the last run, my legs feel like jelly and I'm winded. We return to the car, following the path we forged to the warehouse.

"Again next year?" I say, half joking.

"That was fun, but I don't know. What if there are ravenous gangs out here somewhere?"

"You think?"

"Why wouldn't there be? 70% of the country just abandoned, with *no one* left behind? You really think *that* is true?"

"I guess not. I don't know. I mean I get it—let everyone move down to the Belt and go find a million-dollar cabin on top of a mountain or an oceanfront mansion or something. But to be hundreds of miles away from civilization, from electricity, from cell towers? The fun has got to wear off at some point," I say.

"But it is kind of dangerous being out here, is it not? Imagine you have another adventurous couple like us exploring the Wild and they bring a gun just to be safe."

"Okay…"

"They're camped out on the side of the road in Colorado Springs and we happen to drive by. They get freaked out and they shoot at the car. That could happen, right?"

"Would you immediately start shooting like that?"

"Think about it. The Wild is completely abandoned. *Completely abandoned.* Not another soul for hundreds of miles. You saw how quiet and lifeless it was in the middle of downtown Denver, right? Now imagine how disorienting it would be to see another person in the Wild."

"Ok, I see what you're saying. So, we'll play it cool this trip and then reevaluate later about a return trip next year."

Nova smirks. "Ok, pal."

—

We park underneath the gaudy overhang of Chrystal Peak Lodge and unload our bags. One of the tall windows of the front is shattered, allowing us easy access inside.

The lobby is three stories high, outfitted in classic western mountain resort fashion—cowhide pillows, brown leather seating, a stone fireplace.

"Feel good to be back?" I ask.

"As long as I don't have to clock in," Nova says.

"Weren't you on salary?"

"You get the point."

I pull two flashlights from my backpack and hand one to Nova. The sun is going down, but there's still enough light for us to see our breath as we wander the lobby. I check the little café on the back end of the lobby to see if they left any espresso machines behind. They didn't.

A service bell dings near the front desk.

"Oh, Leo!" Nova calls out, her head popping up from behind the desk, dangling a room key. "How about the presidential suite?"

"They have one of those?"

—

We reach the fifth floor of the hotel and make our way down the cold and dusty hallway to Room 501.

"This place has not changed at all," Nova says, flashing her light on the wild-west artwork still hanging from the wall every twenty feet or so.

Nova opens 501 and we step inside. With enough light still pouring in the floor-to-ceiling, wall-to-wall windows, we turn our flashlights off and look around. The TVs are gone. Same with the dishwasher and fridge. I heard something about the Feds buying appliances from hotels, so I assume that's why.

The dining room still has its vast lodge-style table, surrounded by brown leather chairs. I walk over to the windows and look out on the resort. Our room is situated directly over the Claimjumper ski run—a fifty-foot-wide cut in the thick pine trees snaking down the mountain. The snow falls gently, slowly adding to the thick blanket of white covering the world. The setting sun gives the snow a light pink hue. *Nature can finally reclaim what's rightfully hers.*

"I'm gonna go see if they happened to leave behind any wine downstairs," Nova says.

"I support that."

"Can you fire up the heater? As much as I love staying in

my ski clothes all day."

I move the bags and heater to the bedroom then step onto the balcony.

Breathe in…1…2…3…4…5…

I'm the only person alive in the world.

Hold…1…2…3…4…5…

If only Xan were here, we could make the Chrystal Peak Lodge our home. It would take a little creativity, and I'd have to brush up on my mountain man skills, but we could do it.

Release…1…2…3…4…5…

My daydream is interrupted a few minutes later when Nova returns, swinging the bedroom door open with two bottles of Merlot in tow.

"Alright!"

We pass the rest of the evening eating egg salad sandwiches, drinking wine, and playing cards. As sunlight fades, our solar lights carry us through. We get louder as the evening rolls on. Our conversation bounces between funny Xandra-isms, like how she gives herself flirty eyes in the mirror; to existential questions, like what if mankind as we know it is just some aliens' dorm room experiment gone wrong. It was typical wine-fueled conversation for us.

At one point, I put my cards down.

"What do you think New York is like? Do you think it's empty like this? I mean—Breckenridge is a tiny town. It's bound to be empty. But New York? Think how many good hiding spots there have to be."

Nova smirks, signaling a good hand, and shifts her eyes toward me. "Yes, that's probably true."

"Think about it," I say, throwing my hands in the air. I tend to get more animated under the influence. "The Feds announce they are doing the Move thing. Some guy decides he'd rather try his luck in vacant NYC than race to the Belt. He starts storing food and fuel, collecting generators, etc. Then when the Move happens, he hides somewhere—a storage unit or an office building."

"Yeah but what about the Sweep—"

"That's what I'm saying, if he's a good hider, he could've evaded the Sweep. Especially in such a huge city."

After the Move was supposed to have been completed in a zone, the Guides—a nicer term for military—completed two or three Sweeps of an area, going door to door, business to business, making sure everyone was gone. The Sweeps occurred at random times in random neighborhoods so they couldn't be anticipated.

"But he would've had to check in to the Belt with his social security number."

"I got it—he pays off a Guide. Or he's just friends with one—"

"Yeah okay, maybe it is possible," Nova concedes, then looks back down at her cards.

"My real question is this, if it's not true that 100% of Americans now live in the Belt, then what is the real percentage? 95%? 75%? Exactly how many people are hiding in the Wild? Hundreds? Thousands? Millions?"

Nova puts her cards down and looks up at me, annoyed that we're still on the topic. "Yeah, but we didn't see any sign of life our entire drive here did we?"

"No, but—"

"And can you think of anyone we knew before, from Breck, from Denver, that didn't make it to the Belt?"

"Not that I know of."

I pause.

"Yeah, you're probably right," I say, looking down.

She grabs my hand. "I'm sorry," she says.

"I thought Breck was going to be a thing of my past forever, but being back here—I mean, it still *actually* exists, you know? Unlike Salt Lake."

"Yeah."

"Which, in a way, it's almost easier when the physical thing is gone. It's a kind of forced closure—forced non-attachment—you know?"

"Ah, Buddhist stuff. Attachment is the root of all suffering."

"Exactly."

Nova pauses and runs her fingers along the edge of the table. "I kind of wish my dad were dead for that same reason."

"Burn," I say with raised eyebrows.

"Things become more than they were when they're dead. I think that's true of people *and* places. And, if my dad were dead, he'd get to keep some of his dignity in my mind, anyway. But more than that, if I *knew* my dad was dead, I'd be able to fully move on. It's weird knowing he could show up at any time."

"Do you think about him a lot?"

"I don't know. I was so young when he left. I'd like to think that I see traces of him in me—like I know what he was like because I know what *I'm* like."

"Megan doesn't talk about him much."

"No, she does not," Nova says, looking out the window. The snow is still falling outside. The evening twilight has almost run out.

Nova's gaze out the window intensifies, and she perks up. "Ah, a little family of deer." She stands up and moves toward the window.

"How many?" I ask, avoiding standing up on my wobbly

legs.

"Four—no, five. They're so—" She stops mid-sentence and turns toward me, her eyes wide. She clears her throat. "They're so—" She stops again and holds a finger up like she's listening for something.

"Nova—"

"Shhh, listen."

I hold my breath and listen intently. Then I hear it.

The sound of an engine whirs in the distance.

04

I rush to the window.

"Shhhh," Nova says, her ear against the window.

I stop and hold my breath again. "Do you still hear it?"

"It stopped." She eases away from the window and looks at me, terrified.

"It's probably a—" I rack my brain trying to think of a reasonable explanation that both of us can buy into. "It's probably a tourist. Someone exploring the Wild. Just like us."

Nova moves her eyes back to the window. "That was definitely a snowmobile, right?"

I nod. "Or a chainsaw."

"Maybe we should get into a unit across the hall to give us a better view of the town."

"Alright, just to be safe—cause I *don't* think we have anything to worry about—let's go down to the lobby, you get a key for a unit across the hall and I'll move the car to the garage."

"Okay."

I grab the Victory .22 from my backpack before stepping into the hallway. I wish I had something more powerful, but until now owning a gun was a mere formality.

As we near the stairs at the end of the hallway, it's clear that any playfulness left in Nova has gone. "We shouldn't have come out here," she says. There's a reason it's called the New *Wilderness*—it's lawless out here. Seriously, what happens if someone kills us?"

"Well, let's—"

"Nothing happens. No one would find out. No one would tell my Mom. We would just not show up back home. Search parties wouldn't come looking for us. Have you thought about that?" Her breathing grows loud.

I screwed the pooch on this one. Even if the noise turns out to be nothing, coming out here was a mistake.

We make it to the ground level and I lean against the door, gun ready. I slowly open it and pause, listening for any sign of life.

"I think we're clear," I say, stepping into the lobby.

Nova, now laser-focused, walks behind the front desk and rummages through the keys. I stand with both the front desk and the hotel entrance in view. Nighttime has enveloped the lobby.

"Got it. Top floor, corner unit. That should give us maximum visibility," Nova says, dangling the key above her head. I like this brief resurgence of confidence.

"Good work, space cadet."

The motor whirrs again, louder this time. My heart thuds in my chest and I break out in a sweat.

"God, Leo. Did that sound closer this time?" A wave of hopelessness flashes across Nova's face.

It did—it absolutely did. But I didn't want to add fuel to the fire. "I can't tell. Should we still go up? Should we make a run for it?"

"Why don't we still go up and see if we can see anything first," Nova responds.

"Ok. I'll move the car. You stay here."

She nods and swallows.

I step through the shattered automatic glass door and climb into the car, the headlights cutting through the darkening, snowy air.

I break through the barrier arm at the garage entrance— something a lot less dramatic in real life than in movies—and drive down one level, parking next to the staircase door.

"Thank God," Nova says upon my arrival. "Listen, Leo. I may be overreacting. I think you're right." She grabs my hands. "I'm sure it's just a couple of people like us, going for a wilderness adventure. I mean, this has got to be killer snowmobiling conditions, right?"

"Absolutely," I say, smiling. I hope she's right.

The engine continues whirring in the distance, getting louder by the second.

"I don't want this to ruin the night. Let's go up to our new room and try to unwind a bit. What do you say?" Nova says.

"That would be wonderful."

Stepping back into the fifth-floor hallway, I'm reminded that this place is a fridge. We walk attentively down the hall.

"You keep watch, I'll grab our stuff," I say.

"No way dude, you watch with me!" Nova fires back.

"Yeah but it's friggin' cold in here. Let me at least grab the heater."

"Just come watch for a minute, until the sound stops at least."

I concede and walk with her to the window. We look out on Ski Hill Road, the moonlight diffused through the falling snow. On the hotel driveway, I notice a new track in the snow beside our tire tracks.

"Are those—" I start.

"Oh my God," Nova says, looking down.

"No—"

I look down—straight down—to the entrance of the hotel where a snowmobile is now parked. Its owner appears to have left it behind. Which means—

"He must've pulled up while we were in the stairway," Nova says, her voice trembling. "What do we do?" Nova says, her heavy breathing getting away from her.

"Nov, babe," I put my arm around her, "we're gonna be okay. I've got the gun ready. We'll just hang out in here and stay quiet."

"Oh God, you don't think you'll—"

The door slams open.

We jerk our heads around, our flashlights finding a big—huge—burly man standing in the doorway. He is bald-headed and bearded with a large tattoo across his face. He takes one step into the room and points his pistol at us.

Without hesitation, I whip my gun toward him and pull the trigger. The bright flash of light and deafening *pop* of the gun disorients me. I miss and a portion of the wood door frame shatters.

"Leo!" Nova screams.

The man wipes his face and looks at us, pistol still pointed. He lets out a deep grumble of a laugh and tightens his grip on the gun.

"Who are you?" I scream, cocking my gun.

"That shouldn't matter to you," he says.

I take a deep, trembling breath.

What. The. Hell.

"Leo, what the hell is this?" Nova asks, eyes fixed on the man.

"I have no idea," I say. "Who are you?!"

"I have very simple instructions. And no more funny business, Leo Kline. Nova, you're coming with me," he says.

How does he know our names?

Nova releases her grip on me and steps away. "Why would I go with you?"

"Because you don't have a choice."

Nova looks to me then back to the man.

"You son of a—" Nova screams, her flashlight thudding against the ground.

I fire at the man again. The flash of the gun against the dark, moonlit room stings my eyes. There is a thud of a body hitting the floor.

"Nov—" I say, finding my flashlight on the ground. I pick it up and shine it toward the man. He's lying on the ground, blood spurting from his neck. My ears ring, causing my heavy breathing to reverberate through my body. I flash my light toward Nova, but she's not there.

My heartbeat pounds in my throat as I point the flashlight down toward my feet.

My gun wasn't the only one that went off.

05

Nova is lying on the ground, eyes open, staring at the ceiling, a bullet hole above her right eye. Blood is puddled on the floor beneath her head.

She is dead.

Just like that.

I drop to my knees. My throat closes off and my head starts throbbing. "Nov—babe," the tears stream down my face. "Nova?"

I clench the back of my fist against my mouth and cough violently.

Silence.

Can't be.

This cannot be.

Lifeless.

A lifeless body.

This beautiful woman. This woman I love. The mother of my child. My partner in life. My confidant. My best friend. Now a lifeless body. *A corpse.*

I go from feeling complete, loved, and happy one minute to completely alone the next. Deeply alone. The body is still here, but Nova is gone. Dead. Nova is dead.

She took a bullet for me—she must have. The man was pointing his pistol at me, but Nova is the one who got shot. Not only did I drag Nova up here, but she *took a bullet* for me. And now she's dead.

My trembling breathing turns shallow and the room starts spinning. For a moment, I feel like I leave my body—like I'm floating to the ceiling.

Stuff like this doesn't happen to me. Not to mild-mannered, normal people like Leo and Nova Kline. This is what happens to drug dealers, or undercover agents or—

In a split second, I replay in my head all my missteps starting from the beginning. I shouldn't have pushed moving to Breckenridge in the first place. We were fine in Denver. If I didn't push to move out here, we wouldn't have felt the need to come back. When the government worker told me to *confront it all,* she didn't mean to literally confront it in person. I let Nova think it was safe when I myself had no idea what we were getting in to. The warning sign on the border, why didn't I think about that? Why did I casually drive past it? *One-hundred-percent.* One hundred percent made it to the Belt. I don't believe that, so why did I act like I did? Why did I ignore Nova's repeated questioning—'are you sure it's safe?' 'should we be doing this?'

My thoughts turn to Xandra, now a motherless child. Motherless because of me. Me. My fault. There will be no mom at Xandra's dance performances. No cheering mom on the sidelines of her soccer games. No mom to drop her off on the first day of kindergarten. No mom to be there when she has her first period or gets dumped for the first time. No mom to confide in. Because of me.

I didn't even get to say goodbye.

A gurgling noise comes from the man.

The feeling of utter emptiness and fatigue suddenly turns to fire. I struggle to stand up, my eyes still on Nova. The moonlight pouring in from the windows is stronger now. I direct my gaze to the man, my vision blurry from tears. I wipe my eyes and step toward him. I may have gotten us into this mess, but *he* killed her. It was *his* finger on the trigger.

He's lying in the same position as Nova—laying on his back, staring at the ceiling. Only this animal is alive. Barely.

His chest convulses, blood continuing to spout from his throat. Each second that passes watching him spew blood, I feel pure, thick hate fill my bones, my lungs, my hands.

The questions I should be asking—why he targeted me, how he found us, who he works for—seem trivial. The only thing on my mind is *destroy*.

"You—" I whisper, staring into his beady, bloodshot eyes. His gaze slowly shifts toward me. He has a large, thick line tattoo running from his left temple to his nose, a slash over his left eye. I pick up the pistol laying near him. His glossy eyes follow me.

I look back at Nova's body and grit my teeth. I grip his pistol hard, turning my knuckles white, and kneel down next to him. A flicker of fear flashes in his eyes as I swiftly raise the pistol above my head and bring it down with fury, landing the butt of the gun in the middle of his forehead. He jerks and lets out a grumbly cough. His eyes wince.

"You—" I whisper again, unable to say anything else. Shaky and over fueled by adrenaline, I repeat the motion three more times, raising the pistol and slamming it onto his forehead. The thud gets progressively deeper with each hit. Blood puddles in his forehead, spilling down his face and onto the floor. He continues to gurgle loudly and jerk around in pain.

I stand up slowly and watch him suffer, struggling for air. I think through all the ways I could end his life. I could throw him off the balcony. I could shoot him. I could cut his throat. I've never killed a man before but killing this man does not feel like killing, it feels like doing what was always meant to be done. Is this how murderers feel?

While standing above his body, feeling oddly in control, the sound of struggle is interrupted. I step away from the gurgling man and hold my breath. The faint ringing of more snowmobiles reverberates in the distance. I run to the window and see headlights bobbing through the trees approaching the hotel.

I face the man again. "What do you want with me? What are you doing out here? Who sent you?" I turn back to the window, trying to get a view of the approaching snowmobiles. I'm losing my mind and I know it. I'm watching myself breakdown in real time like I'm a spectator in the stands. I look back at Nova's body, staring up at the ceiling, stiffening by the second. I can hardly catch my breath as the tears roll in.

I could kill myself.

In my moment of despair, I look into the face of the gurgling man, following his slash tattoo across his face. *A slash and a slash,* we used to tell Xandra when explaining how to write the letter X. She would repeat to us *a sash anna sash.*

A pang of guilt sinks deep in my chest thinking about Xandra growing up without parents. I can't take my own life. I need to fight. *I need to fight.*

The man is still gurgling, his eyes following me. I point the pistol at his head and, without a second thought, pull the trigger. Once the initial ringing in my ear fades away, I hear voices outside. They're here.

Gun trembling in my hand, I kneel down next to Nova's body and run my fingers down her face. She's already losing temperature.

Fueled by raw adrenaline, I drag the man's body to the windows across the room. The thought of Nova's final resting place being shared with him is unbearable. I look down and count six more snowmobiles parked outside the lobby entrance. Two men stand outside, the rest must be inside.

Running out of time.

I pick up an oak side table and wield it over my head, the weight briefly destabilizing me. I step back and flex my upper body, regain my balance, and heave the table through the glass. It shatters, cold air rushing into the room. I look down and see the two men shielding their heads from the falling glass.

I drag the dead man to the edge, take one deep breath in, and push him over. The ground below pulls him down with a vengeance, his large frame shrinking as it tumbles through the moonlit winter air. His body lands just to the right of the snowmobiles, sending up a poof of snow. The two men look toward me and shout at one another. I cock my pistol.

"Hey!" Another burly man with the same tattoo appears in the doorway, announcing himself with a deep, raspy voice. He blinds me momentarily with the beam of his flashlight. I fire my pistol, striking the other side of the door frame. The man shields his eyes and turns back to me, a look of determination on his face. He sees Nova lying on the ground and steps into the hallway, shouting something down the hall. For a moment, I'm disoriented again. *Nova is dead and I'm in a gunfight.*

Taking advantage of his inattention, I fire again and hit him in the arm. He drops his gun and lets out a barbaric *arrrrrr* as he falls to the ground. I look one more time back at Nova and whisper, "Goodbye supernova."

This is it.

All my fault.

The man on the ground moans. I step over his body and unload a shot point blank to his face, the impact a splashing thud. I pick up his flashlight and fire a few blind shots down the south hallway at the horde of men rushing toward me. Gunshots explode around me, kicking up dust of burning drywall.

Thanks to a small bend in the hallway, I get to the north

stairwell unscathed. I descend the stairs two at a time, flashlight in one hand and a gun in the other. I make it down two flights before hearing the fifth-floor door open again. Shouting echoes through the concrete stairwell.

Lucky for me, the north stairwell leads directly to the parking garage, a fact that I'm hoping the others are unaware of. As I pass the ground level, I hear a chorus of deep voices in the lobby.

I step into the parking garage and let the door close slowly behind me. Alone in the cold, dark, underground box of a garage, I run to the car, keys fumbling.

I put the car in reverse and step on the gas. The feeling of *I've forgotten something* leaves a pit in my stomach as I realize *what* I've forgotten. As I turn the last corner before the exit, another man pulls up to the parking garage exit on his snowmobile, gun pointed at me. I accelerate up the ramp toward him, ducking as he pulls the trigger. His bullet penetrates the windshield, creating an explosion of white cotton in the back seat. My car grazes a concrete pillar.

I turn on my high-beams and grip the steering wheel. The man throws his arms in front of his face as I blow through him and his snowmobile. His head hits the top right corner of my windshield. Once out of the garage, I slam on the brakes and crank the wheel in an attempt to make the turn onto Ski Hill Road. My car spins around completely before slamming into the curb.

Four more men outside the lobby mount their snowmobiles. I step on the gas, sending the car into a brief fishtail before finding traction. One of the men fires a shot in vain.

I slide onto Ski Hill Road and adjust my rear-view mirror. They're close behind. Gunshots illuminate the night sky with quick flashes and accompanying *pop pop pop*s. Occasionally a bullet strikes the back of the car with a muted thud. The fourth or fifth bullet to hit my car connects with the back window, turning the tempered glass white. I do my best to crouch down while maintaining speed.

I keep my weight on the pedal as I navigate the dark, dusting streets of downtown Breckenridge. The pistol trembles in my right hand. The snowmobiles creep up on my sides. The motors' buzzing echoes off the buildings—the same sound that kicked off this mess hours—no, minutes ago. I check my watch. It's been thirty minutes since we heard the first snowmobile. Thir-ty-min-utes.

Thirty minutes ago, I had a wife. Thirty minutes ago, Xandra had a mother. Thirty minutes ago, we were careless kids on an adventure together. Thirty minutes ago, everything was perfect. Thirty minutes later, Nova is dead—I have no wife, Xandra doesn't have a mother, I've killed three men, and I'm running for my life.

Nova is a stiff, cold corpse rotting in a hotel room. *Dead.*

I glance at my rearview and side mirrors. There are two men directly behind me, one on my right tail light, and one on my left. I slam on the brakes, slowing enough for the two snowmobiles behind me to slam into the back of my car. One of their heads crashes through the cracked tempered glass of the back window, spilling glass pebbles into the trunk. The man on my right veers off the road and bails before his snowmobile crashes into a light pole. The man on the left springs out in front of me. He turns around, trying to get his machine to follow. I fire three shots leaning out of the window, at least one of them making impact and sending him to the ground. In the rearview mirror, I see one of the men on the ground struggling to get up. The other one stumbles back onto his snowmobile but can't get it started. The one I shot on the left side of the road lies motionless.

In a way, I don't want the heist to end. I don't want to face silence. I don't want to think about how I'm driving home without Nova in the passenger seat. I recheck the rearview mirror. I am alone on the road. And alone in this car.

06

Dramatic scenes in movies—scenes where a loved one dies, for example—customarily unfold in slow motion, with real-world sounds turned down and big, weepy music turned up. Lighting dims, cameras zoom carefully. I get it. They need the viewer to invest emotionally in the moment, to internalize its gravity. When a sensitive scene comes on, the elements combine, giving the viewer a good idea of what's about to happen.

When Nova was killed, I was first struck by how lightning quick the whole thing unfolded. Then, I was confused—*No, something can't be right, this wasn't how it was supposed to happen.* Had the scene played out in slow motion, with an underwater soundscape of sad strings and gunfire, I would've understood what was happening—*Ahhh this is the part where my wife dies right in front of me.* But no, I had none of that. All I had were little flashes of future memories, never to be realized—Nova and I holding hands at Xan's high school graduation, dropping Xan off for her first day of freshman year, sitting on our front porch drinking wine as empty-nesters, laughing together, challenging each other. *That* was how it was supposed to be.

Something—someone—has bumped the universe off course. Nothing will ever be the same. The world will always be tainted.

I exhale slowly and realize that I can see my breath against the soft glow of the radio deck. I've driven for who knows how long without heat and I'm just now noticing. I turn the temperature dial and hold my right hand over the vent, feeling the air turn warm.

I'm overthinking it. When you look at the material facts,

it's simple. I brought us into a dangerous situation and Nova was killed. Choices. We made choices—I made choices—that led us to that place. There is no fate. There is no conspiring universe. There are choices. That's all.

I should've stood in front of Nova. I should've pushed her down. I should've fired as soon as I heard the door rattling. We should've left when we heard the first snowmobile. We should've turned around in Denver. We should've turned around in Pueblo. We should've turned around at the border warning sign. I shouldn't have let Adam or Chris talk me into anything. I shouldn't have stopped at The Move Blues in the first place. I shouldn't have let my imagination run with the question: *What if we go back?*

Leo, the responsible one. The one that doesn't take risks. The one that parents of rebellious kids wish they had. Leo got his wife killed trying to be spontaneous. Trying to be fun. Trying to take a risk. *Trying to heal.*

As I approach Highway 50 in Canon City, the elevation drops significantly, a fact I'm reminded of as my tires finally hit the asphalt. It was a transition I may not have noticed if it wasn't for my deflated back left tire combined with snow chains. Did I drive that whole way with a flat tire?

I stop the car in front of a nondescript three-story office building labeled Sunflower Bank. I walk around the car with my flashlight, assessing the damage from the gunfight. I open the hatchback and clear enough of the shattered glass to access the spare tire compartment. A piece of glass slices my finger, drawing blood.

The cold winter will preserve the body for a while, but when spring comes, it will rot. A wave of nausea passes over me. Those cloudy, vacant eyes staring up at the ceiling, a gaping bullet hole in her forehead. It's a haunting image that I don't know I'll ever be able to shake.

The void left by the adrenaline of surviving a heist, the emotional toll of Nova's gruesome death, and my frozen hands combine to make me an incredibly inefficient car mechanic. I muster enough strength to take the jack out of the trunk but fail to move the spare tire even an inch.

I let out an audible burst and throw my lug wrench through the window of the office building. The shattered glass rains down on the sidewalk in front of me.

"I can't—I can't," I whisper through my sobs. After a minute, I try again. I stand up and exhale, looking at the tire, then at the shattered window of the office building.

I break the window around the edges and climb inside. I'm met with a strong, humid smell of mildew. The beam of my flashlight dances around, revealing the empty bank to be mostly cleared out besides some semi-deconstructed cubicles and papers littered throughout.

I walk to the side of the teller's desk, the sound of my footsteps dampened by the carpet below and soggy ceiling tiles above. I move the flashlight back and forth along the ground, looking for the wrench. I shine my light into the open vault behind the teller's desk when a glare on the ground catches my eye. I step forward, my gaze fixed on the object in the vault. It's the wrench, lying neatly on a blanket. I stop dead in my tracks, my heart pounding. The lit candles, notebooks, and empty beer cans tell me that this isn't just a vault, it's someone's home.

I hold my breath, listening for any movement, then clear my throat. "Is anyone in here?" I reach for my gun.

Aside from my heart beating in my throat, the world is silent. I inhale sharply and step inside, retrieve the wrench and turn around. Something moves past my beam of light and disappears into the back hallway.

"I'm just getting my wrench and leaving, whoever you are. I'm sorry to disturb—" My throat tightens, and I swallow hard.

A door slams somewhere down the hallway with a heavy clunk and I run for the exit.

I get back in my car and fire up the engine, not bothering to look around me. I either forget about the flat tire or don't care. I push the pedal to the floor, my tires screeching on the asphalt. I get back on the highway and drive as fast as my three inflated tires will take me.

—

I put in almost nine miles before the car starts convulsing. I pull off the exit for Florence and stop on First Street. I stay in the car long enough for my breath to become visible again, then get out, reassessing the damage.

As I stand outside the car—the car Nova and I have had for almost our entire marriage—I feel pure defeat. This car was our first major purchase together. It was also when I first realized I'm a crappy negotiator. And that Nova is a bit of a fireball. Now I'm abandoning it. *Just like I abandoned Nova.*

I lean against it and drop my head, tears trickling down my cheeks. I want to be angry. I want to destroy the car—to destroy *something*—but I can't. Even if I could muster the strength, I'm too defeated.

Water and a car. That's all I need. Either that or a place to curl up and die. How long would it take to starve to death? I guess the cold would take me first.

I walk a block north past the decrepit commercial strip toward the decrepit neighborhoods, not having much of a plan. *Water and a car.* There are no street lights. No houselights. No headlights creating shadows as cars speed around corners. No garbage cans on the streets. No cars—unfortunately—parked in driveways. The place doesn't feel empty, it feels devoid of life. It feels almost sinister. I look at the houses—the front yards, the porches, the basketball hoops in driveways. Every house I see was once a home. Not anymore. The structures might still stand but they are nothing more than distant memories.

As I walk the blocks, looking for *water and a car,* it starts snowing. The snowflakes are big, the kind that fall on Christmas. The town gets brighter as the moonlight is dispersed across the thick snow clouds hovering above the town. As I approach a new street, I see a minivan three houses down. "Thank God," I whisper.

What am I going to say to Megan?

I move gently through the snow to the driver's side of the car. I look into the windows, my face against the glass, hands cupped around my eyes. No one appears to live *in* the vehicle, which is a start. I tug at the driver's door, but it's locked. I turn around, facing the house it's parked in front of, and cautiously advance.

If not one-hundred-percent, what? Ninety percent? Seventy-five?

With the .22 by my side, I approach the gray brick house and look through the window. Trash litters the floors, holes litter the drywalls, tears litter the furniture. I think I've stumbled upon a crack house. Was this a pre-Move crack house or a post-Move crack house? Lacking evidence of human activity, I go in. The idea that it's a crack house gives me a sense of confidence—like a bunch of crackheads would rather be left in peace rather than kill a passerby. It's probably a false sense of optimism, but I have a gun. *And a taste for killing,* I think.

I try the front door. Locked. I walk around to the back door. Locked. I peek in the kitchen window next to the back door. Still looks like a crack house. Still looks unoccupied. I find a rock in the backyard and hurl it through the kitchen window. After the loud crash of the window shattering, I listen for any stirring—inside the house or otherwise. Still silent.

I clear the shards still clinging to the window frame with the butt of my gun and climb through. Looking for car keys, or really anything, in a crack house is like looking for a needle—no pun intended—in a haystack.

There are no key holders mounted on the walls or magnet key holders on the fridge, so I go through the kitchen drawers. More garbage, coins, pens, receipts. The dates on the receipts suggest that the house has been abandoned since long before the Move. Abandoned by its primary owner, anyway.

While I'm rummaging through a third kitchen drawer overflowing with junk, I hear a loud *pop* outside—like either a firecracker in close range or a gun in the distance. I am not alone in Florence. I continue rummaging with a heightened sense of urgency.

Another *pop* goes off, this time closer.

A jangle sounds from the drawer as my hand makes contact with a jumble of keys. I pull out a large key ring anchored by a pink lucky rabbits' foot—*how lucky am I*—and go through the keys one by one until I find one with a Chrysler logo on it.

I stand up, put the flashlight in my pocket, and run toward the front door, tripping halfway across the living room floor. I break my fall by throwing my right arm in front of my body, forcing me to twist onto my side. I pop back up immediately and step toward the door when I hear a car swerve around the corner, coming toward the house. The *pop* wasn't a gun—or a firecracker—it was a car backfiring. I crouch down, my back against the wall between the front door and window. The headlights shine through the front window briefly illuminating the room and revealing what I tripped over—a dead body.

The car speeds past the house and makes a turn at the end of the street. I shine my flashlight on the body lying on the floor. The face is that of a man in his mid-20s, now cold and pale, eyes and mouth wide open. His lips are shrunk down to almost nothing. A frozen trail of white vomit runs from his mouth to a puddle on the floor. Despite how desensitized I've become, a nauseous feeling sinks deep in my stomach.

This is Nova in what, two months?

I cough intensely for a moment, the cough turning into a violent dry-heave.

Still clinging the car key, I inhale deeply and stand up. I take one more look out the front window, open the door, and run to the van.

On the street behind mine, through a small gap between houses, I see the mystery driver come to a stop. I duck behind the van and hear a car door close. The mystery driver whistles as he leisurely crosses his front yard to his house. I slowly stand up and see the shape of a man walking away from the car toward the house kitty-corner from the crack house. *Is he holding keys?*

The front door of his house opens and shuts and the world returns to silence. I sigh loudly. The Chrysler key gets me into the van, but when I turn the ignition, nothing happens. Dead battery. I don't feel mad exactly—I knew it was too good to be true.

A flashlight beam bobs in the mystery driver's house. I carefully walk toward his car, my feet kicking up the thin layer of fresh snow in my path and crunching the dead, frozen grass beneath.

How did he not see my car on his way in?

As I scale the mystery driver's house, the faint sound of whistling continues inside. The bobbing of his flashlight stops and a gas lantern comes to life in a back room. I turn to the car—a white sedan—and run. The driver's door is unlocked and the keys are in the ignition. *Thought auto theft was a thing of the past, huh?*

I fire up the sedan, throw it into gear, and step on the gas. I make it to the end of the road and look in the rearview mirror just in time to see the man burst through his front door, clearly perplexed. He doesn't fire a gun, in fact, he's not even holding a gun. His moonlit face looks… disappointed. *You and me both, brother.*

I stop the car briefly in front of my bullet hole-ridden car, take the only intact jerry can from the roof rack, throw it in my trunk, and start toward the interstate.

—

After two hours of driving in a dazed silence, I arrive at the border of the Belt. I pull over at the warning sign—the same warning sign I carelessly blew past twenty-four hours ago—in an attempt to compose myself.

Motherless daughter, daughterless mother, I think, smiling at the sing-songiness of the phrase. I look back at the warning sign and laugh. "How long has it been, sign—oh great prophet of doom?" My voice cracks and my throat closes off in anticipation of tears. I pick up a baseball-sized rock on the side of the road through my tear-filled eyes and heave it at the sign. It makes impact with a clink, leaving a small chip below *RISK.*

I assumed the sign was a formality. Maybe the Feds thought so too. Do they even know how crazy it is out there?

The trip to Denver plays back in my mind. Were we being watched? Breckenridge is a tiny town. Canon City is a tiny town. Florence is an even tinier town. I saw other people in them all. How did we not see any people in Denver? Maybe because we weren't looking for it. I don't know.

I close my eyes and take a deep breath. *What's done is done.* All I can do is accept what has happened and move on. Now I have to face Nova's mother and daughter. There is no one more I want to see than Xandra, but it makes me sick to have to explain that her mother is not coming back. How do I explain that to a four-year-old? I wish I believed in God and angels so I could tell her that Nova was still with us—that she was in a better place. But as much as I try, I still know that I'm alone. We're alone. Nova isn't anywhere. She's just gone.

I get back into the sedan and look at the lights of Raton laid out before me. I'll tell Megan and Xandra then I'll go to the authorities. I know they have all those disclaimers about going into the Wild, but they have to be able to do *something.* I'll tell myself that for now.

I fight through the tears on the last twenty minutes of the drive back home. As I pull onto our street, I'm blinded by the incessant flashing of blue and red police lights.

07

"Please don't be 315. Please don't be 315."

They *are* there for 315—something I somehow already knew.

Let's beat him while he's down.

The closer I get to our garage, the slower time seems to move. An ambulance pulls into the alleyway and weaves its way around the cop cars, its siren sounding underwater.

My brain attempts to figure out what the problem could be on its own, but it's weighed down. Like a dream where you know you should be running but can't.

Please be Meg.

I should feel guilty for wishing harm upon my mother-in-law, but I don't. If it's Meg, it's not Xan. *Unless it's both.*

I park as close as I can get to the scene—our home—three houses down.

A stretcher carried by two medics comes around the corner of our garage. The stretcher is adult sized with a body lying on it. It's Meg. No white sheet. She's alive. *And it's not Xan.*

I feel a flash of relief followed quickly by guilt again. I will have to tell Megan that her daughter is dead while she's in the hospital. But what happened? And where *is* Xan? I catch up to the stretcher as the medics get to the back of the ambulance. "Megan!" I yell over the sirens.

Meg turns toward me, her eyes squinting, wincing in pain. "Leo, my God, they took her," she says. "Jesus Christ, Xandra, my baby. They took—"

I grip the stretcher, preventing the medics from sliding it into the ambulance. Both medics look up at me. "Meg—what happened?"

She closes her eyes and grabs her stomach. She's bleeding through her shirt.

"Meg?"

"She's been shot, sir," the medic says, trying to force the stretcher onto the ambulance. "We have to get her to the hospital. Now."

"Meg, what—"

I feel an arm on my shoulder, I turn around and see a police officer, a woman in her early 40s with bleach blond hair pulled back in a ponytail. "Sir, can I have a word? About your daughter."

I swallow hard and look back at Meg, her eyes closed. "Meg, can you—"

"Sir, listen, I know this is a lot right now, but we have to get her to the hospital right now," the medic says. I release my grip on the stretcher. "We'll be at Lakeview Hospital, okay? Officer—" he glances at the police officers name badge, "—Sabine can help you." He glances at the officer and she nods. They close the doors with a hollow thud.

I blink my eyes in delayed reaction.

A bad dream.

That's all this is.

The ambulance navigates through the police cars then turns its sirens on, speeding around the corner onto 4th Street and out of sight.

My world falls silent.

Shadows created by the sirens bounce around the walls of the townhome alleyway. I watch my breath float through the cold air, diffusing the flashing blue and red in blank amusement.

They'll find her. It just happened. They can find her.

…while he's down…

My mind flashes to the man standing in the doorway of Chrystal Peak Room 522, gun held to his side. *And no more funny business, Leo Kline.*

"Sir," Officer Sabine says.

I turn to her, realizing that she's been trying to get my attention. She guides me inside and we sit down in the living room. The *comfort of your own home* isn't a thing when it's swimming with police officers.

"Sir, your daughter, Xandra… We believe she has been kidnapped. Can I ask you a few questions?"

"Yeah, I mean—no, we should be looking for her."

"Mr. Kline—"

"But are they sure that… She was just with her mother-in-law—my mother-in-law—her grandma. It was just overnight. How did…"

"Mr. Kline—"

"How did they take… Who? Do we know who? Where did they go? Why? What is the motive?" I feel as if I'm watching myself from a distance spew words at the officer. I feel another hand on my shoulder. I look up and see another officer, a bald black man with a thin face and slim build. He sits down next to me.

"Mr. Kline, my name is Officer Cooper. I have two daughters myself and I can't imagine what you must be going through. Is your wife—" He checks his tablet, "Nova with you?"

I look down at the ground. My forehead burns. I haven't even begun to process Nova. Now I have to find Xandra. *Is Megan going to die?*

"Sir?"

"My mother-in-law, Megan—is she gonna be okay?" I ask looking up at Officer Cooper.

He glances at Sabine.

"It's a close call at this point. She lost a lot of blood. They'll have to operate. But we'll get an update in a few minutes," Sabine replies. "She was shot in the stomach by who we believe to be the same people who took your daughter."

Obviously.

"Nova is dead," I say, catching myself off guard.

"Nova is de—" Sabine repeats back, turning suddenly to Cooper. Cooper and Sabine share glances.

"Can you tell us what happened, Mr. Kline?" Sabine says, in her well-rehearsed calm voice.

I try to think through how to best approach communicating the mess of the situation I put us in, but my brain is far too cloudy to come up with a coherent strategy.

"Yes. Yes. We went into the—hold on—what happened to my daughter?" I ask. Cooper steps away, putting his phone to his ear. I notice another officer hovering the living room listening to our conversation. He's tall and lanky. Around my same age, possibly younger.

"Of course," Officer Sabine says. "You have to understand, Mr. Kline, that your mother-in-law had been shot by the time she called us." She shifts in her seat. "She couldn't provide us with as much detail about the kidnapping as we would've liked."

I nod, looking past her to a family portrait on the wall. There's me in that dark gray sweater that Nova always liked but I'm not sure why. I'm also clean-shaven even though it makes me look like a child. Nova, her dark hair flowing down past her shoulders, wearing a short yellow dress and jean jacket. I always loved how she looked in that picture. Her green eyes popping against her olive skin. And that smile. I look at Xandra and feel the tears well up. Her and her little pigtails and blue sundress.

She's so happy in the picture. So full of life. Not a care in the world. As long as she's with us, she's happy. She's grown up so much since that picture was taken. Now she's four. God, we have a four-year-old. I feel the corners of my mouth creep up as I think about that day. No one could get Xandra to keep her hands out of her face. In the picture that worked, her hand is in motion returning to her face, but we got it just in time.

"She's just a baby," I say out loud.

Sabine turns around to see what I'm looking at. "Beautiful family," she says, attempting sincerity.

Then my reality catches up to me. Nova, dead. Xandra, missing. Megan, shot. My world goes from color to black and white, comfortable to cold.

"Xandra could've—I mean—maybe Megan was confused about what happened. Maybe Xandra's still here," I say, standing up and moving toward her room.

Sabine follows me. "We've checked the whole place, Mr. Kline. Officers are speaking with neighbors right now. Multiple witnesses say they saw a red truck speed away from the neighborhood at around the same time Ms. Carlota called us."

I stand in the doorway of Xandra's room, half expecting her to be peacefully sleeping in her bed. She's not.

"Listen, I want you to know that we are doing everything we can to find your daug—" Sabine is interrupted by a flustered Cooper who runs around the corner, phone in hand. The third officer—the younger awkward guy—stands behind him.

"Guys, we gotta go. She's not gonna last long," Cooper says, out of breath.

"Not gonna… Who?" I say.

"Ms. Carlota. We have to go to the hospital," Cooper says,

motioning me out the back door.

"I'll meet you guys over there," the awkward officer says before the door shuts in his face.

I follow them to Cooper's car. He turns the sirens on as we speed around the corner and into Raton's commercial corridor.

"All we know," Sabine begins, turning around to face me, "is that, according to Ms. Carlota, two men broke into the house forcibly, one shot her in the stomach, the other took the girl and they left. Our team is trying to piece together the rest."

"And no one has found the car yet?"

"We're looking," Sabine replies.

"The problem is," Cooper says, then clears his throat. "Well, we just have to hope they didn't cross the border."

"To the Wild?" I ask, feeling a pit in my stomach.

Cooper nods. I can tell Cooper is a straightforward, no-nonsense guy, but he's struggling. "It makes things more complicated."

"How so?" I ask, knowing the answer, but not wanting it to be true.

"Let's see what turns up tonight and then we'll worry about it."

Cooper and Sabine sense my distress, which is probably a lot worse than I realize. *One step at a time*, they must be thinking. Let's deal with the Megan situation, then we can address Xandra and Nova. The rest of the car ride passes by in silence.

As we approach the hospital, I think of what to ask Megan, if she's even alive by the time we get there. What did the men look like? What did they say? Did they take anything else? Oh, by the way, your daughter was murdered a few hours ago.

"You ok back there?" Sabine asks.

"Yeah, I'm fine."

We park the car behind an ambulance outside of the

emergency room entrance and I follow Sabine and Cooper through the automatic doors. Cooper checks his phone outside of the elevators.

"Room 336," he says and pushes the up button.

Once on the third floor, we wrap around a nurses station and down a walkway connecting to another building. We pass an elderly man trying to walk on his own, supporting himself with the railing on his right and IV pole on the left. A nurse follows closely behind him.

Just behind him is a new mom in a wheelchair, holding a newborn baby while her husband pushes her. The parents have a look of tired bliss, staring into the baby's face. The scene plays in slow motion.

"Guys, let's move," Cooper says, looking up from his phone. He and Sabine jog down the hall.

Sabine turns back to me, "Leo, we have to go." I realize that I've stopped in the hallway and am staring at the couple with the baby. Here we are, separate people in the same place, but they are here for life and I'm here for death. They are experiencing abundance and I'm experiencing loss and emptiness. And here we stand, mere feet apart from one another. I snap out of my gaze, realizing I'm probably creeping them out.

"Congratulations on your pregnancy—er—baby," I say. The new parents flash awkward smiles and I run to catch up with the officers.

We turn another corner to the sight of doctors and nurses filtering out of a room down the hall. It's 336. As we approach the room, Cooper stops one of the doctors and whispers something in his ear.

The doctor turns toward me with a defeated expression and motions me forward. "She's lost a lot of blood," he says, flashing a glance at Megan's monitors. "At this point, and with her age, there's not much we can do."

I nod and look past him to the motionless woman on the hospital bed.

"We'll give you a moment," the doctor says, signaling for the remaining nurses to clear the room.

I nod again, my lips pursed, and enter the room.

Megan looks like she's aged a decade, but not in a real way, like a movie-makeup way. Her eyes are closed. I pull a chair next to her bed, the noise of the wooden legs screeching across the ceramic floor prompting her awake. She squints her eyes and turns toward me.

"Leo?"

"It's me. I'm so sorry."

"Leo, it happened so fast," she says. "I should've done something. I should've stopped them."

"No, Meg. There is nothing you could've done."

She widens her eyes and looks past me. "Where's Nova?"

I exhale shakily. I briefly consider making up a story so that Megan's last moments aren't filled with dealing with her daughter's death.

"Nova was killed," I blurt out.

"Oh—oh dear God," she says, looking up at the ceiling. Her shallow breathing turns to sobs. After a minute, she turns back to me, her voice frail. "What hap—did she suffer?"

I'm sure she wants more detail but knows her time is limited. "No," I reply.

Tears stream down her cheeks. "Nova, Mom, Dad, Jesus, I'm coming home," she says. Her face turns serious and she slowly turns toward me again. "Leo, my dear boy," she says, her voice getting quieter. "The men, they had matching tattoos."

My heart sinks. "Nova was murdered by men with tattoos on their faces."

She closes her eyes again, freezing for a moment. I wait for the sound of a flatline, but it doesn't come.

Her eyes ease open. "Leo, come here." She looks past me at the police officers in the doorway then back at me. I lean in. "Listen, there's a lot I haven't told you. There's a lot I haven't told Nova. I can't say it here."

"I don't understand."

"Broncos 24," she whispers. "Broncos 24."

"Meg, no riddles. What are you saying?"

Her eyes move to the police officers, then back to me again. Her face transitions from stern to peaceful. She looks up to the ceiling and closes her eyes for the last time. The heart monitor lets out its dull, monotone signal, and her heartbeat flatlines.

"Oh Meg," I say, placing my hands on hers.

—

I imagine Megan floating to heaven, being greeted by Nova. I imagine them reminiscing about the good old days and conspiring to help me find Xandra. But alas, I believe none of this. What I do believe is that she is now a lifeless corpse. Just like her daughter. Just like my parents. Just like Tripp.

A doctor and two nurses enter the room. The doctor walks over to the monitor. "Megan Carlota. Time of death: 4:03 AM." She turns to me. "I'm sorry for your loss. It's never easy losing your mother." She looks down at her clipboard and exits the room, followed by the two nurses.

"In law," I say to myself.

Officer Sabine comes into the room and puts her hand on

my shoulder. "I'm sorry, Leo," she says. Even though it's her job to be here, I appreciate the gesture.

"Thanks, officer."

"Call me Ari," she says.

I feel another hand on my other shoulder. I look up, expecting Cooper, but see the awkward cop. "Sorry for your loss," he says.

I look at his name badge. "Thank you, Officer Folke."

Following Ari Sabine's lead, he says skittishly, "You can call me Jame."

I can't tell if he said 'Jame,' 'James,' or 'Jane' but I don't care to find out.

Officer Cooper, being a man of great confidence, but not so much in the emotionally-trying, clears his throat. "Officers, let's give Mr. Kline a minute."

Ari and Jame-or-James Folke clear the room.

I lay my head on Megan's hands.

I was in my late 20s when my parents died. Old enough to be self-sufficient, but still far too young to have dead parents. Nova and I were still newlyweds. Nova's dad had been out of the picture for a long time—since she was a kid—but Megan was around. Megan took me in as a son. We joked together. I confided in her. I looked up to her. I was mostly happy to have her live with us Post-Move. I loved her relationship with Xandra. Sure, she was a bit churchy for my taste, but she was wise, mature. Now it's over. *Like a lot of things.*

"What do I do, Meg?" I say. "Where do I get the strength? Where do I get the strength to bring my baby home?"

I envision the same men that killed Nova, taking Xandra. My innocent baby. Picking her up in her sleep, wearing her princess nightgown. She probably fell asleep on his shoulder, thinking it was Meg, or Nova, or me. They took her to their truck and drove away. Into the New Wilderness. Xandra will wake up at some point during that drive. She'll wake up in some nasty truck with two nasty men. Why did they take her? Are they going to kill her? Do they know to feed her? She's going to pee her pants. What happens then? Who will take care of her? No one's going to take care of her. She's on her own. A four-year-old child, on her own.

And no more funny business, Leo Kline.

If the whole thing is orchestrated to get at me or Nova, for some reason, I have to believe that Xandra is alive. She is leverage. I don't know what for, but it's the only thing that makes sense.

I whip my head toward the doorway in a fit of rage. I shove the hospital cart with cold turkey and mashed potatoes. "She's only a child. A child!" I scream, directionless into the room. I stand up without a plan and stomp toward the hallway.

Ari Sabine intercepts me at the doorway. "I know, Leo. I know," she says. "We'll find her."

"What happens—" I pause, waiting for Cooper to come closer. "What happens if they take her into the Wild?"

"It makes things more complicated," Cooper says, repeating his earlier answer.

"More complicated like how—as in it's a hopeless cause? The Wild is lawless, right? So, there's nothing anyone can do?"

"Well—"

"Answer the question," I say, looking at him squarely in his face.

A group of three nurses stops their conversation and looks at me.

Cooper glances at the nurses then back to me. "Why don't we go back to the station and discuss our options?"

I'm mentally directing my anger toward Cooper even

though he doesn't deserve it. A group of nurses walks past us and into Megan's room, preparing for her to be taken away.

I look into the room at Megan's cold body and exhale. "Broncos 24," I whisper to myself. The key to finding my daughter is in a riddle. Not practical information or advice, a riddle. I think about the way she looked at the officers before she said it.

"Let us know when you're ready to go," Ari says.

"I'm ready."

The drive to the police station is short and silent.

A man is paying a utility bill at a self-help kiosk outside the front doors to the station. Two separate people, same time, same place. One is paying a bill, checking an item off his to-do list, the other is trying to muster the will to continue living.

The facility is gaudy, the design having gone through several public charrettes I'm sure. Got to make everyone feel included. And you can't skimp on budget. Of course not. The citizens won't respect the police if they don't have a multi-multimillion-dollar facility. What do we want, a lawless community? I can imagine the closed-door meetings preceding its construction. I hate them. All the people who participated in those meetings. Them sitting around plastic white tables with auras of false importance. Their crappy coffee and legal pads and clicking pens and balding heads. I don't know them, but I hate them. I hate the Feds. I hate everyone who promised us a normal life in the Belt—no, a *better* life in the Belt. *You were naïve to believe it in the first place.*

I follow the officers to a conference room on the second floor and sit down. Officer Folke brings waters for everyone.

Cooper begins. "Mr. Kline, I'm sorry for all you've been through today. We just have to get to the bottom of a few things in order to best help you. What happened to your wife?"

Knowing we have a short window to find Xandra before she could be gone for good, I comply with Cooper, telling him the whole story. About my parents and brother dying in the Big One, about my meeting with the job counselor and taking her words too literally, the day trip to Breckenridge. I told him about our adventure, the snowcats, the hotel.

I told him about the man who broke in and shot Nova, about how he called both of us out by name. I described him, the other men, and their matching attributes—burly, bald, bearded, slash tattoos across their eyes. I told him about the men I killed, about the snowmobile chase. I told him about my stops in Canon City and Florence. How I heard someone else in the town. How I took the car.

"Did you and your wife have any marital issues?"

This is a waste of time.

"No. I mean not outside of normal things. The trip was good for us. For our relationship. We hadn't had a chance to be kids like that in a long time." Even though I expected it, I feel disdain at the line of questioning implying *I* killed Nova.

"You knew you were traveling into an unregulated, lawless territory?"

"Yes," I say, guiltily.

"How do you think this looks, Leo? You take your wife into the New Wilderness fully knowing the risks and she gets killed. Her blood is on *whose* hands?"

"Cooper!" Sabine says, giving him a look.

Mine, I think in my head, but don't say out loud. I'm not of much use finding Xandra if I'm behind bars.

Cooper purses his lips looking from Sabine to me. I put my head down. Half a minute passes by in silence.

"Officer Sabine, can I talk to you?" Cooper asks.

Ari looks at me and then back at Cooper. "Sure."

Folke stands up to follow them out of the room when Cooper puts his hand up. "We'll just be a minute, Officer Folke."

The glass door of the conference room closes behind them and Folke sits across from me, leaning forward. "Leo—er—Mr. Kline, listen, I believe you. Your story isn't as outrageous as you might think it sounds. But you have to know that crimes committed in the New Wilderness cannot be prosecuted in the Belt *unless* the suspect is physically in the Belt."

"Yes, but I didn't do any—"

"I know," Folke says, "but the way Cooper is talking, you are the prime suspect. And you are the *only* suspect here in the Belt. The narrative is easy enough to string together."

"I get what you're saying, but I don't care if they think I murdered my wife." I wince at the phrase *murdered my wife*. "What about Xandra?"

"Well, here's the other thing, and I'm sorry to say this, but they won't do crap about your daughter. If she's in the New Wilderness, it's hands off. Same thing for Megan. If the murderer stayed in the Belt and was found, he'd be prosecuted til kingdom come. But as soon as they can determine that he crossed the border, it's over."

I lean back in my chair. "Do they know there are gangs out there?"

Folke nods his head, looking past me to Cooper and Sabine through the glass conference room wall. "We see lots of crap as a border town, believe me. Folks disappear, people are taken, people are murdered, criminals flee to the Wild. It doesn't happen enough to where its widely covered, but it happens enough to freak us out as a law enforcement agency. The bigger problem is that we get no support on the Federal level. It's like the denial runs straight to the top. They don't want to admit that their big Move plan was anything but completely successful."

I feel weak, like I might pass out even sitting in this chair. *I need to get out of here.*

"I'm not saying these kinks won't get worked out eventually, but right now it is a mess," he says.

"So why are you telling me all this?"

He leans in. "If there's any chance of finding your daughter, you have to do it yourself."

"You mean I—"

"You have to leave the Belt behind and go."

"There's no way I'll be effective on my own," I say. *I need to sleep,* I think, my head feeling heavier by the minute.

"Well as much as I'd like to help, and as wrong as I think it is, the Raton Police Force is only going to do you harm. Not only will they not help you find your daughter, but they'll probably nail you with homicide. Then you're of no help to anyone."

I slowly turn around to get a look at Cooper and Sabine. The conversation is tense. I don't know what they're saying, but Cooper is on the offense. He wants results. He wants—needs—a win. And he sees me as an opportunity for that win. Folke is right, my time as a free man in Raton is short. I can feel it.

I lean in. "How do I get out of here?"

"Follow my lead."

I follow him out the door. Cooper looks to Folke, his eyebrows raised.

"Mr. Kline needs to use the facilities," Folke announces.

"Go with him," Cooper barks.

We walk in silence down the hall to the bathrooms. The hallway has a series of glass meeting rooms on the right and a sterile wall with the occasional historic photo on the left. I think for a moment about Ari Sabine and a longing grows in my chest—a longing for my mom, for Megan. Everything slows down, I hear my heels brushing the thin industrial carpet with each step, I hear the clank of Folke's radio and handcuffs tapping together, I hear the distant voices of Sabine and Cooper behind me. I look at my watch. 5:00 AM is a slow hour in the station.

Once we are safely around the corner and out of the officers' line of sight, Jame turns around, looking me square in the face. "My advice is to get in your car and get the hell out of here as quickly as possible. As soon as you cross that border, you are safe." He second guesses himself and rocks forward on his toes. "From the police, anyway. Whatever happens, don't plan on coming back for a while, okay?"

I nod, eyeing the exit sign at the end of the hall. "Why are you helping me?"

"Cause the situation is crap and I can tell you're a good guy. I wish I could come help you but—"

"I really appreciate it, Officer Folke."

"Call me Jame," he says. His name is definitely Jame with no 's.'

I give him a half-smile and walk toward the exit.

"Oh, by the way," Jame adds, "The gang out there—they call themselves *the Reds.*"

PART TWO
THE WILD

08

Six Months Later

The Reds have been on my tail since Elko, maybe before that.

I'm driving ninety miles per hour on I-80, in search of SR-427. My eyes dart between the rearview mirror, the road ahead, and the tattered sticky note in my lap.

456 4th st empire nv

The headlights in my rearview mirror have been reduced to two, the other cars having abandoned the chase a few miles back. I maintain a comfortable lead ahead of my lone follower.

As I stare at those headlights, they narrow for a moment, becoming snowmobile headlights. The desert landscape all around me becomes covered in a blanket of thick rocky mountain snow. For a moment, I'm not fleeing the Reds for the hundredth time, I'm in Breckenridge being chased for the first time, Nova's blood drying on my hands. I glance at the family picture taped on my dash, illuminated by the glow of the dashboard controls.

Hands out of the face, Xan!

The loud whining of my tires making contact with the rumble strip on the side of the road snaps me out of my daydream. A sign announces the exit for SR-427 in one mile. The brief curvature of the freakishly straight highway allows me enough time to exit the freeway and park under the overpass unnoticed. I climb out of the car and lay down in the brush, listening closely. Through the loud—almost deafening—syncopated chirps of the crickets and the gently rustling desert brush, I hear the buzz of the F-150 approach.

Predictably, they are both big, burly, and bearded, with slash tattoos on their faces.

I smile.

I aim my rifle at the driver's side of the car, but don't pull the trigger. Believe me, I'd love to, but I'm smarter than that. I'd love nothing more than to shoot the driver in the throat, spurting blood all over the cabin. I want the truck to veer off into the desert, roll a couple times, and eject both their bodies through the windshield. I don't want them to die instantly though, I want to be there—to be as close to them as possible—for when they suck in their final breaths.

But alas, I watch them roll by and don't pull the trigger.

I've learned a few things in the six months I've been wandering the Wild. I've learned to be cautious. And patient. Sure, most days I'm hopeless, but now that I have this note in my hand, I feel—could it be—hope. Hope that Xandra is out there. The note isn't much, and my interaction with the man who gave it to me wasn't much either, so my hope might be farfetched, but it's something.

I watch the red taillights fade from view. They'll be back this way once they realize they aren't following me anymore. In the meantime, I hop back in my Charger, kill the lights, and coast to the Walmart down the road.

Its parking lot is a sea of graying asphalt with cracks snaking in every direction. Weeds and plants grow out of the cracks like fingers from hell trying to claim the lot for itself. The moonlit building itself doesn't look *too* bad, just neglected. I find it ironic that big box stores—the antithesis of suburban sprawl—almost have more character abandoned than they did occupied.

I drive around the back of the building, park in the

subgrade loading dock, and step out, rifle hanging from my shoulder. The door next to the loading docks is locked. I walk around to the front of the store facing I-80 and climb in through the frame of one of the automatic doors, its glass piled at my feet.

As I step inside, breathing in the stale, musty air, I hear the roar of the F-150 heading back my direction. I turn toward the road and steady my rifle. My finger trembles on the trigger as the truck's headlights come into view. A part of me revels in their failure—they've lost me, and they'll have to answer to someone about that, but that's not enough. I want them dead—to suffer and then to die.

I close my eyes and take a deep breath in. *Stay collected.*

Hold...1...2...3...4...5...

The sound of the F-150 continues to fade.

Exhale...1...2...3...4...5...

My flashlight's beam cuts through the dusty air. I pick up a can of Coke lying on the floor next to a looted vending machine, give it a shake and throw it as far as I can into the middle of the store. It crashes down and fizzes loudly. I ease toward the entrance of the store, my back against the wall, listening for any movement.

Silence.

The further I get into the store, the stronger the mold permeates the air. About half of the store's shelves are intact, the rest are either gone or in piles throughout the main floorspace. Inventory is mostly cleared out, but with enough left that I'm anticipating a relatively successful shopping trip. I grab a shopping cart and head to the coffee section.

I fantasize about the day I can make regular coffee again— the ritual of grinding the beans, brewing in the French Press, the aroma filling the house. *Dad, you're making boffee?* A word that Nova or I didn't bother correcting—boffee—because it was too cute. Our hearts broke when she said it correctly around age three. I'm missing out on a lot of little things like that as Xandra grows up. It's been only six months, but six months is an eternity for a four-year-old.

Stop.

These are the thoughts I have to be careful with. The ones that drive me into a downward spiral of guilt—of regret. I turn my attention back to the present.

The steady sound of water trickling draws my attention. My flashlight finds a large puddle—pond—in the middle of the store, the water coming from a massive hole in the ceiling encircled by spreading black mold. I slosh through the puddle to the coffee section, where I find two 4-packs of bottled lattes near the back of the top shelf. Continuing through the store, I manage to collect almonds, sardines, some canned veggies and bottled water. I pause for a moment and rest my head on the shopping cart.

I need sleep.

I don't sleep much in the Wild. I can't. It's not uncommon for my sleep to be interrupted by the glass shattering, gunshots in the distance, engines revving. If there's one thing I have to my advantage, it's that the Reds are freaking loud wherever they go. If they had one stealthy bone in their bodies, I'd likely be dead by now. But that's not the real reason I can't sleep. It's the scene of that night playing repeatedly in my head every time I try to relax. Suite overlooking the ski lift. The complete silence of the abandoned Rocky Mountains. Her laughter… Her smile… *I have to stay focused…* Megan's dying face clouds my vision. *They took her.*

They.

Took.

Her.

As I make my way to the loading docks, I throw a few last-minute items in the cart, including a flyer advertising tours at the Empire Gypsum mine. I load the groceries into my trunk, taking a coffee with me to the front. I slap myself in the face and look at the bottled latte in my hand. Mocha flavored. I always check the flavor even though they all taste the same. I drive around the store to the main road and get on SR-427 toward Empire.

My watch says it's 1:13 AM.

—

Earlier that day, after waking up from a restless-but-otherwise-uneventful night in the abandoned Owl Motel in Battle Mountain, I heard the familiar roar of motorcycles infiltrating the town. When I exited the hotel and turned the corner, the man with the note was standing there, leaning against the wall like he was expecting me. Out of instinct, I jumped back around the corner and pulled the .22 out of my jacket. I peered around the corner and found him with his hands up.

The man was clean-shaven with curly hair pulled back into a bun. He was my height and build—my senior by five years I'd guess. He had a silver septum nose ring and, most importantly, was *not* a Red. I knew it instantly. Yes, because of his appearance, but also because he didn't shoot me at first glance.

"I come in peace," he said, smiling. He was calm despite the approaching motorcycles. "We can help you, Leo. We're the—"

Gunshots littered the building behind us, raining glass down on us. He handed me the note.

"What is this?"

"I'll meet you there. Just go!"

We went our separate ways and I booked it out of Battle Mountain. Just like that, I had my first non-Red interaction—intentional interaction—since leaving the Belt six months ago.

During my time in the Wild, I've driven a lot. And I've been driven *out* a lot. I left the Belt and went straight for the Pacific Coast working South to North, West to East, in an attempt to cover as much ground as possible. I've learned that any decently-sized city is pretty well controlled by the Reds whereas Rural America is more free-for-all. That's where I spend most of my time, although I have yet to see *any* women or children anywhere.

I know little about the Reds, but I do know that they are trying to take over the Wild and will kill anyone in their way. I don't know why, and I still don't know where they came from or who is behind the whole thing. Oh, and one other thing, a lot of them know who I am and want me dead.

The concept I keep coming back to—the one that keeps me going—is *leverage*. Kidnapping Xandra was leverage to them. Someway, somehow. They killed Megan. They killed Nova, although they were trying to kill me, yet they *kidnapped* Xan.

I'm trying to dampen my expectations, but Empire could be my big break. *We can help you, Leo.*

I take another sip of my latte and roll down the window. I pass a sign that says EMPIRE 30. I look at the picture of Xandra doing her signature tongue-to-the-side silly face taped next to the speedometer.

—

After an hour of driving on this incredibly straight and lifeless desert road, I reach an EMPIRE NEXT LEFT sign. I slow down and turn off the highway onto a straight, narrow road bordered by dead desert trees. As the road curves west into town, I pass a sign for the Gypsum mine.

Slowing to a stop, I turn on the cabin light and scan the flyer I took from Walmart. The mine and accompanying town were built by the United States Gypsum Corporation in the 1920s… The town was abandoned when the mine closed in the early 2010s… The town and mine were then bought in the late 2010s by Nevada Mining Company who restored part of the town and mine… They went belly-up shortly thereafter… Apparently, they did mine tours for a while.

The moonlit town looks as dead as dead towns get. The main road is gravel, having been paved asphalt in a former life. Vegetation grows from every possible crevice in what's left of sidewalks, roads, and building foundations. The manufactured housing is long dilapidated, metal skirts rusted, paint faded, windows broken.

I continue into town, note clenched in my hand.

456 4th st empire nv

C Street takes me past two rows of manufactured ramblers, a post office, a community pool, and a Christian church. I turn onto 4th Street and slow down further. As far as I can tell, the whole town is lifeless. Shouldn't at least the man from Battle Mountain be here? We would've left at the same time, unless—

456. I've arrived.

The beige rambler has a single car garage on the left and a small sheltered patio in front. The roof is a rusted metal. Two of the front windows are broken—the true sign of abandonment, or staged abandonment. No cars, no lights, no sign of recent human activity at all.

I park in front of the garage, walk to the front door and knock. Nothing.

My watch reads 2:32 AM.

The door is locked.

The door on the side of the garage is also locked, but the door hardware is badly rusted, so I break in with relative ease. The scent of stale, musty air tinged with gasoline hits my face. I turn my head, taking one more deep breath from the sweet desert air, ignite my flashlight, and step inside the garage. Its single car slot is empty but neat. I twist the knob of the door leading to the house and push it open. The door doesn't even creak.

"Hello?" I call into the dark house.

Silence.

My flashlight flickers then dims. *Great.*

I pan around the main room of the house with what's left of my light. The room is modestly furnished with a couch, loveseat, empty entertainment center, and some pictures hanging from the walls. A desk with an old computer monitor sits in the corner.

My light flickers again then dies.

I take a deep breath in and exhale, inadvertently closing my eyes.

God, I need to sleep.

I stumble back through the garage in the dark and eventually find the manual pull for the garage. I park the car in the garage and unload the bare necessities into the house, the linoleum kitchen floor creaking beneath my feet.

Home.

For tonight, anyway.

"Anyone in here?" I call out one more time.

Still silent.

I lie down on the living room couch, kick my shoes off, and pull the blanket over me. I don't know what I was expecting, but as of now, this house is just another abandoned structure like everything else in the Wild. As I close my eyes, a familiar dialogue picks up in my head. I'm no psychologist, but I've learned that my post-traumatic psyche generally consists of three players—the Nihilist, the Buddhist, and the Fighter. They come out to play most nights when I'm trying to fall asleep. The more I need sleep, the more likely they are to appear it seems.

The Nihilist thinks I should give up. It has daily existential crises, constantly questioning the point of it all—the search for Xan, life, everything. It wants me to turn around and go back to the Belt, killing as many Reds as possible on the way, and live a boring, routine life with no love, no passion, no family. Prison or free man, it doesn't care. Either that or kill myself.

The Buddhist views all life with value. Even the Reds. *Everything is neutral.* It wants me to be mindful—to listen to my breath, to be aware of my surroundings. It sees life as a game of Tetris—the pieces are always falling; my goal is to make the best of it. The Buddhist looks at the Nihilist in me and doesn't reject him, he welcomes him. The Buddhist believes that we should keep the Nihilist on the team if we keep him in check. The Buddhist keeps me composed. It's my center.

Lastly, there's the Fighter. The Fighter is fuel. The Fighter will find Xan and avenge Nova's death or die trying. During my time in the New Wilderness, I've learned to keep a leash on the Fighter. I've learned that moves made out of pure passion aren't necessarily the smartest. That's where I rely on the Buddhist to slow things down for me and allow me to calculate.

Of course, the Fighter and the Buddhist are often at odds with each other. Where the Buddhist wants me to let go of all attachments, which would include getting Xandra back, the Fighter relies on those attachments to fan the flame. I figure, as long as I can play on the strengths of the Fighter and Buddhist and keep the Nihilist in check, I will survive.

If I was a Red, trying to capture someone like me, someone who is obviously good at not getting captured, wouldn't I devise a trick like this? *Yeah, we've got a whole team of people that want to help you get your daughter back, just go to this abandoned house in the middle of this tiny town in the middle of nowhere…*

Maybe it is a trap, but I don't care at this point, I just need to sleep.

An image of Xandra crying fills my head. We were on Pier 39 in San Francisco. She had just discovered independence, occasionally running off on her own just because she could. We were in the arcade and she climbed in the Jurassic Park interactive game. She loved that thing—I couldn't get her to come out.

"I'm gonna count to five then I'm leaving, Xan." She pretended to ignore me. "One…two…three…four…five… Ok time to go." She continued to ignore me. "I'm leaving."

I waved goodbye and stepped around the corner, close enough that I could see her if she moved, but out of her sight. After thirty seconds or so, I peeked around the corner to find her still sitting in the game, her hands covering her face, crying. But I did nothing. I just sat there and watched her cry. I was being a *consistent* parent. *That's why you listen, Xan.*

I would do anything to go back in time and just hold her. Or not leave her in the first place.

My heartbeat is through the roof. I can't be thinking about this now. Right now, I need sleep. Everything will make sense in the morning. Wishful thinking, I know.

Deep breath in…1…2…3…4…5… "This…"

Hold…1…2…3…4…5…

Release…1…2…3…4…5…"too…shall…pass…"

At around 3:10 in the morning, I fall asleep.

—

Shortly after 5:00 AM, the room lights up.

I jolt awake, rolling off the couch into a drunken crouch.

What. The. Hell.

I come to my feet and scan the room for the source of the light. It's not coming from headlights outside—that's a good thing. It's coming from the old computer monitor sitting on a desk in the corner.

A gentle whirring fills the room.

I cautiously approach the monitor, it's screen blank white and penetratingly bright.

Electricity? From where?

An old office chair lays next to the desk, knocked over. I position it upright and sit down. The whirring grows louder and louder until the whole machine flickers rapidly then shuts off. Silence. Black screen.

The room returns to its natural state—pitch black, silent.

In the silence, I realize how hard my heart is beating.

Then without warning, it comes back to life with a single word on the screen, accompanied by a loud robotic voice over the speakers.

RIPENESS

Then black again.

Another minute goes by with me sitting in shock, trying to decide if I'm hallucinating. My flurry of thoughts gets interrupted by the loud voice and bright screen again. Same word, but this time repeated three times in rapid succession.

RIPENESS

Black screen.

RIPENESS

Black screen.

RIPENESS |

The word lingers on the screen for a few seconds, this time with a blinking cursor, as if it's waiting for a response. I look around the desk and find the keyboard laying on the floor still plugged in. I take a deep breath, then hit a random key with my trembling finger. The cursor stops blinking for a second in consideration, then the machine dies—this time for good.

My watch reads 5:11 AM.

After another minute in dark silence, I flip the light switch next to the kitchen opening. Despite my pessimism, the living room lights up. Since power grids were decommissioned in the Wild, the only homes with electricity are those that are energy independent, and at least somewhat maintained.

I stay seated at the desk another twenty minutes, repeatedly pushing the power button on the CPU to no avail. Must be on lockdown. Someone is trying to contact someone. Someone, someone. Me?

Morning twilight fades in, allowing me a better look at the room. The couch I slept on sits in the middle of the living room, facing a lonely low-profile Cherrywood entertainment center against the wall. There is a collage of family photos scattered across one of the walls. The pictures tell a familiar story. Two parents, three kids. A portrait shows the family of five in front of a house in what I'm guessing is Reno or Elko. The family was young. Bright future ahead.

It looks like the family moved here in the 1960s. The father worked at the mine. The kids went to the company-owned school. The mom stayed home with the kids and had a tight posse of other housewives in Empire. There's a picture of the mom and four other women with glasses of wine taken here on the front porch.

Two of the kids graduated from the University of Nevada, the other from UNLV. All three moved away after college and started families of their own. Two to Las Vegas. One to New York City. I imagine how they describe Empire to their metropolitan friends—tiny, old town, nothing to do. Grateful for their upbringing, sure, but more grateful they high-tailed the hell out of there after high school.

Another portrait shows the elderly couple with a small dog on their front lawn—apparently the last photo taken from the collage.

I find myself locked in a gaze, staring at the picture of the son with his wife and young daughter while I replay the events from the last 24 hours over in my head. The man in Battle Mountain. *I'll meet you there.* This tiny little town. This house. The computer. Ripeness.

Ripeness.

There is a small filing cabinet attached to the desk housing the still-black computer screen. I open it up to a series of folders—taxes, coupons, a folder with pictures of Stevie, their dog. Finally, a folder called "Heartland RIP." I pull it out. The folder contains a collection of articles, some printed, some cut from magazines and newspapers, all related to the decline of Rural America. I pull one of them out and set it on the desk in front of me.

RURAL AMERICA'S LAST GENERATION

EAST LIVERPOOL, OH—A bookshop, a neighborhood market, an ice cream shop shaded by tall trees, American Flags hanging from buildings, families, and folks of all ages greeting each other, kids on bikes racing up and down the streets.

This picturesque scene is the small-town America that most of us know. But, after a new report by the Federal Reserve Bank of St. Louis, the scene becomes tainted.

Advances in technology, shifting demographics, and an increasingly global economy are some of the factors that make many Rural American economies unsustainable in the long-term, according to the new report, leaving many asking the question, "what next for the Heartland?"...

The issue was so simple at one point, when it was all speculative. The big-picture problems of these rural towns had been apparent for a long time. The impending death of Rural America was clear. What wasn't clear was *how* it would happen and *how long* it would take. First came the loss of primary jobs: Mining and drilling towns saw resources dry up and farming towns saw workers replaced with machines. Then came the 'help'—expensive government subsidies and incentives that did nothing but prolong the problem. Then we heard the death rattle—drug overdoses, suicides, teen pregnancy, poverty.

The public perception of Rural America's decline was

noble at first—*we can't let the heartland die!* When it became clear that Rural America was beyond saving, public perception turned sinister—*Stop wasting our tax dollars trying to save something that's beyond saving!*

Daylight spilling through the bedroom doors down the hall reflects off the black computer screen.

I walk cautiously down the hallway toward the bedrooms. The first door on the right opens up to a small office. One of its walls is covered floor to ceiling in cluttered bookshelves. There is a large empty desk in the middle of the room with four chairs around it and a locked filing cabinet attached. A large medieval-era painting hangs from the wall opposite the bookshelves.

The painting depicts an old bearded man in robes sitting on the ground next to a mound of rocks. His arms are thrown up in the air cursing God. A smattering of dead trees populates the background. The sky looks mean, like a storm is brewing. Next to the old man is a goofy looking, jester-like figure lying on the ground, perched up on his elbows watching the distressed old man with amusement.

I pull a loose paper from the shelf and unfold it, revealing a large map of the continental United States, pre-Move. The map is littered with little red slashes covering a majority of listed cities. As I look closer at *which* cities have red slashes, it dawns on me. A Red territory map.

I sit back in my chair and interlace my fingers behind my head. I am up against an enemy much bigger than I ever could have imagined.

The red slashes are most dense in Zone 1, the Eastern Time Zone, which is to be expected because of its higher population density, and because it has been abandoned the longest. *But, God, almost every single city is covered.* Zone 2, the

Central Time Zone, is almost as Red-controlled but with a few more bald patches. In Zone 3, the Mountain Time Zone, major cities and suburbs are conquered, but smaller towns, not so much. Zone 4, the Pacific Time Zone, which has only been abandoned for about eight months, is relatively open. And I thought the last six months were rough.

Who created this map and where did they get their information?

I lose track of time studying the map, tracing my finger along the Zone 3 and 4 roads I've explored during the past six months.

My mind flashes back to the man in Battle Mountain. I wonder if a nose ring like that ever gets infected. Also, shouldn't he be here by now?

I thumb through the rest of the bookshelves hoping to find more maps, but don't. The filing cabinet attached to the table is locked. I look back at the thousands upon thousands of pages, of stories, of *secrets,* resting on those bookshelves.

Thousands of secrets—

I tread the worn brown carpet back into the hallway.

The first room at the end of the hall is bare-walled with two twin mattresses on the ground. The beds are accompanied by two carry-on suitcases, reading lights, and stacks of books. I pull the top three books off one of the stacks: *Tal-Botvinnik 1960* by Mikhail Tal—a book about chess, *Total Diplomacy: The Art of Winning Risk* by Ehsan Honary, and *The Art of War* by Sun Tzu. Beneath the books is a printed white paper from MIT—*The Strategy of Risk.*

His clothes are all size small—neutral-colored button-down shirts, jeans, black socks. I find an ID for Adam Katz from New York, New York in the side pocket of his suitcase. The picture shows a thin geeky-looking man with curly hair, a big nose, and wire-rim glasses.

The suitcase next to the second bed yields a gym membership for a Christian Obi. There are no books by his bed, but there is a yellow legal pad. I pick it up and flip through the worn pages, filled edge-to-edge with tiny, indecipherable black scribbles.

Reds are brutal guys—burly, bearded, inked and dumb as hell. Based on those eerily consistent criteria and my brief view into Adam Katz and Christian Obi's lives, they are not Reds. Not a breed I'm familiar with, anyway.

Educated people who know me by name, semi-working connected computer, books, maps, electricity. *What are you, Empire?*

The second bedroom is in a similar condition to the first, but with some hippie twists. Instead of a mattress on the ground, there is a hammock bolted to the walls. Instead of a lamp, there is a box with incense. There is also a copy of *Letters from a Stoic* by Seneca and *Siddhartha* by Herman Hesse on the floor. I awkwardly dig through the duffle bag of women's clothes and find a prescription bottle for Cherry Sakda from St. Louis.

Team Empire consists of Adam Katz, the strategist; Christian Obi, the big picture guy; and Cherry Sakda, the pacifist. So, what are they doing—or what *were* they doing—in Empire and where are they now? And what about the nose ring guy from Battle Mountain?

I pick up *Siddhartha* and climb into Cherry's hammock, drifting to sleep after a few minutes.

—

On my way back to the living room, I take a peek (and a leak) in the bathroom. The home is on a septic sewage system, which appears to have been maintained. I shoot a glance in the mirror on my way out. I look tired. And old—too old for the ripe age of 32. I sit down on the couch in the living room and look up at the digital clock on the wall. 3:12 PM. A wave of relief washes over me. Even though I know little, I'm not alone. There *are* others out here.

I open the front door of the house and step outside into the dry desert heat. I cross the yellow, crunchy front lawn to the loose asphalt that makes up 4th Street. If I walk across the street between the houses, I can see the approaching highway from the south. If I place two mirrors just right—one in my yard, one in the yard across the street—I could rig a makeshift security system. The mirror across the street could pick up a vast stretch of highway heading into town, sending its feed to the mirror in my yard, through the front window and onto the wall of the living room. It's not a perfect system, but if a car is heading down that stretch toward Empire, it will inevitably give off a glare, which will bounce around the mirrors and end up on my living room wall. During the night, it would pick up headlights.

I stop in the middle of the street on my way back to the house, close my eyes, take a deep breath in, and hold it.

My mind goes back to a time when Empire was thriving. I imagine the excitement of new families moving into town, eager to meet other families—moms excited to meet other moms, kids excited to meet new friends, dads eager to start work in the new mine, and hoping this tiny town will feel home enough for their families.

I imagine a tight-knit community—playdates at the community pool, church on Sundays, barbeques in the evening. Everyone in town knows each other—watches out for each other.

Inhale...

I imagine the day the mine shuts down. Kids crying about losing their friends. Moms crying about losing their little community they've grown to love. Dads stressed about finding new work, about starting over somewhere else.

Hold...

The hot sun on my skin gets blown away by a gentle breeze. A rumble in my stomach reminds me I haven't eaten yet today.

Exhale...

I open my eyes and turn toward home when something catches my eye.

Any calming effect my meditation may have had vanishes. My heart pounds. Something—or someone—is standing in the window of the house at the end of the street.

Instinctually, I crouch down and run around the corner of the house closest. I look down 4th Street to my house. I'm still a couple hundred feet away. I check my surroundings again and slowly peer my head around the corner to get a better look. It's still there—the thing in the window. I see no movement, so I walk toward it, my gaze frozen.

As I peer closer, the shape becomes undeniably human. I continue. *Go get your gun, you idiot.* Whoever is standing in the window would be able to see me by now. And if it's a Red, I'm pretty sure I'd be dead by now. I inch closer.

I get to the house's front lawn and hold my hand up, letting the person know that I come in peace. No reaction. I take a couple more steps forward and figure out why. My new-found neighbor is a lifeless body hanging from the ceiling.

My knees get weak. My breath grows shallow. I lean against the house and put my head down. I've seen a lot of death in the Wild, but it's never easy, especially suicide. I turn around and press my face to the glass. It's a large man in his 40s or 50s, his face purple and bloated, his eyes black, flies swarming. He's been dead less than two months.

I focus on his face to see if he could be Adam Katz or Christian Obi. I look closer at his swollen eyes, specifically his left eye. His eye is not black, it's tattooed. A Red.

The Nihilist and Fighter inside me agree to share a moment of pure joy—pure revenge—together, staring at the lifeless Red hanging from the ceiling. The Buddhist patiently waits for them to finish.

Rot in hell.

I walk hastily back to 456, my mind racing. Who murdered the Red? Adam or Christian or Cherry? Was it meant to be a sign? A threat?

The Buddhist takes brief control over my mind. A life is a life—everyone has a story. Everyone does have a story, the Fighter interjects, and mine is that a Red—just like our hanging friend in the window—killed my wife and kidnapped my daughter. *Death is all they deserve.*

My thoughts are not me, I remind myself.

Clouds passing by.

My thoughts are nothing but clouds passing by.

I return to 456 and retrieve the mirror from the bathroom. With a little effort, I pry it off the wall with a crack. I carry the mirror to the front yard and step on it, slowly applying pressure until it snaps into two large pieces. Shuffling back and forth between my yard, the neighbor's yard, and the living room, I eventually get the alignment just right. I position the couch so I can keep an eye on the mirror's glare and the computer monitor simultaneously. After a minute on the couch, my stomach creaks. I retrieve almonds, sardines, and bottled coffee from the Charger and return to the couch. I eat in silence, my eyes moving between the wall and the computer.

After eating, I lie down and fall asleep.

—

RIPENESS

I'm awoken suddenly, my heart starting its familiar pounding. The word is displayed on the screen accompanied by its loud monotone announcement. I glance at the digital clock on the wall. 5:02 PM.

The message repeats like it did this morning.

RIPENESS

Black.

RIPENESS

Black.

RIPENESS |

The cursor blinks, giving me a chance to respond. No better place to start than the top, I suppose. I type *A* and the computer immediately shuts down. I click the power button repeatedly. Nothing. I pull a sticky note from a pad laying on the side of the desk. I write the alphabet on it, A-Z then numbers 0-9, and put a big *X* over the *A*. I suppose I'll try *B* at 5 AM. God, *that's* an efficient system. What do I do after I get the first letter right? Start at the top again?

I wander back to the library and scan the bookshelves carefully. The titles paint a broad picture of a Pre-Move world becoming a Post-Move world—books on climate change, politics, economics, religion, and a good variety of fiction. There's the *Move to the Belt* government-issued pamphlet and instruction manual next to a thicker *Move to the Belt: A Public Official's Guide*. The guides aren't new to me, even though the latter is technically for elected officials' eyes only—nothing a little five-minute treasure hunt on the internet can't turn up. The bottom shelf is home to the classics—*The Complete Works of Shakespeare, H.P. Lovecraft: The Complete Fiction, The Edgar Allen Poe Collection*.

I breathe in the smell of the books. *Home.*

I face the painting on the wall. The fear in the old man's eyes. The pleading. The frustration. The hopelessness. The jester character and his carelessness. Usually in old age, one grows wise, gawking at the stresses of youth—that at some point, it's all out of our hands anyway, so might as well enjoy what you have now while you still have it. Here, however, it's the old man who's a mess and the young guy who's at ease—entertained by the old man's strife.

I turn back to the books.

Thousands of secrets.

I resume searching the bookshelf for notes left between pages, a key for the filing cabinet, or any more clues that will shed light on the mysterious Empire.

After a while of fruitless searching, I go to the garage for a bottled latte. As I ascend the three stairs back into the house,

I stumble on the top step, sending the latte crashing on the linoleum kitchen floor. The brown liquid shoots in every direction, dripping down the cabinets, the oven, and leaving a trail all the way to the dining area. *Smooth move, Leo.*

I find a couple of small dish rags underneath the sink and start wiping down cabinets. As the mess settles, I notice the liquid draining toward the fridge. I step around the broken glass and inch it away from the wall revealing a slit in the floor. I keep shimmying the fridge from the wall until the slit turns into a square.

A trapdoor.

A portal to hell.

I lift the heavy platform door using the thumb pull and am hit in the face with a horrible stench.

The smell of rotting flesh.

Then lights out.

"You sure we need all this crap? You don't want to just start over?" I yell into the house from the front porch, staring into our packed U-Haul.

"Very funny," Nova shouts back from the kitchen.

Xandra runs past me with her toy dinosaur, bobbing it up and down through the air like it's an airplane. She's wearing her dirty blond hair in a braided bun courtesy of Nova, jean overalls, and a striped pink shirt underneath. Her little gold boots flutter down the wood steps and onto the concrete path from our porch to the yard.

"What do you think, Xan? Should we be bringing this much stuff?" I ask.

"Yep!" she responds, continuing outside. A week ago, she would've responded 'yeah'—now everything is 'yep.'

"See!" Nova says, joining me on the front porch. "We already got rid of tons of crap," she says. "You acknowledge that, right?"

"I know, I know. It just feels like *so* much when it's all piled together like this."

"Hey, I'm with ya. We just kinda need stuff to live normal lives."

"Normal *American* lives."

She lets out an extended exhale, looking out at the front yard.

"I'm gonna miss these trees," she says.

A moment passes in silence, both of us admiring the towering pines.

She turns to me again, her voice a whisper. "This is crazy, right? I mean, the whole Move. It feels so real now." She looks back out at Xan on the sidewalk. "Breck is a ghost town right now. To think that everyone is gone or leaving. That all these houses are just going to rot up here."

"Kinda feels like a dream."

"Ok, I have a question for you," she says. "We've become so accustomed to expecting life to play out one way according to some set of rules. But those rules can change at any time. Think about money. Money isn't backed by anything but the 'full faith and credit' of the United States. It's a collective story that we've all bought into. At any time, the people, or the majority of people, could decide collectively that they don't believe that story anymore. Then, just like that, money has no value. Same thing with the concept of 'home.' What is home? Is the concept of having a home, a refuge, a place to reset—is that a universal principle? Or is it just a story we've all bought into?"

"I think home is what you make it. For some, home is a physical structure. For others, it's the people you're with. For others, it's your breath. It's you. If I were a perfect Buddhist, that's what I'd say."

Xandra runs up to us on the porch, her little chin quivering beneath glossy blue eyes. The look that breaks my heart. The look that triggers my parental instincts—*if anyone hurt you, I will kill them.*

"Mommy, Daddy, the butterfly is hurt," she says, holding a yellow and black butterfly for us to see. One of its wings lays motionless, the other fluttering furiously against her palm. "Can you help?"

Nova and I look at each other, pursing our lips at the same time.

"You know what, sweetheart?" Nova begins, crouching down to her level. "Daddy will take it to the bug doctor in the backyard so it can rest for a while and recover."

"What's 'recover'?" Xandra asks, returning her gaze to the dying insect.

"It means 'get better'," I say.

"Ok," Xandra concedes, handing the butterfly to me. Just then, I realize she's not wearing her overalls anymore. She's wearing her princess nightgown. *Isn't it a bit cold to be wearing a nightgown?*

I get down on my knee and place my hands gently underneath Xandra's. "I'm sorry you got hurt, Mr. Butterfly," I say. "I'll take you to the doctor now."

Nova gives her a hug.

"Ok, you guys stay here. I'll be right back," I say.

Nova and I exchange smiles while she holds Xandra.

I set the butterfly down in the backyard and look up. Man, I *am* going to miss these trees. And we're moving to Raton—the desert. We might not see trees like this ever again.

The empty house feels smaller—and colder—like this.

As I approach the front door, I see Nova's figure through the frosted glass facing me. I open the door to Nova staring at me with a crooked smile, her face flush in dark red blood oozing from a bullet hole above her right eye. Blood puddles at her feet.

I watch the scene unfold not as myself, but as a spectator. "Nova, what happened?" I ask. I glance past her and see Xandra crouched down, sorting rocks on the walkway.

"Xandra, baby, what happened to mommy?" I ask. She continues to play, unfazed by my question, unfazed by her bloodied mother.

I look back at Nova. Her face has changed. The bullet hole is gone. The river of blood pouring down her face is gone, but the puddle at her feet keeps growing. She looks older, her green eyes sunk, her cheeks drooping, her jaw bone accentuated by tightening skin. Her hair changes from rich brown to white before my eyes. Her expression turns concerned. Or horrified.

"They took her!" She cries, staring *through* me.

It's not Nova anymore. It's Megan.

"Meg, Xandra is right ther—"

"They took her!" She repeats, ignoring me.

I look back at Xandra. A man—a Red—slowly walks up behind her. He's a thick build, his face covered by a scraggly beard. A slightly-faded slash tattoo covers his left eye. His eyes are dark and bloodshot like he hasn't slept in months. Or years. He looks demonic.

"Hey, get away from her," I yell. I try to run. I try with all my might, but I can't move. My point-of-view leaves my body, floating away like a balloon in slow motion. I see myself standing on the porch screaming. I see Megan crying, repeating over and over, "They took her! They took her!"

Xandra continues to play with her rocks as the man gets within a few feet of her. I'm now floating above the roof of our home.

Hey, get away from her!

They took her!

Hey, get away from her!

They took her!

Xandra turns to the man and looks up, "Daddy?" When she realizes it's not me, she cries. The man picks her up, Xan kicking and screaming in protest. She looks at me—my body— standing on the porch and screams, "Daddy!"

Hey, get away from her!

They took her!

My view continues floating past the roof line and into the backyard. I can't see the front yard anymore, but the haunting dialogue continues repeating like a broken record.

Daddddddddyyyyyyyyy!

Hey, get away from her!

They took her!

My viewpoint comes to rest on the ground in the trees behind our house. Even though I feel like I can move, I can't. I'm lying in the snow, but don't feel cold. All I can see is the back porch of the house, the trees that surround me, and the snow I lie in.

Daddddddddyyyyyyyyy!

I exert myself and shift slightly. I hear the sound of incessant fluttering against the crisp snow. I adjust my view down toward my body. I see black and yellow butterfly wings.

I am the butterfly.

One wing twitches violently, the other lays unmoving. Nothing I can do but wait to die.

They took her!

12

I wake up with a throbbing headache, my head hanging over the trapdoor opening. I'm quickly reminded of the condition I left this world in when the smell of decay hits my nostrils again. I don't know how long I was passed out, but daylight is on its way out.

Not ready to face whatever died down there, I stumble to the car for ibuprofen and water, trying to breathe through my headache. I return to the living room and sit on the couch. Once my heart rate slows enough, I grip the flashlight and return to the trapdoor.

I direct my light into the void, the air thick with dust. There is a narrow dirt landing three feet below the trapdoor opening, leading to a tunnel. I think about the man with the nose ring. *What the hell have you gotten me into?* Taking one more deep breath, I move my legs over the opening and drop down. The air is cool and stale. I crouch down and begin my descent, scooting slowly down the cobweb-caked dirt tunnel. After a minute, I don't notice the smell anymore.

A butterfly. I'm nothing but a dying, useless butterfly laying in the woods behind my house. Is that what all this is—this last six months of trekking the Wild? I'm trying, but I'm getting nowhere. And I'll never get anywhere. Not as long as I have this broken wing. Broken wing? What is my broken wing? *You're the broken wing, Leo.*

Finally, the tunnel ends and opens up to a small root cellar. I stand up, cobwebs caught in my hair. My speck-filled beam of light bounces around the room, revealing shelves stocked with pickles, pears, and apples in Bell jars against one wall, and an old newspaper-covered desk in the middle of the room with a decades-old vintage bowl and spoon resting on the corner. Did I stumble upon the world's first man cave? In the corner of the room is a narrow closet built into the dirt wall. The door is covered by a rusted metal mesh. I walk up to it, facing it straight on, and flash my light on it.

A pair of white eyeballs stares at me in the darkness.

I stumble back, knocking the desk and dropping my flashlight. I inhale sharply and get thrown into a coughing fit. The bowl and spoon fall of the desk and hit the dirt floor with a muted crack. I pick the flashlight up and point it back at the closet. A tall, black man leans against the mesh door, his bright white eyeballs staring straight ahead. As I get closer to him, the rotting smell gets stronger. His face and body are severely bloated—his skin nearly bursting out of his clothes. A red-white pus leaks out of his mouth and nose. There is a coagulated bullet hole in his forehead.

Seen that before.

A wave of nausea washes over me and I turn away, covering my mouth with my hands. My joints feel weak. My stomach churns and I close my eyes, trying to find a happy place in my mind. I turn back toward the grated closet door and tug on the handle. With some force, the door opens, and the body falls my direction. I jump out the way, my back against the dirt wall. The body hits the ground with a dampened thud.

I step between him and the closet, looking his bloated body up and down. *Three to five days.* The bloating tells me he's only been dead three to five days. Then again, it's cool and dry down here. Maybe it's been longer. My mind flashes to Chrystal Peak Lodge Room 522, Nova's body badly rotted, possibly liquified by now in the summer heat.

Something comes crashing down on my back, knocking

me to the ground. My fall is broken by the waterbed of a corpse, the impact enough to send my flashlight out of my hands again. Whatever crashed down on me is now laying on top of my lower half. Feeling around with my hands for a second confirms what I feared.

Another dead body.

I weasel my way out from under it and crawl to the flashlight across the room. My body feels heavy. A hot pressure builds in my face and forehead. The stench of rotting corpse, now all over my clothes, is almost tangible. The cellar's lack of oxygen doesn't help. I get to the flashlight and sit up against the wall opposite of the bodies, feeling too weak to stand up. I shine the light toward the second body, his sunk grey eyeballs stare at me in the dark. A dried blood trail runs from a bullet hole on his head down his purple face. He is shorter and thinner than the first man, curly hair, big nose. It's Adam Katz.

With some effort, I pull the first man's wallet from his back pocket. A driver's license shows its owner to be Christian Obi. I shine my flashlight into the closet they fell out of, confirming it's empty.

No Cherry.

I crawl to the opposite side of the room and the hot pressure in my face turns to tears. A lot of them. My breath grows shallow. I close my eyes in the dark.

A flightless butterfly, awaiting my death.

Minutes ago, I had a team. I had hope. For the first time since this disaster happened six months ago, I felt *hope*—like I wasn't wasting time anymore, like I was actually getting somewhere.

The brilliant irony of my dream finally dawns on me. Xandra found a live butterfly in winter. Butterflies don't exist in Colorado in the winter. This butterfly, just like me, defied the odds and made it impressively far, but in the end, comes up short.

I turn the flashlight and shine it on Adam and Christian on the ground. I think back to where I said goodbye to Nova. The final goodbye. Her lying face up in a pool of blood, the bullet hole in her forehead.

You're not staring at Nova, you're staring at Xandra.

"No!" I scream, a surge of adrenaline coursing through my veins.

I furiously crawl back up the tunnel and out of the trapdoor opening. I open the garage door and retrieve a jerry can and lighter from the Charger's trunk. Heading back inside the house, I grab a pipe wrench resting against the wall. I stomp through the house to the front door and swing it open forcefully, the doorknob leaving a hole in the drywall. I step onto the street, my path lit by a desert sunset. My eyes are fixed on the house at the end of the street. More specifically, the *man* hanging inside the house at the end of the street.

Xandra is dead.

I run toward the house, the tears now turned to a blistering rage. The gas in the jerry can swishes violently. I get to the front yard, set the can down and run at the front window wielding the pipe wrench above my head. I bring it down hard, crashing through the glass, spraying shards in every direction. I throw the pipe wrench into the house and climb in, not noticing —not caring—about the glass impaling my hands and knees.

"You worthless piece of—" I scream at the body hanging from the ceiling, regaining my footing. I pick the wrench up off the ground, swing it over my head and bring it swiftly down on his face, the impact absorbed by his bloated face. A clouded red liquid drains from his face as I repeat the blow two more times. The force of the last hit pulls the body and the wire he's hanging from to the floor. Pieces of drywall from the ceiling rain down.

Wanted for the murder of your wife.

I march toward the front door and kick it open. I pick up the jerry can from the yard and trudge back into the house.

She was wearing her princess nightgown.

I tip the jerry can's spout over the man, the gasoline mixing with the bloody pus pooled beneath his head. I continue pouring throughout the rest of the house—the drapes, the furniture, the carpet—until the can runs out. I throw the empty can at the man's face.

Burn. In. Hell.

I ignite the lighter and throw it at the body, a ball of flames growing from the puddle of bloody pus and gasoline. I return to the street, the crackling fire behind me growing to a vicious roar. The sudden heat of the fire stings my skin.

Less than one minute later, the entire house is engulfed, the flames stretching twenty feet high. The fire becomes a chorus of wood trusses giving way, the deep thud of the roof hitting the floor, the shattering of glass. The sound of the fire brings an odd nostalgia with it, like a fire in the woods or a fireplace on a snowy day.

I half expect concerned neighbors to fill the streets, for the flashing red and white lights of firetrucks, for wailing sirens. None of that happens. It's just me.

Staring into the flames, I search for a metaphor but don't find one.

It's all useless. I'm a directionless sailboat lost at sea. *I'm a butterfly with a broken wing.*

I lay down in the road and close my eyes, nodding off to the crackling of my oversized desert campfire.

13

I wake up at around two in the morning to the crisp, dark desert night—the fire having run its course. I return to the house and fall asleep on the couch instantly.

At 5:02 AM, the RIPENESS message rings out per usual, jolting me awake. I hit the letter *B* on the keyboard unenthusiastically, sparking another computer shutdown, and fall back asleep.

The mid-morning daylight eases me awake a few hours later. I exhale loudly and for a moment, feel grateful. Grateful for the sun coming through the windows. Grateful for a solid night of sleep, despite half of it occurring on the road. Simple things.

A Phoenix reborn out of the ashes.

Is that what I am? I don't know, but I feel good. Maybe it was beating the hanging Red's face in. *God, what have I become?* Maybe it was the fire. Maybe it was the nearly twelve hours I just slept.

I glance toward the kitchen and am reminded of the trapdoor and my findings in the cellar. My joy vanishes. I walk into the kitchen, sweep the small trail of dirt back into the tunnel, and close the trapdoor. It's not the ideal grave for Adam and Christian, but it will have to do for now. I push the fridge back over the trapdoor.

Occasionally, during my time in the Wild, I do things that make me realize how much I've changed. Shooting to kill, for example. Beating a dead body and lighting a house on fire is another example. Killing is not a natural thing. It takes a certain temperament to kill without it completely destabilizing you. It's this destabilization I worry will get *me* killed. Case in point:

beating a corpse and lighting a house on fire. Lighting a *house* on fire in what is supposed to be a sensitive location. If Empire wasn't on the Reds' radar before, it sure is now.

I get a bottled latte and sardines out of my trunk and wander into the library, pulling up a chair to the table in the room.

Adam Katz.

Christian Obi.

What were you doing here? Where is Cherry Sakda? Did the hanging Red kill you? How did he find you? Why was he looking for you to begin with?

I look over the map spread over the table. How did they figure out which cities were Red territories? I take another sip of my latte and set it on the ground so I can expand the map. I study the areas carefully for the next hour.

I grab *Siddhartha* from Cherry's room and return to the couch. I read for the next hour or so, my legs propped up on the arm of the couch.

> *Truly, no thing in this world has kept my thoughts thus busy, as this my very own self, this mystery of me being alive, of me being one and being separated and isolated from all others, of me being Siddhartha! And there is no thing in this world I know less about than about me, about Siddhartha!*

I set the open book on my chest.

…being one and being separated and isolated from all others… I am separate from Nova. I am separate from Xandra. I am separate from Tripp and mom and dad. I am separate from Leo…*no thing in this world I know less about than about me…*

I drift to sleep.

—

An hour later, I wake up abruptly.

I can't keep sitting around waiting for something to happen. The reason the nose ring man sent me here was to meet up with Christian, Adam, and Cherry. Christian and Adam are dead, and Cherry is nowhere to be found. The nose ring man likely doesn't even know what's happened, or he was killed trying to make it here. Either way, there has been a change of plans. No one is coming for me.

You knew it was too good to be true anyway.

I take the map from the library and bring it to the living room. I get down on my knees and begin mapping out my route.

A flash of light catches my eye.

I look up at the wall in front of me. A brief, but sharp glare flashes on the wall.

"No—" I jump up on my feet and run to the garage. I pull out my rifle and burst through the front door, running across the street to get a better look at the approaching highway. Through the mirage of the desert heat, I see a small red convertible zipping down the highway followed closely by a white pickup truck far in the distance.

Please be Cherry or nose ring man.

I cut through the backyards of my neighbor's houses, trying to get to Empire's main approach before they do. The roar of the engines gets closer. I make it through the last row of houses to the raw desert and continue running, dodging thick desert shrubs and cacti along the way. I hide behind an old auto shop on the highway and peer out from the corner. The cars show no sign of slowing down as they approach the town entrance. I've got one shot.

As they close in, I pop out from the side of the building, gun pointed at the cars, eye to my scope. The driver of the red car is a man in his early 20s. It could be nose ring man, but I can't quite tell. He glances between the road ahead and the rearview mirror frantically.

Holding my gun steady, I move the scope's view to the cabin of the Red's truck. I see two burly men with slash tattoos, the passenger throwing his hands around haphazardly in frustration. I move the crosshairs to the face of the driver, move it slightly up and to the left, and fire. The bullet strikes the driver just over the right eye, blood spattering the back window of the truck cabin. The truck jerks right, sending it into the brush. The Red in the passenger seat yanks the steering wheel but overcorrects, sending it back across the road and toward the auto shop I'm hiding behind. I run out of the way just in time for the truck to hit the corner of the building, firing off an ensemble of shattering glass, breaking bricks, and the deep thud of the engine making impact with the concrete wall separating the office from the service bays. Then deafening silence.

The red sports car pulls off and slides to a stop two buildings up the road.

I slowly creep around what remains of the auto shop, listening for any sign of life. Aside from the occasional glass breaking and remnant bricks falling, the auto shop is silent. I walk to the front of the building and march through the rubble to get a closer look at the Reds. The truck is partially tipped over, the two driver's side tires elevated off the ground, still spinning. The familiar crackling of a fire-starting comes from the office area.

The driver's head—or what's left of it—is folded down

over his seatbelt, blood covering everything. The passenger's head is also kinked over his seatbelt, appearing to be dead, or at least unconscious. As I approach the truck, a portion of the wall behind me collapses, trapping me—us—in the service bay. The area turns pitch black, the only source of light from the fading in and out of the truck's headlights.

With the office now a pile of rubble, my only exit is the small man door in the back of the service area. The yellowish hue of the headlights illuminates the room in about three-second increments.

The headlights fade in and I look up at the ceiling to see if there's a risk of the service bay collapsing.

Headlights fade out.

The engine is dead, so the only noise is the occasional adjusting of bricks in the collapsed portion of the building or under the car.

Headlights fade in.

I make my way to the man door. Only this time, something catches my eye. I turn my head back to the crashed car. *Is that*—

Headlights fade out.

I try to hold still.

Headlights fade in.

The passenger seat of the truck is empty. I whip my head toward the back door and see the staggering silhouette of a man standing in front of it.

Headlights fade out.

Glass shatters in the near-distance. I grip my gun. "Listen buddy, I'm the one with a gun. You tell me—" I start.

Headlights fade in.

The man is walking toward me with a severe limp, his arms outstretched, like he wants a hug.

"Stop walking!" I yell, gripping my gun tighter.

Headlights fade out.

I've got to get to the door.

A flash of light illuminates the space accompanied by a loud crack. A sharp sting shoots down my arm followed by a deep burning. I drop my gun. *Did I just get shot?*

I fall to the ground.

As the headlights fade in, another gunshot goes off, hitting the brick wall behind me. I reach for my gun with my left hand, but the man kicks my arm, flipping me onto my back. Should've taken the shot while I had the chance.

Headlights fade out.

The smell of sweat and body odor intensifies. He's close. I push myself backward and realize I'm lying in a puddle. I initially assume motor oil, then quickly realize it's blood. My blood.

Headlights fade in.

A sinister smile stretches across the man's brutish face as he steadies his gun. I try to move my legs, but nothing happens. *My last sight is a Red's face.*

Headlights fade out.

My life doesn't flash before my eyes. The last six months flash before my eyes. The fact that I've accomplished nothing. The fact that I would've been more effective sitting in prison in the Belt. *I failed Nova, I failed Megan, and now I've failed Xandra.*

I. Failed.

Headlights fade in.

The Red pauses for a moment to let his grumbly chuckle fill the air as he casually holds his gun above my head.

I fade in and out of consciousness. "The Reds…took my daugh…daughter…but…I don't…. why…"

"Heh heh," he grumbles. "Official White business." He straightens his back, bracing for the kick of the gun.

The back door bursts open, the desert daylight illuminating the auto shop. The guy from the sports car stands in the doorway, gun at the ready. The Red standing above me jerks around, but takes three shots in the chest before he can raise his gun. The Red staggers backward then falls.

"Dangit, no! Not right on—" a distant, reverberating voice calls.

Then, for the second time in a twenty-four-hour period, I lose consciousness.

—

I come to rather suddenly, lying on a pile of towels on the floor. The empty Starbucks bottle and dogeared copy of *Siddhartha* next to me tell me I'm back in the house. My arm is neatly wrapped where I got shot. *I got shot.*

Outside, daylight is fading. I sit up, blood rushing to my head.

Who is this kid?

I lay back down and close my eyes, replaying the events from earlier. Shooting the Red. Crash into the auto shop. The wall collapsing. The passenger getting out and shooting me. Then… Then… I'm here.

Official White business, he said. *White business.*

The front door opens and the sports car kid walks in. Seeing another person in Empire is like seeing your school teacher at the movies or grocery store—out of place.

"Hey, you're awake," he says. He has small wire-rim glasses, light brown hair, and a tall, thin build. He's wearing a gray t-shirt that might be a size too big and black pants.

I look down at my bandaged arm and back to him. "You

saved my life," I say, focusing on his face. He looks very familiar. Like one of the last faces I saw in the Belt.

"Jame Folke!" I shout.

14

"So, you just up and left?"

"You have no idea. It got bad. Really bad," Jame says.

"With people fleeing into the Wild?"

"Yeah. I mean, as you figured out, it's not that hard to leave the Belt."

I'm sitting on the couch, Jame is sitting in the office chair. He looks mostly the same as when I last saw him but with slightly longer—puffier—hair, scraggly scruff, and a light tan.

"Theft, murder, rape," Jame continues. "We even had a guy flee over unpaid parking tickets."

"So, what—they just pack their cars and head across the border? No plans, no arrangements, nothing?"

"Yeah. From what I've seen."

"Do any of them come back?"

"For major crimes, I haven't seen anyone come back. The parking ticket guy came back pretty spooked after a week. Totally changed his attitude about his dues."

I try gripping my right arm in a fist and feel a sharp pain shoot up my shoulder then fade away. "And the Feds haven't built a wall or anything?"

"The Feds have asked local municipalities to set up roadblocks on local roads leading into the Belt. The problem is that there are *so many* roads leading into the New Wilderness, and off roading isn't difficult, honestly. We *do* need a wall, but the Feds are concerned about the optics."

"One-hundred-percent made it to the Belt, huh," I say.

"Exactly. The Feds don't want to admit there's a problem. Per usual," Jame says.

"Indeed."

"But, but, but," Jame says, excitedly flinging his hands in the air, "that's just the criminals. There have been people voluntarily venturing out into the New Wilderness and not returning. We don't know where they go or what they do."

"People like me?"

"Certainly, there are people like you who venture out purely out of curiosity. But there are others who are sick of all the people or the blandness of the Belt and just want to go home. They think that things are more or less the same as how they left them."

"What do you hear from people who *do* make it back?"

"That they are happy with the Belt after all. As you know, it takes a lot to survive out here on your own. Finding fuel, food, water."

"All without cell phones and internet, no less."

"Right."

"So how do the Reds do what they do? You have any idea?"

"Probably same things we do—in terms of basic necessities. Not sure on ammo. There's got to be some sort of centralization to their operation."

I try rotating my arm. It's sore as hell but not as bad as I would have imagined a gunshot wound being.

"But gas has to go bad at some point, right? Seems like that would be a day of reckoning for them. And us."

"They could easily get their gas from the Belt. You obviously found the clean border crossing near Raton. I'm sure there are hundreds more. Or, the Reds might have connections inside the Belt."

"Don't you think the Feds expected more workers in the job cycle?"

"I'm sure the Feds anticipated high unemployment for a

while—until people get settled anyway."

Jame walks to the kitchen and comes back with two bottles of water.

"So, what brought you out here?" I ask.

"I don't know exactly. I suppose it all started with your case. With Xandra, I mean. Yours was different. You guys going up into the Wild—which I can't say was the smartest decision."

"Agreed and acknowledged."

"But then you said the guy who shot you—well, Nova—called you out by name," he continues.

I nod.

"He kills your wife when he meant to kill you, it sounds like. Then you return to the Belt; your daughter is gone, and mother-in-law is dead. It's not a typical cross-the-border case. There's something bigger at play."

"Well, in anticipation of your next question, I am no closer to finding answers." I try rotating my arm and wince in pain. "And without being able to get into the Belt, I'm sort of lacking resources."

"Huh."

We both drink from our water bottles and turn toward the front window.

"So, did you come out here for me?"

"That's part of the reason. I didn't think I'd end up finding you, honestly," Jame says.

"So how did you find me?"

"A guy in Elko handed me a note with this address."

"Guy with a nose ring?"

Jame's eyes grow wide. "Yeah—you know him?"

"He handed me a note in Battle Mountain with the address to this house too. He told me he can help find Xandra. He also told me he'd meet me here and that was three days ago."

Jame sits back in his chair and looks around the room in contemplation. "What have you learned so far?"

"First of all, three people were living here recently. Very recently, actually. Like within the last week or two."

"How do you know that?"

"Two dead bodies in the cellar. Bloated bodies."

Jame purses his lips and looks down at the ground. "What about the third?"

"Not here—not that I've found. Her name is Cherry Sakda, though."

"Who killed the first two?"

"I found a dead Red hanging in the window of a house down the street."

"What house?" He walks to the window.

"At the end of the street," I say pointing behind me. "But I burnt it down," I say, avoiding eye contact.

"Why?" he asks, drawn out like an exhausted parent.

"I know what you're thinking, but I don't usually do stuff like that."

Jame clears his throat. "And you don't know what they've been up to in Emp—"

"RIPENESS."

The computer screen illuminates behind Jame, nearly sending him off his chair. Jame stands up and turns toward the screen.

The screen goes dark.

"What the heck is that?"

"*That* is one of the only clues I've got so far. The computer goes off every day at 5:02 AM and 5:02 PM. It just says 'ripeness' and that's all. But then—watch," I point to the screen. "It will come back on three times, then the last time it shows a blinking cursor after the word. Watch it."

"RIPENESS" repeats three times, each time broken up by a black screen. Then the cursor appears.

"It's clearly looking for a password of some sort, but I have no idea where to begin. I've started cycling through the alphabet."

"What letter are you on?"

"C," I say.

"That far huh?"

"I've only been here three days, man."

Jame types the letter *C* and the computer shuts down.

"Now what?" he says.

"Now we wait until 5 AM and try again."

"And you have no clue as to what this is?"

"Not really."

"What else about the house?"

"You saw the library?"

"Yeah—what a weird painting. I saw the map too."

"Red territories, you think?" I ask.

"Yeah definitely. It matches up with what I've seen."

"Me too," I say. "Come with me."

I stand up, feeling much better now, and walk to the library, Jame following. We each pull a chair up to the table and look over the map, comparing notes and swapping stories.

As day fades to evening fades to night, we continue talking.

"The nose ring guy—did he tell you what you were getting into?" I ask.

"He told me he could help," Jame says.

"Help with what?"

"I don't know—he probably figured since I was in the Wild, and clearly not a Red, that I was looking for something."

What is Jame really up to?

"Alright let's think about this," I say, rubbing my eyes. "He's got to come back here eventually, right? I mean, he seems like he's kind of an organizer, or architect of this group."

"What group?" Jame asks.

"Us. The resistance."

"Is that official?"

"No, that's just what I've assumed this is. The people who lived in this house were sophisticated. They thought a lot about strategy. One guy has a white paper about the board game Risk. He also has a book about chess strategy. I mean, chess, seriously? These guys were clearly up to something that had to do with counteracting the Reds."

Jame sits up in his chair and looks over the map again.

"Do you think we're all there is? Resistance-wise, I mean."

"God, I hope we're not the only ones."

Jame stands up and turns around, looking at the mural on the wall. "Looks like something out of a Shakespeare play," he says, putting his hand up in the air like the man in the picture. "Why, God?! Whyyyyyyyyy!?" he says mockingly, shaking his hands. As quickly as it came, it went. He puts his hands down and continues scanning books.

He may have saved my life twice, but he is still quirky as hell.

"I mean, the bigger question is what the heck are the Reds up to? Why all the kidnapping and killing? Why the land grab?"

"I don't know," I say in a hushed tone. I look past him to the mural. *Why, God? Why?*

—

At around midnight, I lie on the living room couch, staring up at the ceiling, trying to create some separation between my racing mind and my breath.

Resistance.

A team. A team of like-minded people who want to take down the Reds. But why? Is this as simple as a good versus evil? Light versus dark?

No. To think that way would be naive. We have no idea what the Reds want. We can only fight our fight based on material facts. For me, they killed my wife and mother-in-law, and they kidnapped my daughter. I have cause to fight them. But what about other resistance members? What about Jame? The material facts are that the Reds are murdering innocent people, and we, the resistance, are morally opposed to it.

But *why* are they killing innocent people? Why did they kidnap Xandra? Are they kidnapping other children?

Do the Reds even know why they do what they do? Someone has to know. Nose ring guy from Battle Mountain— he's got to know what's going on. Cherry. She has to know. Right? Christian Obi and Adam Katz *used to* know, I'm sure.

What if they're all as clueless as we are?

—

"I got it! I got it!"

I sit up suddenly to Jame yelling from the bedroom.

"What the hell," I whisper to myself. It's one thing to be awoken by someone yelling, it's another to be awoken by someone yelling who you've forgotten exists. Living with another human again will take some getting used to.

Jame runs into the living room, his mouth and chin covered in blood.

"King Lear!" he yells.

"What the hell happened to you?"

"The painting!" Jame runs into the library and digs through the books.

I follow him, my arm feeling like a sack of soggy newspapers dangling from my torso.

"What time is it?" I call down the hallway.

"It's 4:30, we still have time!"

Jame rummages through the Shakespeare collection on the bottom shelf, his fingers running up and down the imprinted play titles on the book spines. "King Lear, right here," he says, slamming the heavy book down on the table.

"No, your face. You're bleeding."

"King Learrrrrr, right herrrrrrrrrrre," he sings, ignoring my concern.

"Do you not care that you're bleeding everywhere?"

"Oh," he says and wipes his nose with his shirt, not breaking his gaze on the book. "Uh, I pick my nose in my sleep. When I'm stressed. Gets bloody sometimes."

I take the flashlight from him and hold it above his head. As he flips through, we stumble upon a familiar visual. An old man cursing God, a jester amused. We look at each other, a mixture of *ah-ha* and *you sly devil* looks on our faces.

"What time did you say the ripeness message shows up exactly?"

"5:02, I think."

"Five-oh-twooooooooo," he says in a half-whisper. "Act five scene two," he says, stopping on a page. He finds the line and reads the passage aloud.

"What, in ill thoughts again? Men must endure
Their going hence even as their coming hither.
Ripeness is all. Come on.

He looks up at me, my mouth agape. "Ripeness *is all.*"

—

At 4:55, we move to the living room. I sit at the chair pulled up to the desk, and Jame gets a chair from the kitchen. The next few minutes pass by in silence.

I'm tired as hell but my mind races on. I'm finally getting somewhere. Whatever 'is all' brings us, it *will* be something. It has to be. And *something* is a lot more than the sea of nothing I've been aimlessly floating through the last few months.

Morning twilight slowly creeps into the room. Both of us watch the faux silver digital clock on the wall move from 5:00 to 5:01. I inch the chair closer to the computer screen, my left fingers hovering near the letter 'I' on the keyboard.

Even though I'm expecting it, my heart jumps a little bit when the screen finally flashes on.

    RIPENESS

Black.

    RIPENESS

Black.

    RIPENESS

Black.
I try to steady my breath waiting for my cue.

    RIPENESS |

The cursor blinks and I nervously type 'I' on the keyboard. Nothing shuts down. I carefully move my left pointer finger to the 'S' key and press down. We're still in business. I finish the phrase and the computer makes an upbeat *ba-ding* sound. The message disappears and takes us to a new blank screen with only a flashing cursor next to 'emp:'. I glance at Jame.

"Try typing something," he says.

```
emp: hello?
```

15

We wait.

And wait.

And wait.

Ten minutes pass with Jame and me both staring intensely at the screen, waiting for something to happen.

"Well, is that it?" I say.

"Let's think about this," Jame says, standing up and walking toward the window. The morning twilight is much stronger now.

"Maybe whoever handles the chat room is dead now. Or maybe when they didn't get a response for such a long time, they abandoned the post."

"Maybe they realized that Christian and Adam were killed, and Cherry disappeared, so there wasn't a point in communicating with Empire anymore."

A flicker of light from the screen catches my eye.

"Jame! Look!"

He runs back to the desk.

Underneath our greeting, the words appear:

```
pao: who is this?
```

I start to reply when Jame stops me.

"Hold up, play it cool, man. Play it cool," he says.

"Right," I say.

```
emp: you tell us first
pao: cherry
```

I sense Jame looking at me, but don't care.

```
emp: it's leo and jame
pao: ok
```

I look at Jame, we share surprised glances. "Ok Cherry, tell us what the hell is going on," I say, turning back to the screen.

```
emp: you used to live here, right?
pao: yes
emp: where are you now?
pao: you have to understand, it's not safe
there
pao: empire has been compromised
emp: cherry, you need to tell us what the
hell is going on
pao: i know you've had a lot thrown at you
the past few days
pao: i'll explain when you're here.
emp: when we're where?
pao: can you guys make it to the midwest?
```

I look at Jame. We shrug at each other.

```
emp: where?
pao: paoli indiana
```

Jame grabs the map, lays it on the ground next to the desk and circles his finger around the state until he finds Paoli, a little town in southern Indiana about 40 miles northwest of Louisville, Kentucky.

```
emp: why?
pao: this is leo typing?
emp: yeah
```

```
    pao: I know your story. about your wife and
daughter
    pao: we can help you
    emp: how do you know?
    pao: we work with ryan
    emp: who is ryan?
    pao: I'll explain when you get here
    emp: how do we know we can trust you?
```

Another minute passes.

```
    pao: broncos 24
```

I lean back in my chair and break out in a sweat.

"Broncos 24," Jame says. "What the heck does that mean?"

My mind races a thousand miles an hour trying to think of the possible connections between Megan and Cherry or the Reds.

"Leo?" Jame says.

"It's—" I start, "it's something my mother-in-law said to me on her deathbed."

"What the—Leo, what are you not telling me?" Jame asks.

"I didn't think it meant anything. I have no idea what all of this is. The fact that these people know me by name—I have no idea." I go back to the keyboard.

```
    emp: any parting advice?
    pao: the reds are on to empire so hurry.
    pao: theres a roadmap in the filing cabinet
in the library that shows the cleanest route to
paoli.
    pao: the further east you go, the more
dangerous it gets. BE CAREFUL
```

A reflection flashes on the wall for a split second, right

above the entertainment stand.

"Oh—" I yell, stumbling to my feet.

"Geez, what the heck man!" Jame says, startled.

"That reflection, that's my—the Reds are coming. Or someone is coming."

"Crap—the drawer!"

"The drawer, the drawer, the drawer," I say, desperately looking around for keys as if they'll be laying in plain sight. "We have maybe two minutes before they get to Empire, another minute til they find the house."

Jame runs to the kitchen and begins frantically opening and shutting drawers and cabinets. I go to the library and start pulling books off the shelves. I catch a glimpse of the King Lear mural and look closely at the jester character. He kind of reminds me of…

"The bodies!" I yell from the library.

Jame runs around the corner. "What do you mean, *bodies?*"

"The bodies in the cellar, do you think the key could've been in one of their pockets?"

"Yeah, but wouldn't Cherry have told us?"

"I think there's a lot she would've told us if we had time."

"Wait, is the chat still open?"

We move to the main room. My arm is throbbing in pain, interrupted by brief bursts of adrenaline. The computer screen is black. Jame hits the keyboard a few times, but it's dead. Then we hear a sound—*the* sound. The sound that haunts my dreams. The sound that says *your wife is about to be shot in the head, murdered in cold blood.* The sound that says *your daughter is about to be kidnapped.*

An engine rumbles in the distance.

"How long?" Jame says.

"A minute?"

"Show me the cellar."

We dart down the hallway and into the kitchen. I pull back the fridge with my left arm, Jame helps.

The cars pull onto 5th Street.

"We don't have time," I say, peeking around the corner toward the front window.

"You go, I'll hold them off," Jame says.

"No way, we don't know how many there are."

"I got this. Go!" Jame says. He grabs an automatic rifle from off the ground in the main room and cocks it.

I open the trapdoor and am welcomed by the stench of rotting bodies again—not as bad the second time around. I hang my legs over the opening, take a deep breath, and jump in. I turn the flashlight on and close the trapdoor behind me, scooting down the tunnel much faster this time.

As I get to the room opening, I hear a thud above my head and a gentle trickle of dust falls on my head.

Adam Katz's bloated body accentuates everything left in his pants pockets. I find a knife in one, nothing in the other. I maneuver the knife out of his pocket and put it into mine. I go to Christian's body, lying face down in the dirt, and feel around the outside of his pockets. I find a pack of gum, a pen, and a small spiral-bound notepad. No keys.

Another thud from above. The ceiling rattles, releasing another layer of dust. God, let's hope Jame survives whatever is happening up there.

As I pan the room again with my flashlight, something on Adam's body shimmers. I step closer, running my light up and down his body—his body resembling a seal more than a human—and find the source of light. His finger. Buried deep in his bloated finger is a wedding ring.

I step toward him to get a closer look, only it's much too

narrow to be a wedding ring.

It's not a wedding ring.

It's a key ring.

I lift his arm, twisting it toward me, the small key standing erect against his ballooned palm. I try prying it out from under his flesh, but there's no use.

I exhale, knowing what I need to do.

With a trembling hand, I take Adam's knife out of my pocket and flip it open, resting the blade against Christian's finger. The knife is small but has enough teeth to saw through the spongy flesh. I put pressure against the skin until it gives way.

The liquid that pours from his flesh is a cool, foul-smelling, oily red pus. It runs down my arm and drips onto my legs. A puddle forms below me. My gag reflux seizes. I turn my head with the back side of my hand pressed against my mouth, trying to breathe. The wretched smell fills my nostrils, and I vomit on the dirt floor.

I'm brought back to a road trip Nova, Xan and I did across the Great Plains two years ago. We ate at a Greek place in North Platte, Nebraska that didn't sit well with Nova or me. We had to pull over about ten times on the drive home, Nova and I taking turns vomiting on I-80. Xandra in the backseat, confused out of her mind.

I dig through my pocket for Christian's gum and throw a piece into my mouth. I hold my breath as I cut away enough of the flesh to dig my fingers in and pull the key ring apart. The key drops into the puddle of pus and I force my mind to go to a sunny beach while I dig my fingers through it and find the key.

I make my way up the tunnel as footsteps cross the main room and stop. As I get to the landing, crouched directly under the trapdoor, the footsteps plod through the kitchen and stop above me. I grip the knife tight.

The tunnel fills with light as the trapdoor opens from above. The contrast from total darkness to light stings my eyes.

"All clear," Jame says.

"Gosh, Jame," I say, climbing out.

Jame looks unscathed. The rest of the house does not.

"Man alive, you smell," he says, scowling.

I dangle the key above my head.

"Nice."

"I really hope that was worth it."

"Yep, me too." I walk around the hallway to go to the library.

"Oh hey, Leo," Jame says, running after me.

I turn the corner into the library and see a large man—bald, scraggly beard with a long black tattoo across his eye—sprawled across the table. His glossed-over eyeballs stare up at the ceiling. Blood is puddled on the table beneath his chest.

I smile.

—

Jame and I lay the roadmap flat on the living room floor. Each highway is meticulously marked noting demolished roads, roadblocks, and Red checkpoints.

A muffled drone comes from the library accompanied by the creaking of the table the Red lies on.

"Woonbeehaaaad," followed by a loud thud.

"What the hell? I thought he was dead," I say.

"Me too."

Jame and I run into the library, firearms at the ready.

The man is on the floor, face in the carpet. "Woonbeehaaaad."

I turn his face with my foot.

"Won't be had. Won't be had."

"Hey—"

"Won't be had," he grumbles.

Without a second thought, I kick him swiftly in the head. He opens his eyes slightly, still staring straight ahead.

"Won't be had."

"I get it. You won't be had. Who sent you here?"

"Won't be had."

I slam the table. "Who sent you?"

He reluctantly looks toward me. Not quite *at* me, but toward me, a smile slowly creeping up his worn face. He coughs hard, then convulses. He struggles for breath and claws at his throat.

Jame and I look at each other.

The man lets out a final breath and his eyes gloss over again.

"Won't be had? Is that their little motto?" I ask.

"Yeah, I've seen it around."

"You think he's dead-dead this time?"

Jame points the gun at the man, while still maintaining eye contact with me, and pulls the trigger. The man's body jumps with the bullet's impact, but his expressionless face remains the same.

"Yep," Jame says.

"Ok, psychopath," I say.

I notice a small metallic canister next to the dead man on the ground. "What's that?"

Jame nudges it with his foot and a needle and broken syringe falls out. "Either heroin or—"

"Or steroids? Maybe that's why they all look and sound like animals."

"Hm."

I return to the main room and change my clothes. As I pull a fresh shirt over my head, another glare against the wall catches my eye. And then another. And then another. And then another.

"Jame!" I yell, still staring at the wall, which is still glaring repeatedly. "Jame, hey come here!"

He turns the corner to the front room, eyes growing wide at the stream of glares hitting the wall. "Leo, what's happening?"

"They're sending an army."

16

We sit in the Charger, engine idling, at the end of Circle Drive, watching the highway in silence. I'm in the driver's seat, Jame's in the backseat with a rifle. We count twelve cars coming down the highway, most of them small pickup trucks. *Twelve* trucks for *two* people. We knew we didn't have a chance beating them to C Street—the only road in and out of Empire—so we have no choice but to hightail it through the desert. The only problem is that the stretch of desert we need to cross is very flat and very visible, so we wait at the edge of the desert until all cars have made the turn into Empire, giving us a meager head start to the highway.

Jame tries to steady his breathing. I do too. I've outrun plenty of Reds in the past, but not an entourage of twelve. And my luck has to run out somewhere.

The cars slow down as they approach Empire.

One turns on to C Street.

Two.

Three.

I realize that they are all getting a great view of their fellow Reds that chased Jame into town, now crashed into the auto shop near the town entrance.

Four.

Five.

Six.

"Ok when?" Jame asks.

"We have to wait until the last one turns onto C Street. They'll head straight to 456 I assume," I say.

"There's enough of them that they'll probably patrol the whole town too," Jame says.

"Yeah. Good point."

"This is gonna be another high-speed chase isn't it?"

I look at him. "Yes, but you've never done a high-speed chase in a Charger and with a gunman," I say, smirking. "This'll be fun."

Jame lets out a nervous chuckle, his gaze fixed on the desert before us. He has his rifle at the ready, another at his feet, and an entire arsenal in the back seat, including grenades.

The last of the cars turn onto C Street. The roar of the engines spreads throughout the whole town. I let out one last exhale and punch the gas. Dirt flies up behind us as we navigate the jarring terrain. My eyes dance between the side and rearview mirrors even though all I see are clouds of red dirt. Jame has his gun pointed out the back window.

"Onto the road," I announce, easing onto the highway. The tires screech and the car jerks momentarily before settling. *Has asphalt always been this smooth?*

"We have a visitor," Jame says.

I look in the rearview mirror. Two pickup trucks are on the highway behind us.

"Can this thing go any faster?"

"What's going on?"

"The truck in front—they have some sort of gun attached to the bed of the truck."

"Are you kidding—like the Taliban?"

"The what?"

I look in the rearview mirror again just in time to see a small red-tipped missile followed by a trail of white smoke ripping toward our car.

"Turn! Turn!" Jame yells.

I yank the steering wheel sending us into the desert, only this time at ninety miles per hour. I slam the side of my head on the steering wheel, Jame hits the back of my headrest.

The missile whistles and crashes with a vengeance against the asphalt twenty feet behind us. The explosion rumbles our car and leaves a ringing in my ears. I feel the immensity of the impact in my chest.

"Holy—" I say, realizing I can't hear myself talk.

I ease the car onto the highway again. The rearview mirror shows a thick black cloud around the missile's impact zone. That's a shot in the foot if I've ever seen one.

"Something tells me no one's gonna repair that road, am I right?" Jame says.

I roll my eyes.

In the side mirror, I see the two trucks slow down and veer into the desert to avoid the crater in the road. The first truck swerves too far and falls into a desert wash. The second truck maintains control and pulls ahead of the first, eventually finding its way back onto the road.

As the highway curves west, we hit 120 miles per hour. The trucks fade in the distance—a sight that never gets old. The next few minutes are driven in silence, Jame on his knees, facing the rear of the car with his hands gripping the rifle; me paying more attention to the rearview mirror than the road ahead.

The drive is peaceful now but won't be for long, not with two thousand miles of Red territory ahead of us.

Jame eventually turns around in his seat and puts the gun down by his side. He folds the map so the western third of the US is visible. "Empire, empire, empire," he mumbles as he gets oriented on the map. "Get on I-80 in Fernley, I guess."

"There's a Walmart in Fernley. We can stock up there," I say.

Jame sets the map down on his lap and looks out the

window.

—

I park on the back side of Walmart, out of view from I-80.

"Meet back here in ten?" I ask.

"Where you going?"

"To get gas. I'm not sure how long we have here."

"Ok. Any special requests?"

The thought of drinking another bottled latte makes me sick. I always wondered when I'd hit that wall. "Green tea or something people drink when trying to curb a caffeine addiction."

Jame laughs and climbs out. I watch him in the rearview mirror pick up a rock and hurl it through one of the intact windows of the storefront. I laugh to myself.

I head west out of the Walmart parking lot toward a clump of houses a street over.

Most garages are still filled with crap, so finding a jerry can or two of gas is generally not a difficult undertaking. I pull into one of the driveways and get out. The house's garage has a manual pull but is locked. I give it a swift kick with my heal and knock it loose. After a good tug, the knob cracks, and the garage door loosens enough to pull open. The humid air smells of grass clippings, gasoline, and mildew.

Digging through old lawn mowers, trimmers, and fertilizer, I spot a little red canister in the back and blaze a trail to it. My mind wanders to the two-thousand-mile trip ahead of us. It's a lot of time to think about my girls. *Who puts Xandra to bed? Who feeds her? Does anyone talk to her? Does she know her mom is dead?* A tear drops onto my hand.

If anyone has laid a single finger on you, I will destroy *them.*

Obliterate. Mutilate. Chop up into tiny pieces. One finger. My heart beats in my throat. My breathing grows shallow. I clench my fists.

You can't find Xandra if you lose your mind.

After a minute, I feel level again. I lift the jerry can, it's heavy.

A gift from Nova.

Xandra's dead.

I empty the jerry can into my tank and toss it in the general direction of the garage.

———

Jame is sitting on the curb outside Walmart clenching something in his lap and rocking back and forth. I roll down the window and kill the engine. "Jame, you okay?"

He looks at me, pulling a Minnie Mouse stuffed animal from his lap. Tears streaming down his face. He tries to smile, but his body convulses through the sobs. He looks back at the stuffed animal and closes his eyes. A golf club lays on the ground next to him.

"Oh my God, Jame. I didn't—do you have a daughter?"

He shakes his head.

"Did you lose someone?"

He nods and attempts to slow his breathing.

"I'm sorry—we don't have to talk about it. I guess—I'm sorry—I've been so selfish talking about my problems when I don't even know much about you at all."

His gaze meets the asphalt in front of him. He takes a minute to compose himself. "Oh boy, I'm sorry about that," he says. "Gosh, I'm a mess."

"Don't feel stupid," I say. "I break down all the time. I

broke down like two minutes ago looking for gas."

He closes his eyes for about ten seconds and then jumps up with enthusiasm. "I hope you like sardines," he says.

17

"Ok but we *know* that Battle Mountain is a Red territory," Jame says.

"Yes, but I still think we have a better chance of high tailing it on I-80 through Battle Mountain than getting off on some state highway that might lead us to a Red territory anyway. Then we'll be in Red territory *and* stuck on a crappy road. You have the map there, we don't have many options to go *around* Battle Mountain, right?"

Jame throws his hands up in the air in defeat. "Battle Mountain it is."

I nod. "Alright, the approach is extremely straight. You have a scope, don't you? We can scope it out as far out as possible. Sound good?"

"Ok," he says.

A Minnie Mouse doll, yet he doesn't have a daughter. Could be a niece or a girlfriend. Or a wife? I pretend to look at the map but sneak a peek at his ring finger. No ring. God, what a weird thing to do. I look back to the road. He probably got married and went on a honeymoon to Disneyland. Then his wife died somehow. Could she have gone into the Wild? Well, we have two thousand miles to figure it out. I shouldn't be so concerned, it's none of my business. If he wants to talk about it, he'll bring it up.

As we approach the Valmy rest stop, Jame adjusts his scope on his rifle and pulls it up to his eye. From my view, it's unobstructed desert road as far as the eye can see. Nothing but desert brush, tumbleweed, and fence posts. Mountains lay far in the distance, topped by wispy clouds. The sky is a rich blue.

"I don't see anything," Jame says.

"We only have about two miles of visible freeway left. We'll just zoom right through."

"Ok, but I'm still gonna have my gun ready."

"I wouldn't suggest anything otherwise."

As we close in on Battle Mountain's only exit, I grip the steering wheel tighter.

"Someone's on the overpass," Jame says, his face pressed up against his scope.

"Just one?"

"Yeah, sitting in a chair. He has a gun, but he's not paying attention. He looks like he's nodding off."

"Do we take him out?"

"I don't see a need to," Jame says.

"Ok, just stay ready." I step on the gas.

As we approach the overpass, the speedometer hits 110 miles per hour. Jame steadies his gun pointed at the man. "It's not him," he says.

"It's not… who?" I ask.

"It's not—he's not, um—he's—oh crap, he's up."

We come out on the other side of the overpass. I watch the man in the rearview mirror stumble from his chair and stand up, leaning his head into a walkie-talkie fastened on his shoulder. He holds his rifle erect and fires a couple of wild shots at us.

And just like that—like ripping off a band-aid—we were in and out of Battle Mountain in less than a minute.

—

With the huge map spread across his lap, Jame mumbles the names of interstates and no-name towns to himself.

"You're from Salt Lake aren't you?" Jame asks.

"Yeah—did I tell you that?"

He looks up. "I may have gotten that from your record. Sorry, that's creepy," he says.

"Haven't been back there since the Big One."

"You ok passing through it?" He asks.

"I guess so."

"You had family die in the Big One?"

"My parents and brother died. I was living in Colorado at the time."

"I'm sorry," Jame says, briefly looking out the window before returning to the map on his lap. "I had some cousins die," he says. "Lived all the way down in Nephi, the south end of the destruction. I'll never forget hearing about the Big One, thinking this can't be right, this is America, not a third world country."

"You and me both. Ya know, they had been talking about 'The Big One' for decades. Like since my grandma was in elementary school. I think everyone just assumed it wasn't gonna happen—at least not in anyone's lifetime. It was a hypothetical event. Not to mention, *if* the Big One hit, it would be a 7.0 only in the worst-case scenario. Maybe a couple thousand people die, power is out for a week, roads need some repair, but that's it. A 7.9 wasn't in the cards. No one was prepared—not that there's a good way to prepare for a 7.9."

"Did you find the bodies?" Jame asks.

"No. They were missing for two years then we gave up. You?"

"Yeah, they were found. Nephi's a rural town, so it was a bit easier. Less concrete to dig through."

"Did you know anyone in the other Bigs?" I say.

"No, just Salt Lake. You?"

"Same."

—

Thanks to Cherry's map, we took county roads around Elko and Wendover and found ourselves crossing the Utah border unscathed. We took Highway 93 through Tooele then linked back up to I-80 as it hugs the Great Salt Lake. Well, it used to hug the Great Salt Lake. Now it runs *through* the Great Salt Lake. The earthquake caused the lake to swell, permanently altering its footprint in several areas. As the Wasatch mountains come into view, my heart sinks.

Home.

Gone.

My mind wanders to the story of Siddhartha. He left behind his wife, baby, and lush lifestyle in his father's kingdom *voluntarily*. To him, his attachments were preventing him from finding himself. Since the Big One happened, I've lost my parents, my brother, my childhood home, my wife, and now my daughter. I didn't choose any of this—of course, I didn't—but this is the setup that Siddhartha *needed* to find enlightenment. So, what does *that* mean?

When the Big One happened, I went through all the stages of grief. For my mom. For my dad. For Tripp. For my childhood home. For the foothills Tripp and I would explore as kids. The road I got my first speeding ticket on. The ski resorts. The movie theater. All of it. Your experience of growing up, your past relationships, the places you love—they all play a role in shaping you. They contribute teeny tiny droplets to your ocean of a lifetime. And even though they don't need to keep existing for those droplets to continue swaying inside your ocean, there's something meaningful about knowing these people and places are still alive in the world.

But when those people and places cease to exist, do they really continue living on in you? Anyone would tell you yes—that they continue living *through* you. But I can tell you it's not the same. My day-to-day life as a financial analyst in Denver should've been the same whether my parents were alive or dead, whether the house—the city—I grew up in still stands, right? Wrong.

When those things disappear from the earth, you feel something. Something missing. A little bit of emptiness. Their influence lives on, but in a less concrete way. These are things that people don't acknowledge, because losing loved ones sucks. It's hard as hell. I can see why there were seven thousand religions on the earth at one point—we need stories to cope. But when you throw the stories in the trash, take all your clothes off, and stand in front of a mirror, what do you see? No, stop. What do you *really* see? *Who are you?*

When it comes right down to it—when death is surrounding you like you're on a canoe in the middle of the Pacific—*who are you?*

When your wife is murdered, when your only child is kidnapped, *who are you?*

When you're out here in the Wild being chased out of every town you venture in to, the question gnaws at the back of my neck—*who the hell are you? Who are you doing this for? Who are you trying to impress? What are you trying to get out of this? You think you'll get Xandra back alive? Really? You're just killing time.*

It's a feeling that breaks you down to the dirt. The realization that no one living cares about you. Your family is gone. Your close friends are gone. Your dad is gone. Your wife is gone. The ones whose expectations you were living up to. All gone. Now it's just you. No one else cares.

When you realize this—when you are lying face down in

the dirt almost wishing you could inhale enough dust to fill your lungs and end it right there—that is when the darkness either swallows you or you start to see a pinhole of light a hundred miles away. If you can see the light and get up on your feet and move toward it, that is when the world slowly starts coming together.

Xandra is that light for me. Call it instinct, call it a made-up story in my head, but that girl is what keeps me going. I will either find her and give her a true shot at life, or I will die trying.

And I probably *will* die trying.

"Oh my God," Jame whispers, looking out his side of the window.

I snap out of my train of thought realizing that my hands are tired from death-gripping the steering wheel. I take a deep breath in and out and lean back in my seat. We have arrived at ground zero. The home of the first Big One. The first major natural disaster credited with tipping the nation's scales. There's not a good final death count to the first Big One, but estimates range from 250,000 to 1,000,000—the high-end representing half of the Wasatch Front's total population.

I-80 winds around a large open mine on the east side of the road and then reaches what used to be civilization, now just an endless expanse of rubble. I think about the building inspectors, the sophisticated architects and engineers, building codes, design standards. All of it goes out the window when you're hit with a 7.9.

The closer we get to Salt Lake City, the nastier the destruction gets. Piles of concrete. Trees uprooted. Billboards leveled. Powerlines scattered. Rebar sticking out of seemingly every pile. The air still seems dusty, but that could be my imagination.

We drive on an elevated two-lane version of I-80—the

stretch of freeway rebuilt after the earthquake. It used to be four lanes each direction, but when you eliminate the two million people living in the Wasatch Front and are only accommodating cross-country travelers, two lanes does the trick.

The Wasatch Faultline snakes through the foothills like a crack in a windshield. I see crushed trains, cars, trucks, piles of blue glass shards where fancy modern buildings used to stand. I see a lot of junk too—trampolines, strollers, bikes, headphones, coffee cups.

Once we move past the destruction, a deep sense of relief washes over me.

"Evanston, twenty miles," Jame says, pointing at the road sign now behind us. "I don't think—" he runs his finger along the map again, "—yeah, it's not a Red territory."

"At least not at the time the map was made."

—

We arrive in Evanston around midnight. The stars are bright, the night sky taking on a dimension of its own. We find a Holiday Inn Express quickly and park under the valet overpass. *Just like Chrystal Peak.* We unload onto the sidewalk and I park the car around the corner, hidden from the interstate. I watch the sky as I walk back to the main entrance hoping to see a shooting star—which I do after thirty seconds or so. These stars never get old.

Novae and Supernovae are rare events that occur when a star goes dormant for a while and then surges back to life, emanating a flash of light that can last weeks or months until it fades to black again. They are rare for astronomers to see, let alone a casual observer with his naked eye.

Six years ago, I got the itch to find a Nova or Supernova for Nova. According to my research, the next known Nova to be visibly seen from earth wouldn't appear for another five years, so I had to turn to plan B—a meteor shower that was going to happen that next week. I had the whole thing planned out. I'd wake up a few minutes before and set up a blanket and bottle of champagne, then I'd wake Nova and carry her to the front yard just in time for the show to start. It'd be romantic. It'd be fascinating. It'd give us that feeling of being so incredibly small.

The night came and I was prepared. I woke up ten minutes before 3:00, put my clothes on, got the champagne ready, laid the blanket out, and woke Nova up. She got up and, very groggily, followed me to the front yard, where I told her to look up. For all we know, the meteor shower was amazing, but the cloudy sky had other plans for us. We laughed and returned to bed.

I laugh to myself in the silent and dark Evanston streets at my naivety. My blind hope. My unpreparedness. It's like trying to read a book when you have a smudge on your glasses. The meteor shower is up there. It's happening. It's mind-blowing. But these clouds will never let you know it.

By the time I make it back to the hotel, Jame has made his way in, as evidenced by the automatic doors peered open. We pick rooms near each other on the second floor of the three-story hotel. We stop in the hallway between our rooms and chat briefly about tomorrow's route before parting ways.

We're both overwhelmed, tired, and a little amazed that we're still alive, but that's just how it is out here.

I lay down on the bed with my sleeping bag opened and sink into the mattress, the tension in my arms, my calves, my ankles, melting away. I close my eyes and count myself to sleep.

18

I wake up to sunlight a few minutes before 7:00 AM with the itch to go for a run. I wear what I have on—a dark grey t-shirt, blue basketball shorts, and Converse—and take the stairs to the colorful but comatose lobby. I prop the wheelchair accessible door open with a rock and step outside, taking a deep breath of crisp morning air. It feels good.

I look to my left at the row of rundown Main Street buildings. Little towns generally have one redeeming quality, in my opinion, and that is the quaint, charming downtowns that call back to simpler times. Times when kids ran free, rode bikes to the corner store for an ice cream cone. Not in Evanston. They protested quaint here, I'm sure of it. It's just one brick box after another lining the street.

Oh well, I'm here for the exercise anyway. I touch my toes, stretch my quads, and hit the road.

The sound of my feet hitting the pavement, the chirping birds, the gentle wind. I trot along, my breath picking up. Trash and moldy leaves run up and down the sidewalks, shattered glass scattered in front of looted storefronts. A large puddle from a backed-up street drain runs halfway into the road. Whatever windows are left intact are layered in dirt. I hurdle a downed power pole.

The window of a building next to me shatters, stopping me dead in my tracks. I crouch down and survey my surroundings, carefully reaching for the pistol in the back of my shorts.

A loud voice reverberates from behind me. "Fore!"

I turn around and stand up slowly, my hand shielding my eyes from the sun. In the distance, on the roof of the hotel is a man holding a golf club. It's Jame.

"Are you *trying* to hit me?" I yell back.

"Sorry—didn't see you down there."

From here, I can see his white shirt is stained with blood around the collar. Must have been one of those nights.

I laugh to myself and continue running.

Further down the road, I approach St. Paul's Episcopal Church, a Victorian white-washed brick building topped by a modest spire. It's a textbook small-town church except for one disturbing deviation. The Celtic Cross on top of the spire is not white like the rest of the building, it's black. And it's upside down.

A brush with the Occult. There's a first for everything.

My jog slows to a walk as I near the building. The windows are intact but boarded up from the inside. One of the Medieval front doors is slightly ajar. I cautiously move toward it, listening for any movement inside. I nudge the door open and step inside. It's dark and silent. As light fills the chambers revealing its tall ceilings, intricate chandelier, and rotting pews, I notice the smell. That familiar acidic, rotting smell of drying blood.

Oh my God.

I freeze in my tracks as light falls on a second inverted Celtic Cross on the wall behind the stage, but this one is painted in blood. Just in front of it is a charred makeshift altar.

This is the problem with religion.

I step backward into a puddle. *Please don't be blood.* I move under the door frame and lift up my right foot, a splotchy scarlet footprint left behind. I break out in chills.

"Is someone there?" a timid voice calls from the chapel mezzanine.

My heart sinks another level, my heart pounding in my

throat.

"Someone's there—who are you?" the voice continues.

I hold my breath.

"WHO IS THERE?" The voice shrieks, reverberating through the cavernous chapel. As the echoes fade, there is a loud crash on the pews just in front of me.

"Damn—oh holy—" the voice mutters. This time much closer.

Did he just jump from the mezzanine?

"Sorry—I don't mean any trouble. Just stopping through," I say.

"Stopping through—oh God, why the hell did I— stopping through Evanston, huh? Our garbage little piss-cowboy town?"

I slowly push on the door behind me allowing more light into the chapel. That's when I see people. Well, bodies. Motionless bodies staged, sitting in the pews. Probably twenty. All sitting up with kinked heads. I feel another round of chills run down my spine.

"You like our art project, mysterious stranger?" The light finds the man speaking. He flinches when it reaches his eyes. "Oh, man. Too bright."

I know I can leave at any time. I can run right through the door and he probably wouldn't be able to catch me, but part of me is fascinated—like trying to avoid staring at a car crash as you roll on by. This idiot just jumped from the mezzanine level on top of pews filled with dead people just to get a closer look at me.

"You from Evanston?" I ask.

He lets out a booming, maniacal laugh. "I've never met such a talkative—what do you call yourselves—oh yeah, Reds. Red like bloody bloody blood. Say, have you ever been to a slaugh—" He exhales loudly and winces in pain.

"Are you okay?"

He inhales loudly through his teeth. "Yes. Born and raised. This junk tiny town. A bunch of good Christians here. That's what we are. You know there's like twelve Mormon churches here? That's like a Mormon church for every three people."

"I'm not a Red by the way," I say.

He gives me a double take. "Well, then what the *hell* are you doing here?"

"Did you kill these people?"

He lets out another maniacal laugh and steps closer into the light. His hair is unnaturally black, his skin unnaturally white. His eyes are red. "Did I kill—" he stops in his tracks and looks down at one of the sitting corpses. "Actually—no, no I didn't."

"So, who did?"

"Well, my friends and I, we always liked the idea of the Occult—Devil worship. Thought it'd be funny to turn one of the churches into a Satanic temple."

"What's the goal? Summoning demons?"

"The funny thing about Satan is that he believes everyone deserves to be in hell. It's not that he—oh hell—" He rubs his knee, wincing in pain. "He doesn't just *want* everyone in hell, he legitimately believes everyone *deserves* to be there. When someone goes to heaven, he thinks he's being ripped off. And I happen to agree." His smile creeps up, revealing horribly yellow stained teeth with brown splotches. He seems far too young to have teeth like that. "I think you deserve to be in hell, my sweet, mysterious stranger. You think you just *happened* to wander in here today? You don't think you were guided?" He hobbles closer. "Do you agree, Dark One?"

A women's voice drifts from the front of the chapel. "Who

do we have here, my son?" I swing the door open further, the light finding the source of the voice—a woman in her mid-40s, black hair, pale skin standing at the front of the chapel next to the altar.

A golf ball bounces down the road past the church.

The woman slowly walks towards me, a long knife hanging by her side.

All at once, a feeling of nausea washes over me, the walls close in. "All right, psychos, I'm outta here," I say, stepping back toward the doors.

A hand touches my shoulder. I jerk around to find a zombie-looking woman, probably late 20s. She has dark, sunken eyes, with blood-streaked blond hair.

I swat her hand off me and step through the door.

The corners of her mouth creep up to form a smile.

Another guy comes around the corner of the building. "What shall we do with him, Dark One?" he yells, ensuring his voice reaches the woman in the chapel.

I continue toward the street, trying not to show my panic. I look over my shoulder. Four others have appeared from the back of the building.

"I don't know about all of you, but I haven't eaten in three days, and I've kinda missed the taste of charred human flesh," the 'Dark One' says, now standing in the doorway. "Get him."

I run toward the hotel as fast as I can, the clapping footsteps and ravenous breathing following close behind. I pull the pistol out of the back of my shorts and cock it mid-stride. I turn the corner of a block of buildings a street away from the hotel and lean against the wall. One by one, they run past me, all seven, yelling at each other. I try to steady my breath, my heartbeat beating through my still-bandaged right arm.

Realizing they've lost me, their conversation calms down.

I hear things like "couldn't have made it far" and "he'll turn up—it's Evanston." I count five heading back.

Just then I feel a tap on my shoulder from behind me. I turn around and find one of the women hunched over with that voracious smile across her face. Her eyes are sunken, dead. She put on eyeliner at some point in the last month I'm guessing.

These observations occur in a split second, because then she kicks me swiftly in the gut, scissoring me in half. My gun drops but she doesn't notice. From the other direction I take a kick to the face from someone else.

"Lousy tourists," one of them says, snickering.

The other one brings her face down to my level and grabs my hair, jerking my head upward. "You look like you come from money. You ever been to a Luau, rich boy?"

I try to open my eyes, and only successfully do so with one of them.

"You know how they roast a friggin' pig over a fire?" The girls chuckle. "That's what we're gonna do to you. Except for you're gonna be alive." Another chuckle. "Just have to wait til sundown."

"God, I can't wait that long. You think she's gonna make us wait that long?" The other girl says.

"I didn't make the rules, sweetheart. You know that."

Still in the crouched position, I slowly pick up the gun and kink my hand to point at the first girl's torso. My arm is shaking in pain, but this is my only chance. If any of the others come back here, I'm a dead man. A burned-alive-in-a-ceremonial-satanic-ritual kind of dead man.

I take in a shallow breath and pull the trigger, hitting the first girl in the arm and sending her back hard against the brick wall behind us.

"What the—" the second girl yelps before I swing the gun toward her and connect with her face, sending her to the ground. I turn back to the first girl, she is crouched down with her back against the wall gripping her arm, blood trickling onto the ground.

I stumble to my feet and step over the second girl lying on the ground holding her bleeding face. With my gun pointed at them, I slowly back out of the alley and into the street. Neither of them has any interest in continuing the fight, but the others do. The remaining five sprint toward me, yelling. I fire two shots toward the group, neither bullet making contact.

A car honks behind me. I turn around and see Jame in the driver's seat of the Charger rapidly approaching. Thank God. I fire one more shot at the group and climb in the car. I watch out the back window as the group and the church fades from view.

"How have you survived out here this long without being killed?" Jame asks.

"I was just going for a run. An innocent run in Evanston, Wyoming. Is that too much to ask?"

Jame laughs.

19

Jame and I quickly learned to travel by night.

A couple of miles before Rock Springs, a known Red territory, we got off the freeway to take county roads when we were attacked. By the time we turned around, I-80 had a whole crew of men waiting for us. Rock Springs is desert, but rocky, so cutting through the desert wasn't an option. Only through an act of amazing luck did we finagle our way through the sea of cars alive. Jame was muttering a prayer under his breath the whole time, so it could've been God watching out for us too. Also, we threw a grenade.

Luck, God, and grenades aside, best we can figure is that Reds aren't anticipating intruders. They are used to busting into towns on the offense and conquering, but they're not used to being invaded. They're not trained for it. Nevertheless, Jame and I realize we've been too lucky too many times in situations like Rock Springs. We stopped in Rawlins that afternoon for Walmart and gas then took Highway 30 to evade a supposed roadblock on I-80 in Elk Mountain.

State highways, particularly in wild west states like Wyoming, are in rough condition. The winner-take-all nature of the Pre-Move economy meant that good places did better, and bad places did worse. Towns accessible only by state highway tended to be in the latter category. Highway 30 is the poster child for this notion.

Right now, we're chugging along the highway both silently calculating how long it will take us to cross the country if we're forced to take back roads that mirror the surface of the moon the whole way.

"Right there." I point to a pothole in front of us and Jame

slams on the brakes, swerving around it. We do this a lot—speed up, hit the brakes, speed up, jerk the wheel, hit the brakes.

We stop in Medicine Bow for the night at the best, and possibly only, hotel in town, The Virginian. It's a four-story, cowboy-era brick building, void of any character. Its placement adjacent to the highway is its only redeeming quality, making it an effective watchpoint. Jame and I follow the same protocol, dropping our stuff off then taking the car to a discreet parking area—this time to an alleyway between the post office and the Old West Saloon, a block away.

Independent hotels like these don't have fancy design and security standards like the chain hotels, so breaking in and making our way around is easy. Well, for one thing, there is no *breaking in* to The Virginian because the main door is unlocked.

The lobby sports a decades-old maroon carpet with Victorian floral patterns throughout. The smell of cat urine is strong, which means either cats live here, or this was once a meth-house. Maybe both. The cramped, nine-foot ceiling of the lobby doesn't help. After a few minutes inspecting the common areas—the one hundred square foot fitness center, the kitchen, the dining area, the back office behind the front desk—the coast appears to be clear.

Jame and I find a conference room in the back equipped with empty, built-in bookshelves, a large wood conference table, and a handful of worn tweed office chairs scattered around the room. I lay the territory map and roadmap flat on the table and Jame pulls up two chairs. We study the map in silence for a couple minutes.

"I-80 is clearly off limits once we cross into Zone 2. That's tomorrow," I say.

"We'll take 385 south to I-70," Jame says matter-of-factly,

tracing his finger along the path.

"Well, then I-70 becomes off limits in Colby. That only gives us like twenty minutes on I-70." Another minute passes by in silence. "You know, we almost named Xandra Colby. That was Nova's top choice, but I ended up convincing her."

"385 to 36 then. I don't care," Jame snaps.

I sit back in my chair. Jame's eyes stay fixed on the map. "Listen man, I know it's exhausting," I start.

"Do you? Do you know that, Leo?"

"I'm sor—"

"Why don't you—" Jame cuts himself off by putting his hand up to his mouth. He moves his gaze from the map to me. "You have Xandra out there and that's great, but do you know anything about me? Do you even care? All we ever talk about is your perfect little family. Why do you think I'm out here, Leo? You really think I'm just here to help you or just because I'm curious? Is that what you think? That's probably what you think. You know other people have lives too, not just you."

The image of him sitting alone in the Walmart parking lot in Fernley holding the Minnie Mouse doll comes to me. He became a child to me then, and he's becoming one to me now. Not in an immature or childish way, but in a fragile way. He's a broken kid.

He stands up and paces the room then returns to the table, leaning forward on his arms. He puts his head down and sobs uncontrollably.

I watch him for a second then turn my head, feeling suddenly invasive. This is the Wild, we're all entitled to our breakdowns from time to time.

After another minute, he settles down.

"I'm sor—sorry," he says.

"It's okay. Jame, listen, you are completely right, I talk way too much about my problems and I haven't taken the time to get to know you and why you're here. I'm sorry."

He nods, his hands up to his face.

"You okay?"

"Yeah," he whispers.

"You don't have to tell me anything, but—"

"I'm sorry. I didn't mean to come off like that."

"It's okay. You know how grateful I am for you. You've saved my life on more than one occasion. I owe you more than you'll ever know. I won't pretend to know what you're going through, but I know that dealing with loss sucks."

He looks up at me, his cheeks wet. "How do you deal with it? How do you even function?"

"I'm not sure. The only real thing I've learned is to accept that death is all around us, as odd as that sounds. The reason loss feels so painful is because we spend our whole lives pretending it doesn't exist. But of course, it *does* exist. It touches every single person in the world. Death is as natural as breathing and it *always* wins. No amount of religion or fairytales can prevent it."

Jame chokes a laugh through his tears. "If you can't beat em, join em."

I smile sympathetically. "I know it's counterintuitive, but death is not the enemy. Loss is not the enemy. They are life."

If only I could get myself to believe that.

"I tried, Leo, I tried. We had something. 'Brecken Brown turn that frown upside down,' I used to say. It's not easy for people like me, Leo, you get that?"

I nod, trying to follow.

"For people like us, I mean. Not when you grow up in an uber-religious household, an uber-religious community. The rest of the world moved on long before. The gays were not a subculture anymore—I mean, not nearly like they used to be. But in religious circles, time stood still. Homosexuality was the second worst sin possible both 2,000 years ago *and* today. The only thing worse is murder. The *only* thing worse, Leo. You remember that?"

I nod again.

"And why? Because to them, it's a choice. To them, everyone is born the same as them. If you're different, something's wrong. You made a bad choice. An evil choice. For all the progress and innovation in the world, you'd think there'd be a bit more empathy. And like it takes that big of an imagination—to imagine what it would be like to be born gay. Born without a choice. To be born poor, or not white, or Muslim."

I sit back down across the table from him.

"I had a boyfriend. *I had a boyfriend.* Do you know how long it took me to even allow myself to *try and find* a boyfriend? I knew I was gay when I was thirteen. I mean, deep down I knew it, but I didn't really admit it to myself until I was twenty-five. Just lived in limbo for twelve years. I know that's shorter than what a lot of people deal with, but—" He pauses and looks up at me, almost as if he forgot another person was there, then continues. "But then I met Brecken. Tall, strong, bold, confident. It was meeting him that allowed me to step up to the plate. Ya know, my mom always told us kids to *rise to the occasion.* I never knew what that meant until meeting Brecken. I knew that this was a once-in-a-lifetime chance. Not only to be with an amazing guy—or at least pursue it—but to embrace myself as I truly was.

"And I did it. It was hard. Hard as hell. My mom rejected me. My dad erased me from memory. My brothers and sisters pretended to be understanding at first but then faded away. My entire support system, my community left me. Well, according to them, I'm the one who left. I'm the one who chose—*chose*—this sinful life, therefore, I deserve to have everything ripped from me. That's how it goes, right?"

"Gosh, I'm so sorry, Jame."

"All I had left was Brecken. It worked for a while. A year. But then it was too much for him. I get it. How does one individual replace an entire family—an entire community of support? He essentially replaced God for me. Not to mention, he had his own crap to deal with. He also grew up with a religious family that rejected him too—that was part of why we connected so deeply. But as time went on, the pressure we placed on ourselves and each other was too much. We fell apart."

"Gosh," I say, shaking my head sympathetically.

"When I first came out, people told me it would get better. You'd grow comfortable in your own skin. You'd make friends. Your family would realize you were still the same person you've always been. After Brecken and I split, I realized that all that advice was crap. Maybe it's valid advice for 99% of people, but not for me. I'd be the exception, the one to be permanently destroyed. Stay in the closet and live a life with my shoes one size too small, or come out and lose—" He pauses for a minute to catch his breath. "—lose everything."

He pauses for another minute, quietly crying with his head down.

"Did the Minnie Mouse have anything to do with Brecken?" I ask.

Jame quietly laughs. "Yeah, one of our things was Minnie Mouse—how we both felt we identified more closely with Minnie than Mickey growing up. It's stupid, I know."

"Hey, I'm an expert in emotional triggers."

Jame smiles.

"Then what happened?" I ask.

"The Move was the nail in the coffin for us. I decided to become a cop. Classic tough guy job. And he—he chose a different path."

"What did Brecken do?"

"He joined the Reds."

20

Jame and I continued traveling by night, circumventing Red territories and flagged roads on Cherry's roadmap as much as possible.

A bullet blew out our back left window in Wall, South Dakota. Our front right tire was shot outside Sioux Falls causing us to drive on a flat tire twenty miles to Beaver Creek, where we found a replacement car—a red F-150. Jame thought he saw Brecken manning a post in Worthington, Missouri which turned out not to be him after a very emotionally-charged and dangerous U-turn on the freeway.

We stayed in hotels along the way, sleeping during the day. Motel 6 in Kadoka. King's Inn in Kennebec. Hampton Inn in Oacoma. The flipped schedule took a while to get used to. Well, to be honest, I'm still not used to it.

Jame screamed during the night in Austin, Minnesota because a raccoon was rummaging his room. I cried when we passed a defunct carousel at the Olmstead County Fairgrounds in Rochester, Minnesota. We picked up some night vision binoculars at an old hunting store in Waterloo, Iowa.

We met Peter, a pre-Move homeless man—*king of the Shell station*—in LaCrosse while trying to satisfy a sudden craving for whiskey. 'We should be drinking more,' Jame had suggested. He talked with us for a half hour about how the Big Ones and the other natural disasters were signs of the times and how the Move got rid of the sinners and left the chosen ones behind. Jame and I had fun with the conversation until Peter told us he thought the Reds were anointed, causing Jame to storm out of the station kicking a Pringles display on his way out.

I talked about Xandra and Nova ad nauseum on our drives.

Jame talked about Brecken ad nauseum. We talked politics and conspiracy theories. We placed bets about what Cherry and Ryan look like. We argued about what car we should try to find next should this one break down. Jame had two more stressed-induced nose bleeds.

I finished *Siddhartha* and immediately started it over—*spoke of peace, spoke of completeness, sought nothing, imitated nothing, reflected a continuous quiet, an unfading light, an invulnerable peace.* I meditated morning and night. Sometimes it helped, sometimes all I could see was Xandra's big blue eyes. Sometimes all I could think about was Nova's body temperature plummeting while I held her. I think about dragging the first Red I ever knew to the window, I think about pushing the big blubbery body out, watching it fall, disappearing into the snow with a poof. I think about returning to Raton in a blur. I think about my first few months in the Wild. Wandering aimlessly. Learning how to survive. Getting lost.

All until meeting nose ring man in Battle Mountain. How that would change everything. I think about how far we've come since Empire. How lucky it is we haven't been killed yet. I think about our chances of making it to Paoli, now that we're entering Zone 1.

My mind still wanders to dark places. To dusty, dark basements dimly lit by pool lights filtered through cigarette smoke. Places where the Nihilist invites me to sit down, passing me a very simple message: *Nova's dead, Xandra's dead, and you'll be dead soon.*

Now I'm sitting in what used to be the food court of the long-abandoned Southlake Mall in Merrillville, Indiana. I'm surrounded by dated tables and chairs, moldy paper menus, and plenty of broken glass. Its mildewy aura brings nostalgia of foraging Royale Center with Tripp as a kid.

Jame is exploring the mall while I sit here, maps spread across a couple tables pushed together. Tomorrow is a new day. The day we enter Zone 1, the longest abandoned area of the Wild—the birthplace of the Reds.

Jame comes back from his walk and picks up a chair from off the ground, turning it right side up.

"Find anything good?"

"There's an old Foot Locker back there. I found some rejects in the back of the store." He swings his leg around the side and slams it on the table revealing a fresh pair of bright green Nike running shoes.

"Those… are very bright."

The sound of a crashing store rack reverberates from the other end of the mall.

"What the—" I stand up looking toward the sound.

Jame negotiates his leg off the table and stumbles trying to catch his balance. "Also, someone lives here," he says.

"What the—who?" I say, walking around the corner to get a better view of the long stretch of stores leading to the former Macy's (well, Macy's before it was laser tag before it was the Montgomery Aquarium) at the end of the mall.

"Just a mall dweller, that's all."

"Cool," I say turning back toward the food court.

"There's *two* handsome young men?" A jovial voice rings out.

We turn toward the voice. An elderly, overweight black woman wearing a bright purple shirt emerges from the mezzanine level of the Macy's. She moves slowly, methodically.

"Hi," Jame says, waving his arm.

"Are we—do we need to talk to her?" I say, nudging Jame.

"No, of course we don't. Just trying to be nice."

"Yeah but, is she crazy?"

"Shh, it's okay."

"My name… is Zara," she says.

Before she even gets to us, I feel her presence. She isn't like anyone else we've met in the Belt. She has a warmth to her that I haven't experienced in a long time.

I think you're tired, Leo.

Still about six or seven stores away from us, Zara starts her speech. "You know, the Reds have been through here. A while ago now. Maybe a year. No matter how good their intentions, I think they are pure evil. Broke in here, killed a whole bunch us. My best friend Tara—we loved introducing ourselves together, Tara and Zara—she died right there." She points to a destroyed kiosk on the floor below. Sunglasses4Less, now a pile of rubble coated with dry blood.

"I'm sorry to hear that, Zara," I say, hoping them not to be my last words. She's now standing right in front of us.

"We had a whole community here. Almost a hundred fifty people. We used the food court as the cafeteria—what else, of course! Church service in the aquarium's amphitheater. We even had a doctor's office, Dr. Barton, General Practitioner, down in the old LensCrafters. Stitched my little Rose up once upon a time. Tried to take her little bike down the stairs, that silly girl." Zara points to a sleek glass staircase in the atrium.

Ambitious kid.

She puts her hand on her heart and looks up to the ceiling. "They killed Tara. They killed Pastor Jim. They killed Dr. Barton. They killed everyone except me and the GA—as far as I know. But they took Rose. My sweet grandbaby Rose."

Jame looks at me.

"Ya know, Zara, my little girl was taken too," I say. "That's why I'm out here. Trying to find her."

"Lord Jesus," she says, grabbing both my hands and looking into my eyes. "May Jesus deliver our two girls back to us."

"That would be ideal," I say, glancing over to Jame.

"So, what kind of community was here, Zara?" Jame asks.

Zara breaks her gaze and lets my hands go.

"Pentecostals of Southlake. We had a church just down the road but decided it'd be easier to operate as a united community here in the mall. We could choose anywhere we wanted, you know."

"Sorry, if we're not supposed to—"

"Please, it's been so lonely here. I'm just thrilled to have two handsome young men like yourselves come and visit."

"So why stay behind in the Wild? Why not move to the Belt with everyone else?"

"That certainly would've been easier. But *easier* rarely means *right*. Us Pentecostals have a strong belief in the Rapture, meaning that we believe Jesus is going to personally carry us believers up to heaven Pre-Trib. Are you two familiar with Tribulation?"

Jame nods his head yes, I shake my head no.

Zara faces me, switching to ministry mode. "Well—what was your name again?"

"Leo."

"Well, Leo, a lot of Christians believe that there will be a seven-year period called Tribulation before the Millennium. Are you familiar with the Millennium?"

"I think so, the time when Jesus will rule the world?" I say, hoping I'm remembering right.

"Yes, Leo, exactly. Well, there's fierce debate in the Christian community as to *when* the Rapture will occur. Everyone agrees it will occur during the period of Tribulation, but some think it's supposed to start at the beginning—or right before—Tribulation begins. Some think the Rapture will happen during the middle of Tribulation. Others think it happens at the end of Tribulation, right before the Millennium begins."

I nod my head. *Like rearranging deck chairs on the Titanic,* I think to myself.

"Now here, Jame and Leo, is where things get complicated for us Pentecostals. You see, Pentecostals are generally firm in the belief that the Rapture will occur Pre-Trib—meaning *before* the seven-year Tribulation begins. Our community was adamant that the Move was the start of Tribulation. I mean, everyone knew that President Lussier was the Antichrist. And I don't mean to bring politics into this, but that one was obvious to most religious communities. An atheist president? Please.

"So, then the next question was *when* exactly the Tribulation would begin. When the antichrist is elected? When the natural disasters happened? When the Move is announced? When the Move rolls out? This question is particularly important to those who believe in a Pre-Trib Rapture cause we could be taken up at any time without warning, really."

Jame straightens his back and inhales like he's going to say something, but turns his head and sneezes.

"So, we resisted the Move. We planned for months. We prepared food. We scoped out locations. We hid from the Census Workers. We were confident that this was the start of the Tribulation which meant we only needed to hang out for a couple of weeks at most, then the Rapture would happen. Well, those couple weeks turned into a couple months then almost a year. Things grew tense. Now we were questioning if the Tribulation had truly begun. Pastor Jim and some of us bible scholars scoured the scriptures in all humility to see if maybe the Rapture could, in fact, be Mid-Trib or Post-Trib, as many other Christians believe."

"Then the Reds came?"

"Not quite yet. Lucky for us, we stayed a unified community for the most part. There were a few who lost the faith and moved to the Belt. But everyone else who stayed behind—even though there were differing beliefs on some of these things—stayed united. We were a family. Whether Tribulation had begun, we were a family of saints and we were gonna stay that way."

She puts her hand on her hip and looks out on the food court. "Then Pastor Jim commissioned a group of eight young men and women, called Gods Army or GA for short, to scope out the rest of the Wild and see if there were other religious groups out there. They were out for a week when they came back and warned us of the Reds. Said they were possibly a radical religious group and very violent. They almost didn't make it back to us alive. Our leadership team immediately started to identify other locations we could move to in fear that the GA had been followed. That fear was confirmed when the Reds raided us the next morning."

Zara cries again. I look around carefully, noticing the aftermath of the raid around me. The overturned tables, the broken glass, the bullet holes in the walls. What I had assumed was the work of vandals was probably the result of the Reds.

"I was in the bathroom right over there." She points to the bathroom sign placed between two empty storefronts about thirty feet away.

"See, my hearing isn't the best. While I was in the bathroom, I heard noises out here, but assumed it was the kids playing, jumping around the food court tables. When I came out, it was a war zone. I don't know how many Reds were here, but it was enough to wipe everyone out in five minutes. I came out just as the last of the Reds were leaving. The kids were gone at that point. One of them saw me but turned around and left when he saw that none of the other Reds noticed me. Makes me think Jesus intervened."

Jame looks down.

My eyes burn thinking about the kids, playing one minute, gone the next. Their lives turned upside down just like that. "I'm so—so sorry, Zara."

She nods, trying to compose herself. "I saw Tara lying in the crashed Kiosk and ran to her. Her head and part of her face was smashed in. The blood, oh Lord, the blood was everywhere. I asked her where Rose was, she said the kids were taken. That was it. I never got to say goodbye to Rose. Tara passed on seconds later. I scoured the mall for the next few minutes, there was smoke in the building, almost like a fog machine. Dead bodies everywhere. But not just bodies; my friends, my family, my community. We were gonna be taken up to Jesus together. There were no survivors besides me and the GA. They were out getting food at the time of the raid but haven't come back since. I spent the next two weeks dragging the bodies to the basement and praying the whole time. For an old gal like me, it's only through Jesus that I had the strength to do so."

"Are you gonna stay here?" Jame asks.

"I don't know where else to go. This is my home. I have food, I have working restrooms. Besides, I don't have any other family and I'm old. Either the Rapture is gonna happen or I'm gonna die, but going to the Belt ain't gonna change nothin'. And if the GA comes back, or if Rose comes back, God willing, I want to be in the place they last saw me."

"Listen, we are meeting up with a kind of resistance group in rural Indiana. They say they can help me find my daughter. Do you want to come with us? We will take care of you," I say.

Zara smiles. "I appreciate you boys, I really do, but I'm comfortable here. I would be no help there. You go on your journey and find your daughter. Oh, and keep an eye out for my Rose." She pulls a picture out of her pocket and extends it to me. The girl looks about Xandra's age with thick dreads pulled into a ponytail. She has a wide, bright smile, and a comically cute oversized forehead just like Xandra.

A few seconds pass in silence. The three of us awkwardly staring at each other.

"I'm sorry—is there any chance we could crash here for the day? We've been sleeping during the day and traveling at night."

"Boys, of course, I should've offered it in the first place. There're some bunks in the whole block of stores directly below us."

Jame and I stand up. Zara stays seated.

"Thank you, Zara. We'll probably be leaving late tonight. Is there anything we can do while we're here?"

"Turns out supplies for 150 people for two weeks lasts a long time for one 70-year-old woman," she says, smiling.

Jame and I find our way down the stairs and to the bunk zone. The scene is gruesome. There are no bodies but there is plenty of blood—blood splattered on walls, glass storefronts, the floor. There were paths of blood leading to a narrow hallway off the main concourse. Must be where the freight elevator goes to the basement.

And I thought the cellar in Empire was bad.

We split up, and I find a clean bunk in what appears to be, ironically, an old mattress store near a side entrance of the mall.

I ascend a small ladder to the top bunk near the glass storefront and lay flat on my back, sinking into the mattress immediately. I breathe deep and start mentally preparing myself for what's to come tomorrow. To think that we've come all this way because of a two-minute chat on an antiquated computer terminal literally in the middle of nowhere. The amount of blind trust we're putting in Cherry and Ryan and the nose ring guy is nauseating.

But it's the only thing we have. And it's gonna be good.

A waste of time is what it is. It's a miracle you've made it this far.

Death is as natural as breathing and it always *wins.*

My inner dialogue puts me to sleep.

—

I wake up feeling hollow, thinking of all the moments I wish I could take back. The times I scolded Xandra for leaving her bed too many times in the night because she 'wanted to snuggle.' The times I told her we could only read *one* story even though she wanted more, because *I* thought I had better things to do. The times I could've kept holding her, the times I could've kept listening to her stories, the times I could've been more patient.

What I wouldn't do to have her back.

I roll over to face the entrance of the store, the long shadows of early evening spilling down the hallway. With no setbacks, we should be able to make it to Paoli in five hours. Depending on how brutal Zone 1 is, we may have to break the trip up into two days.

"Oh Leo, are you sure you want to cross the border—to Zone 1, I mean?" Zara's voice makes me jump, partially because the silence she interrupted was so deep, partially because I couldn't see her coming from the top bunk.

"I mean—the Reds are everywhere there. At least that's what the GA told us, and they're gone now. I saw what those Reds can do, they're vicious."

"I know."

"Why don't you and Jame stay here with me? We can be our own little community. It doesn't have to be religious. I—I have food, shelter, supplies."

"Zara, the offer still stands for us to take you with us. But you have to understand that if I'm alive one second on this earth without fighting to find my daughter again, I'm wasting time. I have to do this."

She looks down, then pulls a school picture from her pocket and hands it to me. "Please, keep an eye out for her."

I look carefully at the photo of Rose and smile, feeling a tear form in the corner of my eye.

Zara puts her hand on my shoulder and bows her head. "Please God be with these two young men. My baby Rose is gone and so is Leo's. Please give them the strength and vision to find these two angels."

I turn and see Jame standing just outside the store entrance, a tear rolling down his cheek.

Zone 1, here we come.

21

"Zone 1 has been abandoned for what, four years?" Jame asks.

"Yeah—well almost five at this point."

Before meeting Zara in the mall, Jame and I mapped out potential routes along state highways and county roads to Zone 1.

"Not only is it the most densely populated area in the country, but almost the whole time zone had to move, right?" Jame asks.

"Winter freezes in the Northeast and Midwest, hurricanes along the entire east coast, then Florida is its own thing," I say.

"Sea level rise?"

"Yeah sea level rise, but when you combine sea level rise with warmer water that means superstorms. *And* the state is built on limestone. Limestone is porous. I'm shocked there's anything left of Florida now."

"I guess I never paid attention to any of this. I mean, I was in high school when the Move was announced. Then it became normal. I never cared why—not in any meaningful way, I guess. All I cared about was where we'd end up and whether any of my secret crushes would be there," he says.

We both laugh.

"I bet the Feds wish they would've done the Zone 1 Move in phases. I heard there were just as many people in Zone 1 as there were in the other three zones combined."

"Now *that* is a land grab. I mean, there's what, 70 or 80 million households that just got left behind in Zone 1?"

"Yeah."

We pass through San Pierre, a tiny rural town that appears to be deserted. *But probably isn't.*

I exhale loudly. "'Bout an hour out," I say, a pit in my stomach.

—

The next hour goes by much too quickly and much too quietly. As we approach Monon, Indiana—the first town in White County, and Zone 1—I slow the car down.

"See anything with those hawk eyes?" I ask.

"No. This is good though. Let's take it slow."

A half mile out, I see something in the road, illuminated in the distance by my headlights. I slow down further. "You see that?"

"You got those binoculars?"

"Glove box."

I stop the car. Jame takes the binoculars from the glovebox, clicks on night vision, and puts them up to his eyes, leaning forward. "Roadblocks. Military grade." He pans around. "The buildings are like ruins. I mean, the whole scene looks like a war zone."

From where we are, I see charred buildings half torn down, piles of rubble.

"Oh God," Jame says, handing me the binoculars abruptly, closing his eyes.

I watch him for a second then put them to my eyes. I see now that some piles are rubble. *Some* piles. The other piles are of dead bodies. Bodies piled ten feet high. Primarily men. No, exclusively men. No women or—thank God—children from what I can see. There are men of all sorts, white collar, blue collar, white, black, Asian, Hispanic—they all bleed red. But that's not all. Some are Reds—*were* Reds. Beefy stature, beards, slash tattoos across the eyes. There are almost as many Reds as there are others. From here I see one pile in front of the roadblocks and two more behind.

"God," I whisper.

Jame opens the car door and hurls onto the road.

The sound startles me. "You okay?"

He sits back up in the car and closes the door, exhaling loudly. His face is drained of color.

"You think there's anyone else here?" I ask. "I mean, alive?"

"Give me a second."

I pan the landscape with my binoculars. I see dead fields in all directions, downed power lines to our right, abandoned farmhouses to our left. A large Victorian-style house two streets east from the main highway has the word *UNICORN* painted in red on the side.

"Unicorn," I say out loud. "Does that mean anything to you?"

"No."

I hand the binoculars back to Jame. "There were a lot of Reds in that front pile there. I don't know if you wanted to look for Brecken still, but—"

Jame sets the binoculars down. "I know it's probably nothing, but could you check?" He hands me a picture, one that I've seen a couple times before. Brecken has a strong jaw, wide shoulders, and fire red hair.

"Yeah, of course." I put the car in drive and pull as close to the piles as the roadblocks will allow.

The thick cloud cover diffuses the moonlight, giving us decent visibility as I stop the car and kill the headlights. I step out and taste the dust from the dead fields blowing through town. Besides the howling of wind—unnaturally cold for this time of year—it's silent.

Zone 1.

In the seconds between the wind shifting directions, the all-too-familiar scent of rotting bodies touches my nose before being blown away again. I cock my gun, hold it by my right side, and walk. A loud creaking noise from behind me catches my attention. Three bodies hang from a wooden beam that spans a half-burned down building, the lifeless corpses swaying in the wind. One is a Red, one is in a tattered suit, the other is a younger guy in his twenties. All men. All transitioning from the bloated phase to the shriveling phase. I pan the scene again when my light glimmers on one of the hanging men. I step closer. The man has a silver septum nose ring.

The nose ring man from Battle Mountain.

I exhale sharply.

A government sign sits atop the roadblock tagged with *UNICORN* in red spray paint. Underneath the paint, I make out familiar PSA messaging:

ZONE 1 IS PERMANENTLY CLOSED
THE AREA BEYOND IS WILDERNESS
NO SERVICES AVAILABLE
ENTER AT YOUR OWN RISK

The second pile's occupants are a similar makeup to the first pile. All men, a decent number of Reds, no women or children. The town is small, ending just a quarter mile beyond the roadblock. I turn around, catching a glimpse of another large red tag on the building to my right, *WON'T BE HAD*.

"You ain't welcome here," a drunken voice calls out.

I spin in a circle trying to find the source of the sound.

A man stands on the roof of a two-story hotel across the street from the hanging bodies. He's older, bearded, and has a tattoo across his left eye. His rifle swings around his body as he stumbles toward the fire escape stairs on the side of the building. He's drunk.

I tighten my grip on the pistol as he stumbles closer.

"This is Red country, boy," he says.

"What does that mean?"

"Boy, have you been livin' under a frickin' rock?"

He trips halfway down the first flight of stairs and is forced to jump the last few to the landing. "Hoooooeeeeey!" he yells.

I hold the pistol steady and point it at him. I look over my shoulder and see Jame watching me with the car door open.

"Hell boy, you gonna shoot me?" Miscalculating his coordination under the influence, he reaches for his rifle and fires it toward the ground, the bullet making a loud ricochet noise against the metal fire escape. "Ah damn," he yells.

"Are *you* gonna shoot me?" I ask.

"I will if you try to pass through here. I might either way, honestly," he says and steadies his rifle. He shifts his jaw back and forth then twitches suddenly.

"Yeah, I think we're gonna pass anyway," I say, gripping the pistol.

"So what, you get past me and then what? You're in Zone 1 now, boy. We won't be had!" He tenses his trigger finger and braces for the kick.

Before he can fire, I pull the trigger of my pistol, the bullet striking his leg. He drops down the remaining stairs and spills onto the road, screaming.

I hear shuffling from the building next to me.

"Will, what's goin on?" Another drunken voice calls.

"It's a frickin' Belter!" The Red yells.

"Oh hell." Another Red appears around the corner from the neighboring building. He's skinnier, but still white and bearded. And shirtless. "Yo, don't shoot, man," he says as he scrambles back around the corner.

Is this all they got? Two drunks patrolling Zone 1?

He appears around the corner again and fires a shot before I notice he's even holding a gun. The bullet zooms past my hip striking the building behind me. I fire two shots toward him and sprint toward the car.

As I run, I hear an exchange of gunfire. I look up and see Jame standing outside the car firing shots past me. The Red laying at the bottom of the fire escape moans in pain. "Call it in, Tommy!" he yells.

I hear the static of a walkie-talkie in the distance behind me. "This is Monon—come in—we've got a Belter trying to come through, over."

Through the gunfire, someone responds on the walkie-talkie, although I can't make out what was said.

"We need backup—Will's been shot," the Red says.

Jame and I jump into the car and slam the doors shut.

"They got the nose ring guy," I say, stepping on the gas and flipping the car around back to Zone 2.

"No—the guy with the notes?"

"Yeah."

"Ah, gosh."

"No Brecken though. From what I saw."

Jame exhales.

"What's our plan B?"

Jame opens the map on his lap. "We'll try a re-entry at Remington."

We drive north, transferring to CR-114 west. The fifteen-mile trip takes forty-five minutes, thanks to the utterly-neglected county road.

"They're expecting us now," I say as we approach our second attempt at entering Zone 1. "You heard them call us in?"

"Yeah."

"They have to know that we're gonna try other routes. 231, 55, 71."

"Yes, but how much work are they gonna go through to keep two guys like us out?"

"Belters."

"What?"

"The two Reds back there referred to us as Belters," I say.

"Ok, I still don't get it. How would they know we're from the Belt? And why isn't anyone interested in recruiting us? I mean, all those hundreds of thousands of Reds had to have come from somewhere, right? Someone had to have recruited them."

"These are the things that keep me up at night."

"Nothing keeps you up at night. You sleep like a rock."

I turn to Jame. "Well, I have vivid dreams, how's that?"

We pass signs letting us know we're entering the town of Rensselaer, population 1,629.

"Leo—car!"

I slam on the brakes, avoiding an unmarked white van with its headlights on, stopped crooked in the road. Jame loads his rifle and points it at the van through the windshield. The wind gently rocks our car, the blowing dust tickling our windows.

I slowly back the car up and stop about twenty feet back.

"Is this a trap?"

"Forget it, let's drive around."

We pull around the van when the driver's door pops open. Jame holds his rifle steady. I reach for my pistol. We see one hand—an open palm—reach through the narrow opening of the door. The door opens further, and another hand appears. Black hands.

"Is that—"

"Zara!"

She steps out, nearly falling onto the sidewalk. Jame and I jump out of the car.

"Zara, are you okay?"

"Oh God—praise Jesus I found you boys!"

"Are you okay?"

"Someone shot at the van a few minutes ago," she says.

"Are you hurt?" Jame asks.

"No—thank God no. I didn't even see where the gunshot came from. I haven't driven a vehicle since—well, longer than I care to admit. That's how I ended up on the curb here."

Jame and I look at each other.

"The gunshot was so loud, and it broke the glass of the back window here," she says, gesturing toward the van. "At first I didn't know if I had been shot. There was just this bang followed by loud ringing. I must have worked myself up. By the time I got here, I could barely breathe."

"You need to sit down," Jame says, grabbing her arm.

"No, I feel better now. After you left, I got to thinking about my life there in Merrillville. I'm 70 years old. I'm all alone. Sure, I'm in decent health, but I won't be for much longer. Not as long as those statistics stay true!"

She laughs, and I feel a physical weight being lifted off me.

"I started thinking about my sweet Rose. My baby Rose. She's out here somewhere. I can't give up on her. Her mama already gave up on her once before, and I am not gonna make the same mista—" Her sentence is cut off by a crack of lighting, which briefly illuminates the heavily overcast skies, followed by an onslaught of rain.

We load into Zara's van, which is in much better shape than our F-150, and resume our path to Highway 231.

She's wearing a large black Purdue hoodie, her face is glazed with sweat. She's closing her eyes with her arms resting behind her head—not in a relaxing way, more of a fighting-a-headache way.

"You sure you're ok back there? Need any food or water?" I ask.

"I'm good for now. Thank you, son."

"Where'd you find this van?" Jame asks.

Zara attempts to sit up but opts for resuming her laying position. "We had a couple vans hidden in one of the mall service bays. We had three vans. GA had one. Well, *still* have one, God willing."

"How did you find us?" I ask.

"To be honest, I eavesdropped a bit on your conversation while you were mapping out routes. I knew you were gonna be on 114 at some point, I just hoped and prayed that I wouldn't miss you."

"Well, you almost did. We had a run-in with some Reds in Monon and had to turn around. And thank heavens in hindsight," I say.

"You know how to shoot a gun?" Jame asks.

"Oh God, that's one thing I won't do. Drive a van through abandoned America, sure. Fire a gun, no way mister."

"That's perfectly fine," I say. "I wish I never had to shoot a gun. If my life ever returns to some form of normalcy, I hope I never have to touch another gun as long as I live."

"Guns are a lot more fun when you're not being shot at. And not shooting at people," Jame says.

"Jame here is a cop," I say.

"Ya know what, that makes me feel safer. And what did you do before this fiasco, Leo?"

"I worked at a ski resort in Colorado."

"Huh," she says.

"What, does that not make you feel safer?"

"Ha!"

We all share a much-needed laugh.

"I never tried skiing. Maybe I should someday," Zara says.

"You definitely should," I say, the smile quickly leaving thinking of the last time I went skiing.

"Tell us about your family, Zara."

"Well, I had one daughter. Excuse me, I *have* one daughter. She's not with us anymore. Jasmine JoAnn is what we called her. Either that or Jazzy-Jo. She was such a bright spot in my life. My husband could never be relied on, so I was essentially a single mother. Her daddy, Randy, was the love of my life at one point. We fantasized about getting out of the suburbs to live the city life. This was Indianapolis we're talking about.

"We both had work. Well, I had work. He was in and out of jobs. I loved him the same. Eventually, we started fantasizing about living back out in the suburbs, living the family suburban life. And we did just that. Moved up north to Anderson. I worked at the Anderson University bookstore, Randy worked for the city as a maintenance guy. He also ran the snow plows in the winter.

"We were doin' okay. We had been trying to get pregnant as soon as we moved there. Eventually one of the swimmers stuck, if you know what I mean, and nine months later Jasmine JoAnn was born.

"A few years after that, news came that my dad had stage four bladder cancer. They didn't detect it until it was too late. They gave him weeks to live. He had been an alcoholic since he was a preteen. My mommy left him when she couldn't take it anymore, so as a result, he had no one to take care of him. My mom wasn't gonna. My sister wasn't gonna. Only me. It was my duty. Besides, deep down, I loved him. My dad lived in Merrillville, which you boys are now familiar with. So, Jasmine and I drove down to spend some time with him. AU was very generous to give me time off. They are owned by Church of God—not my church, but good Christians none the less.

"Once we got to Merrillville, we decided to stay as long as we were needed. Weeks turned into months and he kept hanging on. At this point, Randy didn't feel like the love of my life anymore. That had faded. For both of us, honestly. He started hitting the bars more frequently with his buddies. It started out with just Colts games, then it became Pacers games, then it became just about every night. He stopped caring about me, stopped caring about Jasmine it seemed. I wasn't gonna kick him out or anything, but we grew apart, ya know. Like dying a slow death. Anyway, Randy said my daddy was a horrible father, so he didn't want to come to pay his respects. I didn't disagree with his assessment, but it was funny how he didn't see the irony in sayin' that.

"Well, the months turned into years. Jazz and I visited home every so often, but we basically lived in Merrillville. Then Jazz got to be school age and we realized that we needed to set down roots. I had grown comfortable in Merrillville, so had Jasmine, so I got a new job in town. Randy visited once, we fought basically the whole time. When he left, I knew that was gonna be the end. We didn't ever divorce or even have an *it's over* moment, it just fizzled out. In the end, my daddy lasted three years from when he was diagnosed until he passed."

"I'm sorry to hear that, Zara."

"It's been so long now, but yes, I do miss him. You know, I learned a lot from him—I learned a lot about myself during those three years. When you are basically taking care of someone who could die at any moment, it's kinda like staring death in the face every day. Forces you to set your priorities straight. At one point, I even wrote a letter to Randy and thanked him for what he did for me. For the time that we were in love. For the fun times we had. For giving me our daughter. It was a nice letter. I didn't expect anything back, just wanted to express it."

"Did he write back?"

"Nope. Don't know if he ever got it, but at least I put it out there."

"So, Rose is Jasmine's daughter?"

"Yes, I'm sorry, I get rambling like crazy—I'm sure you've figured that out by now."

"This is actually great. Leo and I have been together way too long," Jame says. We laugh.

"Jasmine and I had a good life after moving to Merrillville. She went to college, Purdue. Got a degree in Economics. Smart girl. Then she got pregnant fast after college. It was a one-night stand thing. Totally not like her, but it happened. Shortly after that, Rose entered our lives. We all lived together—us three—in my daddy's old house.

"You know, back in my daddy's day, a college degree meant something special, it meant that you were guaranteed a good job for life as long as you didn't get a DUI or launder money or something. Well, that's not really the case anymore. Even though Jazz worked hard, the stress of holding multiple jobs while being a mom eventually got to her. I was doing all I could to help. Of course, I could've done more. I *should've* done more. First, she turned to prescription painkillers, then meth, then heroin. Before I realized what was going on, she was hooked. We tried rehab. We tried Narcotics Anonymous. We tried Jesus. She never made it longer than a couple months clean at a time. She died at age 27. Far too young."

"I'm so sorry," I say.

"You've been through a lot, Zara," Jame says.

"That's what makes me strong. Although, since my community fell apart and Rose was taken, I've lost that strength. I thought I was just gonna live out my days in that shopping mall. Then you boys came and I let you just walk out the front door. I realized my mistake not an hour after you left. And I say again, it is a blessing from our Lord and Savior that I found you boys."

"Well, we're glad you did. We're gonna find Rose."

"And Xandra," Zara adds.

23

Zara's life story helped the time fly by on our drive to Remington. It also must've taken a lot out of her cause one minute after finishing her story, she announced that she would rest her eyes and zonked out. Once she fell asleep, the butterflies returned. Monon was a war zone. We're expecting the same for Remington.

We slow down as we approach the town. Another military grade roadblock is set up in the road, this time it's about a quarter mile before town. Above the roadblock is the familiar government warning, and just beyond it is a wooden ligature with two hanging bodies. Both men, both decaying. One has a red X spray-painted on his face. A large spray-painted sign on plywood is affixed to the top of the ligature.

RED TERRITORY

Belters <u>not welcome</u>

Lions <u>not welcome</u>

X <u>not welcome</u>

<u>WONT BE HAD</u>

On closer inspection, the Feds' sign is tagged, but this time it's a red spray-painted stencil of a lion.

"God, now who are the lions?"

"Beats me," Jame says.

"And X?"

"No idea."

We stop the car.

Jame and I step out to get a better view. The scene is

familiar—charred, half-standing buildings, cars upside down burned to a crisp. There are no piles of dead bodies in the streets here, thank heavens. On the second floor of a half-burned building is a recently-deserted patrolling station—a canopy with a Rubbermade table, two folding chairs, and an entire arsenal of guns. A metallic box holding syringes, similar to the one the Red had in Empire, sits on the table.

"Maybe these guys were Monon's backup," Jame says.

"They had to have known we were gonna try other border entrances," I say.

"Maybe. But maybe not. I mean, this place has been abandoned for a long time. They probably think they have a good hold on the territory now. Maybe they're not as heavily staffed as they were at one point. Besides, they are moving far beyond Zone 1 now."

I think back to Empire and finding the *Risk* strategy book by Adam Katz' bed.

"Have you played Risk?" I ask.

"The board game? Maybe once," Jame says.

"I mean, I think you're right. In Risk, when you are getting ready to expand to a new territory, you fortify your borders with armies, then spread them out as you conquer new territories. And that's how you can lose—by expanding too fast," I say.

"You spread yourself too thin," Jame says.

"Exactly."

"You might have a small but well-fortified piece of the map one turn, go on a rapid takeover next turn giving you control over a much larger area, but then lose it all the next turn. Just like that."

"So maybe the Reds are in their third turn here in Zone 1."

"Maybe, but we haven't made it into Zone 1 yet ourselves."

"Speaking of which, if it's true that the backup is coming from Remington, we probably don't have much time until the Monon group realizes we're on the loose."

We get back in the car.

"This Remington?" Zara asks, sitting up.

"Sure is," Jame says.

We navigate around the road barrier and make it back to the grid of county roads.

We are officially in Zone 1.

—

The mile-by-mile grid through farm country means that our options traveling south are virtually limitless.

The thickest section of *Move to the Belt: A Public Official's Guide* is a step-by-step guide to decommissioning key infrastructure. Critical tasks—dismantling cell towers, distribution lines, etc.—were done by the Feds themselves, while less critical tasks were handled by local municipalities. One of those less critical tasks was dismantling road infrastructure. The Feds asked that local municipalities lay roadblocks or cause irreparable damage to key arteries and intersections to make travel in the Wild *inconvenient*. While many municipalities obeyed, many did not. Logistically, I don't blame those that ignored the Feds, and frankly, I'm grateful too.

The randomly-placed roadblocks force us to snake through the back roads. Cherry's map helps, although it is outdated in a few spots. Eventually, we come to a T in the road signaling that we've reached the Wabash River. We follow the road fronting the river two miles east to a crossing. As we approach the small, two-lane bridge, we realize that it ends halfway over the water.

"Work of the Reds?" Jame asks.

"I don't know, could've been the county trying to fulfill their duty of disrupting traffic."

"I was hoping we'd get to follow these quaint country back roads all the way to Panoli," Zara says.

"It's Paoli," I say.

"Pay-oh-lee," Zara repeats. "Right."

"Can you see where the nearest crossing is?" I ask.

"Hmmm," Jame fumbles the map on his lap. "Nearest I can see is Lafayette a ways further east, but that's a known Red territory, and it's pretty big. Or there's Attica a couple miles west. That's also a known Red territory."

"Well, the Reds would've left bridges intact, or rebuilt where possible, right?" I say.

"How so?"

"Cause they want to move around the country. I'm sure they are taking it upon themselves to do whatever it takes to mobilize."

Jame folds the map further and brings it close to his face.

"Lafayette may be big, but it has *four* crossings. Attica has one," he says.

"Lafayette it is. You cool with that, Zara?"

"I've been to Lafayette dozens of times. Remind me what we're looking for in Panoli?"

PART THREE
THE X

24

Panoli.

Remind me what we're looking for in Panoli?

Then what happened?

Then. What. The hell. Happened.

I feel like I'm dreaming, but I know I'm not. At least I think I'm not. It's usually not this hard to breathe in dreams. Even the vivid ones.

Jazz went to Purdue.

Feeling comes back in my fingers and toes, but with a burning sting. Like frozen fingers by the fire after a snowball fight.

I've been to Lafayette dozens of times.

Am I in the car? Maybe, but why would I be sleeping in the car? I don't remember pulling over. Also, I can't hear anything. I try flexing my body, a trick almost every kid learns at some point to get out of bad dreams, but nothing changes. Just another case of sleep paralysis. All I can do is wait it out.

I try desperately to recount the events preceding me lying here in—wherever I am. A car crash? Ambush? Did I fall asleep at the wheel? Did we run into trouble in Lafayette?

First bridge is officially down, folks.

The first bridge in Lafayette was down, so we went to the next one. Did something happen on the second bridge? It was closer to the middle of town, and we knew Lafayette was a Red territory. Did Reds attack us?

As the fog lifts, it becomes clear that I'm not asleep. I'm either drugged, paralyzed, or in a coma. I can't seem to will myself to move or even open my eyes.

I hear the muffled, underwater sound of a door opening.

Is this how all coma patients feel?

Footsteps tap on the floor. A computer keyboard clicks. A machine beeps. A hospital. I have to be in a hospital. But where? Was I taken back to the Belt? Now the muffled sound of people talking—a man and a woman—though I can't make out what they're saying. I try with all my might to flex again. I must have done something because the conversation pauses for a moment. Footsteps come closer.

"He'll be okay," the man says, his voice muffled.

Well, at least I know I'll be okay. But what about Jame and Zara?

Where am I?

I try to talk, but my throat seizes. The tingling sensation moves from my fingers to my wrists to my arms. Then the cold, tingling feeling is replaced with a deep, burning sensation. I twitch again. Footsteps approach me again and stop. I must be breathing, cause I'm still alive, but I don't *feel* like I'm breathing.

For the next couple of minutes, I'm in and out of consciousness until a weightless, euphoric feeling passes over me, washing away the pain and putting me to sleep.

—

I gasp for breath and try to see through the penetratingly bright lights. My lungs and ribs are incredibly sore, like I've been in an underwater chamber for days. I look around me. White walls, white floor, white ceiling. Clean. I'm in a hospital alright. I'm hooked up to an IV and monitor. I can't be in the Wild, can I?

Then comes a throbbing headache. I squint my eyes and look through the small window on the door of my room. I see no movement from here. Morning light spills into the room from the large window on my left.

Did whatever series of events that brought me here happen only last night? How long have I been out?

I fumble around for the chair remote and bring it upright, its motor whirring quietly beneath me. The further up I go, the more I feel the pressure in my lower abdomen and back. I close my eyes and exhale through pursed lips.

I swing my legs to the side of the bed and throw my momentum forward. I stand up for a brief second before the lightheadedness catches up to me. I stammer forward and fall hard against the door, bringing the IV pole down with me.

The pain comes from all directions.

I pull myself up to a sitting position, my back against the wall. I close my eyes and try to breathe through the pain. That was stupid.

I'm running out of time.

Footsteps click-clack down the hall and the door swings open. A bewildered doctor steps in, his eyes first glancing at the empty hospital bed to the toppled-over IV pole then to me. There's a small trail of blood following me from the bed to where I sit now.

"What in the hell?" he says.

The doctor is a portly man in his early 60s. Strong face, thick mustache. He'd be completely gray if he wasn't desperately staying on top of dyeing—both hair and mustache.

"Where am I?" I say between shallow breaths.

He shuffles to my side and helps me up. I try to stand on my own, but my legs are still numb. The mere act of *trying* to stand makes me lightheaded again.

"I'm gonna pass—" I start.

He gets me back to the bed before I crash again. I lay down and break out in a sweat. My body temperature feels like it doubles.

"Let me get you some water. Try raising your hands above your heads. It helps."

I don't even attempt to raise my hands. I just sit and breathe, trying to maintain consciousness.

The doctor returns a minute later with a plastic cup of ice water. I lift it to my mouth with both hands and get a sip before spilling it.

"Damn," I say, slurred, the cold water trickling down my chest.

"To answer your question, you are in a hospital, in case you haven't figured that out. I'm Doctor Adler, by the way," he says.

"Am I in the Belt?"

Looky here, a van full uh Belters.

"You are in a little town in the New Wilderness called Paoli. Welcome to Rural Indiana."

25

"Thank God," I say, allowing my body to sink into the hospital bed.

"I understand that you traveled here from Nevada, is that right?" Doctor Adler says.

"Yeah."

"Well, you're lucky you made it alive. I mean, especially after what happened to you guys."

"Yeah—what exactly *did* happen?"

"Looks like you took a heavy hit to the head. Possibly a rock or butt of a gun. You don't remember anything?"

I touch the tips of my fingers to the back of my head. It's shaved clean with a long set of stitches running through the middle of it. I run my fingers up and down the stitches, intrigued by the lack of pain.

"Yeah, let's leave those stitches alone. You're pretty numbed up. We don't want you to accidentally pull them out."

"Sorry," I say, quickly returning my hands to my lap. "And no," I continue, "I don't remember much. I remember that we were trying to cross the Wabash River in Lafayette. Well, we were planning to, anyway. The first bridge was down, so we went to the second one. And then, we must've—" I rub my temples and close my eyes. "We must've—I don't know—ran into trouble on or near the bridge I guess."

"The important thing is that you made it here. I'll let Cherry fill you in on the details since she was actually a part of the rescue. She should be here later today."

"There was a *rescue?*"

"Yes, by the XD—they're sort of our military defense."

"Who is *our?*"

"Us, Paoli, The X—wow, this really *is* all new to you, huh?"

"Completely," I say. Under my hospital gown, I feel the healing bullet hole on my arm. "What about Jame and Zara?"

"Who?"

"I was traveling with two other people, a skinny tall white dude and an old black lady."

"I'm sorry—yes, Zara is here. She's upstairs. Still unconscious but she's being treated. The other fellow, I'm not sure, we can look into that. Or I'm sure Cherry would know."

"Oh God," I say, closing my eyes and rubbing my temples again.

He sits on his padded stool and rolls closer to the monitors. "The memories should be coming back over the next couple days. Just give it time." He types on his keyboard, his thin glasses resting low on his nose.

"Ok."

He pushes out from the computer monitor and faces me again, looking over his glasses. "You'll recover just fine. You got a concussion. We had to stitch a couple places on your head and it looks like you have a few bruised ribs. We'll have you stay in a wheelchair for the next couple days, okay?"

"Thank you for your help."

"Of course. And, hey, no more superhero moves, K?"

I laugh. And it hurts. "Yeah, sorry about that. I didn't expect to collapse like that."

"They never do," he says, sticking his tongue out to the side, barely visible beneath his thick mustache. "No—it's okay. It's not every day that you black out and wake up in a hospital a hundred miles away. In the Wild, no less. I'll give you a free pass this time," he says, raising his eyebrows and smiling. He stands up and walks toward the door. "A nurse will be by with breakfast in about an hour. You good with bacon and eggs?"

I snort a laugh. "Oh heavens, yes please." I can't even think of the last time I had bacon and eggs, or a warm breakfast. Or just a decent meal.

"Holler if you need anything."

"Will do. Thanks again," I say, still smiling. That feeling—something I haven't felt in a long, long time—is safety. I feel safe here.

I look straight ahead at the wall. There is a distinct outline where a wall-mounted TV used to sit. The clock on the wall appears to be stuck at 2:22. A sign reminds patrons to wash their hands for thirty seconds in warm water. Another tells us this is a non-smoking hospital. *Good to know.*

Sometime between observing my bed remote and wondering if we're alone in the universe, I drift to sleep.

—

"Bridge is destroyed up here," Jame says and returns to the passenger side of the van.

We drive another couple of miles into Lafayette to the next bridge. Only, the closer we get, the darker the skies get. Then the sky turns dark red with orange streaks, like it's on fire.

I roll down my window. Sounds of gunfire, explosions, glass shattering, and yelling surround us. The ground shakes lightly.

Bullets hit the van seemingly from all directions. I speed up, swerving around a pile of bodies. Then around another one. Our tires splash through puddles of crimson blood.

"How far out?"

"We've gotta be close. Turn here—wait no, the next one," Jame says, fumbling with the map.

"Lord be with us," Zara mutters from the back seat.

Buildings tumble in the distance. The shaking of the ground intensifies. One of the back windows gets shot out. An intense burst of hot air rushes into the van.

"Ohhhhh Jesus, please Jesus," Zara says, ducking down.

There's a roadblock on the second bridge, but not military grade, just plywood paneling spanning the bridge. My peripheral vision fades until the only thing I can see is a narrow cylindrical shape in front of me.

I take a hard right turn, screeching around the corner. Our back left tire is flat.

Hordes of Reds eek into the street, guns pointed at us. The plywood roadblock says WON'T BE HAD. I ignore it and put the pedal to the metal, bracing for impact.

"Hold on."

My body floats above the scene. I again become a spectator to my own life, watching the van sway back and forth on the bridge, continuing to be littered by bullets. A calm voice speaks above the chaos below.

"Leo... Leo... Leo..." the voice says.

Nova?

—

"Leo?"

I open my eyes. My tunnel vision is gone. And God, those lights are bright. It was all a dream. At least some of it was, I think. I regain focus and see a woman standing above me, she has shoulder-length wavy dark hair and olive complexion— possibly Southeast Asian. She smells good, clean. Like shampoo. *I remember shampoo.*

"I'm Cherry," she says, stepping closer. "I'm sorry that our first virtual meeting was less than ideal."

I sit there staring at her for a few seconds. "I'm a little shocked that I'm actually here with you." I try sitting up. "I should thank you. I don't know exactly what happened, but I know that you saved me in Lafayette."

"No biggie. We're thrilled you're finally here."

"Uh, the nose ring guy—" I say, then succumb to a coughing attack.

"Huh?"

"The nose ring guy—the guy that sent me to Empire. He's dead. We found his body in—" I scratch my head as close to the sutures as I can manage. "We found him in Monon."

Cherry exhales. "Damn," she says and looks out the window. "That's Andre. He was one of our scouts. It got dangerous out there real fast. I almost didn't make it back from Empire myself. It's a miracle you guys made it, to be honest."

There's a plate of food on the tray sitting on the side table. Real eggs, real bacon, and real coffee. All very cold. I look out the window and realize it's late afternoon.

"Man, we drove all this way and put our lives on the line hundreds of times based on a two-minute chat with you."

"Empire was compromised literally a day before you got there." The light from the sunset glares off her thin, gold-rimmed glasses.

"Ok—I have a million questions for you, but first of all, Shakespeare?"

"Ripeness is all. Yes—well, it wasn't supposed to be a riddle. It was a simple password that our Empire team used for communicating with Paoli. It was set up to ping Empire twice a day automatically," she says.

I nod and take a sip of coffee. I look up at the clock stuck at 2:22.

Running out of time.

"Listen Cherry, you said you can help me find my daughter—" An itch in my throat causes me to cough heavily into a clenched fist, my head throbbing. I close my eyes in pain for a few seconds. "I would like to know *why* you want to help me and *how* we can get my daughter back. It sounds like you know my background, which is another question for another day, I suppose."

Cherry leans forward and opens her mouth like she wants to talk but doesn't know what to say. "Any chance you can hold your questions until tomorrow? Ryan wants to meet with you in person."

"No!" I say, slamming my hands on the table, rattling the utensils. "Do you—I don't even know if you can help me, Cherry. I know nothing about you, about Ryan, about this whole damn thing. Why would I waste another day here if you can't do anything for me?"

Cherry's eyes soften and her head darts toward the doorway.

Dr. Adler stands there, out of breath. "Everything okay?" He asks.

Cherry looks to me then back to the doctor. "I think we're okay."

I close my eyes and exhale deeply. *Give these people a chance. Like you'd be able to do any better on your own.*

Dr. Adler nods, darts his eyes back and forth then steps out of view.

"I'm sorry," I say, closing my eyes.

"You're going through a lot right now, and clearly don't know what you've stepped into here in Paoli. I promise that everything will be explained to you. Ryan just asked the big picture stuff be left to him. I promise it will be worth the wait. And I promise that we *are* on your side."

I nod. The hot emotion has now reached my face. Funny how your mind is half a step ahead of the body with emotions. "I understand."

Leo, you prick. These people saved your life.

"I'd like to walk you around town tomorrow, show you what we have going on here. Maybe after you talk with Ryan."

"That would be great." I take another sip of coffee, trying to act more composed than I am. "Can you tell me how I ended up here? I don't remember what happened."

As I set the cup back down, I notice someone else has walked into the room. A tall, fit man probably around my same age. He's wearing black pants and a long sleeve black shirt. He has thick brown boots on.

"Great timing," Cherry says. "Leo, this is Joseph. He led the XD rescue mission in Lafayette."

"Hi Joseph."

Cherry pulls up a chair for him. "Leo doesn't seem to remember what happened in Lafayette. It might be best if you fill him in."

"Sure thing. First of all, how are you feeling?"

"Well, I'm heavily medicated, so great. Doctor Adler said I got a concussion and bruised some ribs. Oh, and I have these," I say, and turn my head around to show my stitches.

"I don't know how much you've heard, but XD stands for X Defense. We are sort of the military arm of the X. Anyway, Cherry has kept us in the loop about you guys coming to Paoli. Given when you left Empire, we had an idea of when you'd arrive in the area. We have a drone surveillance program that normally runs a twenty-mile radius around Paoli, but knowing you were coming, we expanded the program so we could watch for you—particularly around the Wabash River crossings. We know things can get hairy there. We saw the Reds mobilizing heavily toward Lafayette, so we sent a team to intercept you. Your van tipped over after it was partially hit by a grenade. There was a bit of a gun battle, but we were able to get you out quickly."

"And Jame?"

Joseph looks at Cherry.

"Leo, Jame was taken by the Reds," Cherry says.

"God," I say, bringing my hands to my face.

Joseph continues. "Jame was ejected from the vehicle when it tipped. Two Reds immediately grabbed him and made a move for you and the woman."

"Zara," Cherry says.

"Yes, Zara. Our team was only able to get you two. It was too dangerous to go for Jame. We had to get out of there," Joseph says.

I drop my head and close my eyes.

"I'm sorry. We did what we could," Joseph says.

"I understand. And I should be thanking you. You saved my life. Did they kill Jame?"

"Not that we saw."

I pick up the mug and swirl it around, watching the mug move around the coffee. Cherry and Joseph exchange a glance.

"Well, that's probably enough for today. You need to rest, Leo. I'll pick you up tomorrow morning and we'll go for a spin around town. We're meeting Ryan at ten," Cherry says.

They stand up and step toward the door.

"Joseph, thank you again," I say. He turns around and smiles. "Cherry, thank you. I don't know much about this whole thing, but you've given me hope. And for that, I thank you," I say.

She smiles. "Welcome to the X."

26

WON'T BE HAD, the sign warns. I laugh to myself at the irony—y'all are about to be had alright.

I put the weight of my foot down on the pedal. The thud of gunshots continues to pepper the van on all sides.

It's only a matter of seconds before one of us gets—

I wake up to the familiar scene of the TV outline on the worn wallpaper illuminated by morning daylight. Not more than two minutes after Cherry and Joseph left the evening before, I crashed hard. The empty plate of bacon and eggs on the side table has been replaced by a ham and cheese sandwich with a bag of Lay's potato chips. I wolf down the first half of the sandwich and bag of chips just in time for Dr. Adler to walk through the door, absorbed in his clipboard.

"Feeling okay?"

"Not bad. Sleepy. Sore."

He sits down on his rolling chair and wheels over to the side of my bed. He looks between my monitors and his clipboard, jotting notes.

"How is Zara?" I ask.

He looks up at me, his head tilted back to see through his glasses. "She's still unconscious, I'm afraid, but stable."

"When can I see her?"

"Well, you could see her whenever you want. She's obviously nonresponsive right now."

"Can I see her now?"

"Sure."

Dr. Adler leaves the room and returns clipboardless, pushing a wheelchair. We roll out of the room and I'm immediately reminded that I'm in a *former* hospital in the Wild.

About every four or five lights are burned out or flickering. Most rooms are deserted, including the nurses stations, the floors and shelves gathering dust. I run my hand along the counter of a nurses station as we pass, my mind jumping back to the day Xandra was born—I was so elated, I bought doughnuts for the nurses. They loved it.

The elevator announces its arrival with a muffled digital *ding*. The doors slide open and Dr. Adler waits a second to allow the elevator to level with the floor. Nice. The third floor is almost identical to the second but darker. Entire wings are decommissioned. I feel a draft of wind passing through an intersection of hallways.

"Right in here," he says, pushing the door to Room 3114 open and rolling me in.

The room feels colder than mine. The air is stale.

Zara lies motionless on the hospital bed, her mouth gaped open. Fluid has been drained from her face giving her dark skin a gray tinge. She has stitches running along her jawline and a swollen left eye.

"Oh, Zara," I say under my breath.

Dr. Adler rolls me to the side of her bed then steps back to the perimeter of the room. I hold her cold, papery hand. Even though she's unconscious, seeing her alive offers a much needed moment of respite.

———

I wake up the next morning to a fresh plate of bacon and eggs and a steaming mug of coffee.

Cherry is sitting cross-legged on the ground facing the window, large black headphones covering her ears. I hear her steady breathing and the muffled sound of a pipe flute.

I clear my throat. "Morning Cherry."

She doesn't move.

"Cherry?"

Still nothing.

I take a sip of coffee and set the mug down with a clank.

Cherry whips her head around and takes her headphones off. "Leo, hi, good morning," she says and stands up. "You wanna go for a ride?"

"Let's do it."

We follow the desolate hallway to the elevator, this time taking it down to L. The lobby, once a bright and vibrant all-is-welcome space, is bleak. Cherry pushes me down the sidewalk that runs through the middle of the empty, sun beat parking lot. As we wheel through the neighborhood outside the hospital, I find myself skeptical that we're in the Wild—kiddie pools and trikes are scattered across lawns, sidewalks are lined with skateboard ramps and chalk drawings. These homes are occupied.

"How many people live here?" I ask.

We turn the corner onto Main Street.

"About 1,600. The town was originally built for about 2,200," she says.

She eases me down a curb, and we cross the street. Although only about a third of the stores are occupied, the storefronts are mostly clean. We pass a pharmacy, a diner, a bookstore, a coffee shop, and a 'resource center'. I don't think I've ever seen something so quaint outside of the movies. We walk for a few more minutes in silence, the wind blowing gently, bringing with it the smell of fresh flowers. People—normal, nice looking people—walk by occasionally, greeting us.

A group of kids rides their bikes in the street and park

outside the pharmacy. They are loud and rowdy, just as you'd expect them to be, gawking about what flavor ice cream is best. I smile, then feel as if I've truly stepped back in time. It dawns on me that I have yet to see a car in Paoli.

"No cars?"

"No cars in Paoli. We have a fleet available for the Scouts and XD."

We turn on Washington Street and the sidewalk disappears, forcing us onto the tattered but manageable asphalt road. Several potholes appear to have been recently filled.

"So, what's your background?" I ask.

"My mom is from Thailand, my dad is from Maine. I grew up in Florida, where my dad was in investment sales."

"How did your parents meet?"

"Well, my dad had ambitions to be a chef when he was younger. He traveled the world with a couple of friends. They tried to become internet stars by seeing how the rest of the world ate."

"Didn't pan out? No pun intended."

"Ah, a pan pun."

We laugh.

She continues. "No. I mean, I'm not sure how serious he took it to begin with. But, in that process, he met my mom. She flew back with him and they got married weeks later. They had a baby boy—my oldest brother—almost immediately. It forced them to settle down and find jobs, which is what brought them to Florida. Then another boy thirteen months later. Then me three years after that."

"Any after you?"

"Nope, I'm the baby."

"How did you get mixed up in all this X stuff?"

A basketball rolls out into the road. A young girl with

pigtails and denim overalls runs after it, smiling at us along the way.

"I've known Ryan for years, I was one of his research assistants back in the day, but the real reason is because of my parents. My parents defied evacuation orders and stayed in Florida through the Move. They moved inland a bit to avoid the flooding, obviously, but they stayed. I went down there, tried to move their stuff. I set them up with a nice single level house outside Atlanta but they didn't want it. I don't know what it was—the independence, the rebelliousness that followed my dad back to his youth. They said they had enough friends staying behind that they'd be fine. I kept in touch as best as I could. There was that messaging service for a little bit when the Move was underway—since cell towers were in the process of being dismantled—but once Zone 1 was done, that was it."

We stop outside a three-story Victorian house, green ivy running up its red brick front.

Cherry continues. "I kept expecting them to show up in Atlanta, but they never did. I checked the Move Census Bureau but they just gave me the runaround."

We both look at the house for a moment, Cherry in self-reflection, me wondering what lies behind those dark, ornamental doors.

"Anyway, I went back to Florida to find my parents. They weren't where I left them, so I had to search around. Eventually, I found them, only my dad was dead. Bullet hole in the head. My mom was still with him, traumatized. Said it was a botched robbery. She said she was out of the house when it happened just a few days before. I was crushed, of course, but I had to be the strong one. I put on a front like I always do. I packed my mom in my car, and we drove to the Belt. And that's when I first encountered the Reds. We came upon a newly installed roadblock on I-75. When we tried to reroute, there was a gang of Reds waiting for us. I'll never forget those ugly slash tattoos."

"You always remember your first."

"They ambushed us. I plowed through the group of them, but their gunfire was too much. My mom got hit in the throat. I got hit in the arm. By the time we were in the clear, my mom was convulsing. Blood was spurting from her throat. I thought the movies were dramatic, but that's literally what it was like. I tried putting pressure on it. It didn't work. She had lost too much blood. She died in my arms. I didn't even notice that I had been shot until a few minutes after she died." Cherry coughs and I can tell she's fighting tears. "Just like that, I had no parents."

"Did Ryan recruit you?"

"I got in touch with Ryan shortly thereafter. I was looking for answers—specifically about the Reds and the Wild—and he filled me in on everything he knew. He told me about his ideas for the X and I jumped on board. Had nothing better to do."

"What happened in Empire?"

She exhales loudly. "We had something special there, Leo—in Empire. We were attacked, as you saw I'm sure. Christian and Adam were killed and I barely made it out alive. I killed the Red that killed them and hung him in that house on the end of the street."

"I saw that."

I also burned that house to the ground.

I turn my wheelchair ever so slightly and it gives off a glare that shines off the stained-glass window above the front door. I'm reminded of my makeshift security system in Empire.

"You haven't heard anything else about Jame have you?"

"Nothing yet. We're still looking into it."

I nod.

"To be honest, when someone is kidnapped out here in the Wild, it can be like falling into a black hole. We have scouts that are keeping eyes out for prisoners and travelers like yourself, but the Wild is vast, to say the least. We have fifty full-time scouts sneaking around the country at any given time and we really haven't scratched the surface yet."

I nod again.

"Anyway, enough about that," Cherry says, clearing her throat. "Let's meet Ryan Urban."

27

Tall topiaries line the front yard, standing guard. Cherry opens the front gate and pushes me through. We cross the long, lonely concrete path to the front door. The small details come into focus—the cracked cement path lined by decorative brick, the overgrown, weedy lawn, the antique windows, some open, most closed. The rumbling of a tense conversation comes from a second-floor window. Cherry's pace is slow and calculated as she pushes me down the path in a daze.

I imagine this house's previous life—a second home for a Louisville-based doctor, or businessman. I imagine kids excited to get back to their bikes and balls, kayaks and water toys to be used on Patoka Lake.

Cherry secures the wheelchair's brake and helps me up the front stairs. She turns the ornate doorknob, swinging one of the sun-worn mahogany double doors open. I lean against the doorway while Cherry retrieves my wheelchair and hauls it back up the stairs. She sets it down just inside the house and holds it steady while I ease into the seat.

"Alright, let me see where Ryan is," she says, her eyes darting back and forth between the hallway leading to the back of the house, the living room to the right, the nook to the left, and the staircase. She pokes her head in the nook then heads up the stairs.

I cautiously roll my wheelchair forward to get a better look of the front room. The wood floors creak below me. A polar bear rug lays beneath a copper coffee table between two yellow couches—décor from a lost era.

"Betcha feel like you've stepped back in time," a voice calls from the staircase. A middle-aged man descends the staircase.

He sports round crystal framed glasses, short salt and pepper hair and gray scruff. His blue eyes are framed by crow's feet. Cherry stands behind him.

I let out a chuckle. "This whole town feels like a step back in time."

"When you don't have the internet in your face all day, that tends to happen." He gets to the bottom of the staircase and sticks out his hand. "Ryan Urban," he says.

"Leo Kline," I say, shaking his hand.

"It is great to finally meet you. I can't believe you're here." He pauses for a minute, staring at me. "Well, please step into my office," he says, gesturing to the entrance of the nook. "Or I guess roll into my office."

I park in the middle of the nook. Ryan sits on a blue chair in the corner, Cherry sits on an olive-green couch and clicks the overhead lamp on. The wallpaper is of Victorian flowers and symbols, maroon with gold accents. Mahogany bookshelves frame a stone fireplace behind me.

"I know you must have a lot of questions," he starts.

"Really, my request is simple. My wife and mother-in-law were murdered, and my daughter was kidnapped all on the same night about nine months ago. I've been in the Wild trying to find my daughter since."

Ryan nods sympathetically.

"Honestly, I had been spinning my wheels for about six months until I met— "

"Andre," Cherry finishes my sentence.

"Andre in Battle Mountain, and got the address to the house in Empire."

He nods again.

"Of course, Empire was confusing. *Really* confusing. I'm not sure why you sent me there. Then Jame showed up."

Ryan and Cherry exchange glances then turn back to me.

"I'm sorry to hear that Jame didn't make it," Ryan says.

"There's obviously a lot more to the story, but—" I pause, feeling a lump in my throat. "*Why* do you want to help me?"

Ryan leans forward, glances at the floor and then back up at me. "Leo, thank you for coming to Paoli. We can help you find your daughter. We have the resources, or at least we are working toward that. We are in great need of folks like you to help build our cause. I know you've been working in the dark and our whacked communications in Empire didn't help. I want to set everything straight."

Cherry sits up.

"I was a university professor, Leo, before the Move. My specialty was authoritarianism—specifically authoritarianism within a Utopian ideal. Just about every Utopian society dreamed up by novelists, poets, screenwriters, you name it, I've read it. I've studied it. About fifteen years ago, in response to the increase in natural disasters, social unrest, the economic crisis, etc., the government funded a series of committees to come up with solutions."

"How have I never heard of this?"

"Top secret. As top secret as it gets. Despite there being tens of thousands involved."

"The president knew?"

"Presidents knew but Congress was kept in the dark."

"Huh."

"Well, I was recruited by one of these committees to serve as research lead. I assembled a team—mostly grad students, including Cherry—and got to work. It was a full-time job for me. We'd check in with the committee every month or so to share our findings and receive feedback."

"So, you set out to structure an American Utopia?"

"We called it the Unicorn Project. It might be hard to believe, but the government was pretty forward thinking at the time. They knew we had to approach things differently, had to think outside the box. The economic model we built fueled by *unlimited* future growth proved bust. Everything had to be thrown on the table. After months and years of research and planning, we had come up with a pretty good idea of what a modern-day utopian society would look like. The only problem was getting there. How do you take a country so diverse in ideology and get them to fit into a Utopian society? We concluded that you can't. Not without taking drastic measures."

"Drastic like what?"

"Well, let me say this. One of the other committees came up with the idea for the Move. They came up with zone maps, the moving schedule, the housing plan, the cash incentives for businesses, the Move Census, the dismantling of key infrastructure, everything. They even had a PR plan. I'm sure you've heard that the Move was 100% successful—that there was no one left behind?"

"Wait, the *100%* lie was planned?"

"From the beginning."

"Shoot."

"As you can imagine, the committee that came up with the Move had the most buy-in from the Feds. The Feds thanked all us other committees for our years of service and that was that."

"So, ten years of your life research was basically flushed down the toilet once the Feds decided on the Move?"

"That's what I thought at the time."

"What happened?"

"I listed my DC townhome for sale and bought a small

house in Atlanta. I figured I could get ahead of the Move by a few years and lay down roots. Not to mention I had a fat savings and could afford to take a couple of years off before finding another University gig."

"Sounds like insider trading to me."

"Well, I never ended up moving. About a month after our committee was decommissioned, I was approached by an individual named Ray Ward. I didn't know him, but he was familiar with the Unicorn Project. He said he was a big fan. I wasn't used to having 'fans' and, to be honest, I was flattered. He offered to buy me a drink and discuss a proposition. He said he had a group—a well-funded group—that was interested in hiring me full-time to implement my Utopia plan in real life. But there was one catch. The Utopia had to have a kind of Anti-Authoritarian slant. They didn't want a centralized government forcing people to do anything."

"Don't you kind of need that in a Utopia—rules, laws?"

"Well, yes. But it's really a matter of perception. We couldn't let the people—the participants—*think* they were in a controlled environment."

"How did you navigate that?"

"Well, that's what we were paid to figure out."

"Where was this Utopia supposed to be?"

"The part of the United States that was left behind. The Upper States or New Wilderness, as it would later be known."

"And you went with it?"

"To be honest, I was intrigued. I'm a Utopia nerd. The opportunity to actually try and build a Utopia was fascinating to me. And not a science fiction Utopia that made everyone horrified of Authoritarianism or Fascism, but a more realistic, less sinister version. One built on community, ethics. Having a common shared vision."

"Did you think it would really be possible? I mean, *really*?"

"I didn't know what was possible, but it sounded more fun than going back to a University job in the Belt. I figured I'd give it what I could then find my way back to civilization after a while." He takes another sip of his water and sets it down. "So, I accepted the job and resumed the research."

"Where were the people for this Utopian society supposed to come from?"

"Ray hired leaders of some less-than-stellar groups to help recruit members."

"Less than stellar?"

"Anti-government groups, motorcycle clubs, hardcore Libertarians, gun-loving hunters, ex-military, anything that had a strong history of offline recruiting. They were looking for people that were inherently anti-establishment—people who had rebellion running through their blood. They recruited people mostly through word-of-mouth. If they did anything online, it was heavily coded. They had to be very careful."

"You don't think the Feds picked up on anything?"

"They had to have picked up on *something*. I mean, millions were recruited. But secrecy was key to the process. And with most of the recruiting occurring offline, I'm sure whatever the Feds did discover, they just thought they'd let them have their fun. I mean—I saw one of the early presentations promoting the Move. They had anticipated people staying behind. That's why they planned to make it Wilderness. It would be every man for himself in the Wild. Wouldn't be the Feds' problem."

"Would the Feds have shut it down if they knew the extent of the recruitment?"

"They probably would've intervened, but who knows."

"After knowing all this, you were still on board?"

"Ray was very serious about keeping all the architects in

their own lanes. He was the only key master, as far as I knew. I simply didn't know what was happening with recruitment. Or several other aspects. Funding for example. I didn't connect the dots until I was on my way out."

"Then what happened—you quit and started the X?"

Ryan rests his hands in his lap, interlocking his fingers. "Ray was adamant that we controlled the entire Upper States, coast-to-coast. He didn't want to execute the Unicorn Project until the Move was said and done—for all zones. And this was a good thing for me because we still hadn't figured out arguably the most important thing about our plan—how to get from point A to point B. How do you essentially train our recruits to live under this new format? But then, things got a bit more complicated as the zones started moving. The number of people staying behind, that weren't our recruits, was staggering. Several hundred thousand more than we ever anticipated."

"100%," I say, scoffing.

"It's close to 100%, but with how big the US is, anything less than 100% is *a lot of people.*"

"So how many people are left behind?"

"Our best guess is about 2.6 million people. About a million of those were our recruits."

"And the other 1.6 million?"

"Old people not wanting to leave, rural folks thinking they could do it on their own, a lot of religious people thinking that the Move was a sign we were near rapture."

I nod, thinking of Zara's church of 150 people. There are probably thousands of similar groups out there.

"And to be honest, there were a lot of people who were just curious. I mean—San Francisco or New York City abandoned? For a lot of people, that's incredible. If you can find a way to break into some luxury condo building and take an abandoned penthouse unit for yourself, that'd be amazing, right?"

"How did that jive with your plan?"

"Not well. And that's where the real disagreements between myself and Ray began. In one of our earlier drafts of transition plans, someone on my team suggested that should there be a significant number of people left behind—enough to disrupt our plans—there could be a 'mass removal' of those left behind, giving us a clean slate coast-to-coast. Once I saw that suggestion, I had it removed. I knew that such an idea was toxic. And was one that Ray could potentially cling to. And he did. Somehow, the first draft leaked and Ray found it."

"Mass removal?"

Ryan looks to Cherry then back to me.

"The report didn't specify, but Ray took *mass removal* to mean *slaughter.*"

"So, the Red's purpose is to slaughter everyone left behind that's not a Red."

Ryan takes another sip of his water.

"After the Move started with Zone 1, we conducted heavy field research and discovered that the number of folks left behind likely outnumbered our recruits. That threw Ray into a full-on rage. He started shouting 'We have to cleanse! We have to cleanse!' like a madman. Of course, he *was* a madman. He stormed out of my office and I didn't see him for a week. Then I started noticing our recruits driving around, heavily armed, with these goofy slash tattoos across their eyes. Referred to themselves as Reds, saying their job was to cleanse the Wild— to conduct a mass removal.

"I demanded to speak with Ray, but of course he only comes to you, no one comes to him, that's part of his act. I finally got him on the phone and asked him what all our recruits were doing calling themselves Reds. He said that the only way to create our Utopia is by cleansing the Wild. I reminded him that he's talking about a lot of people—hundreds of thousands, maybe millions when the Move was complete. He knew. I asked to see his plans. He told me, as usual, to *stay in my lane*. He told me to give him a couple of years before my establishment plans would kick in. He thanked me then asked me to leave. I was physically sick. What had started as a fun challenge had resulted in a plan to murder potentially millions of innocent people. I hated myself. I don't know why I didn't get out sooner or try to put an end to it earlier. I knew that Ray was crazy from the beginning."

Ryan pauses for a moment and looks at Cherry, then back to me. "So that's when I split. I packed my crap and got out. I hid in the Wild and tried to come up with a plan to stop this. I immediately got a couple of my old colleagues and grad students to help. Cherry being one of them. Two others—Christian and Adam—are now dead, as you know."

He pauses for a moment as if to pay respects to the deceased. I imagine the acidic stench of their bloated bodies in the cellar.

"Our mission is simple: to stop Unicorn—Ray and the Reds. We've tried and failed several ways. We originally tried to spread out a bit—set up regional offices in each zone. We were quickly found out, as you saw in Empire. Since then, we've decided to build a strong base here in Paoli *then* branch out, being strategic in our attacks."

"How much cleanse is left to go though? I mean, it seems like there's death everywhere you turn," I say.

"The Reds have spilled far too much innocent blood, no question. However, we have reason to believe that the majority of those left behind are still alive. We know, for example, that the Reds have a good hold of interstate towns, which I know you've gotten a taste of. But the people who stayed behind had to have dodged Move Census Workers, which means they know how to hide, and that means off-interstate, generally. The best we can do is try to put an end to the cleanse and save those that are left. But, honestly, it's more than that. I think there's a reason Ray keeps his cards close to his chest. I believe he and whoever funds him have bigger plans. I think they are going to make a move for the Belt at some point."

"You mean attack the Belt? Why?"

"I'm speculating, but I worked with this man for nearly five years, and he's… different. He has no ideology, only a strong, insatiable thirst for power."

There's a moment of silence between the three of us.

"I'm sorry—I'm still not sure what I have to do with any of this. I mean, you know my story, right? You've said you can help me find my daughter."

"Of course," Cherry begins. "The Reds are only one component of Ray's operation. There are also Blues and Whites. The Reds are the military front, conducting the cleanse and conquering territories. The Blues are the women and children, raising up the next generation of Utopian citizens. The Whites are the ruling class. While the Reds are spread out, the Blues are far less prevalent, located in only a few camps around the Upper States. The Whites are based just outside Washington DC."

"Red, white and blue," I say.

"We believe your daughter is in one of these Blue camps," Ryan says.

"So, what do we do? How do I get to the Blue camp?"

"It's not quite that simple."

I maintain composure, even though my face is burning up.

I let him continue.

"For one," Ryan continues, "there are multiple Blue camps—that we know of. We don't know which one Xandra is at."

Xandra. Does everyone know Xandra's name?

"Which one is closest to Raton, New Mexico?"

"At the time she was kidnapped, Salem, Indiana. About twenty miles east of here. There's a good chance she's there. Since then, however, we know they've set up camp in Panguitch, Utah. But, Leo—"

"Well, let's try Salem. Can't you just do your drone surveillance?"

"I know a lot of the Red territories look like they're patrolled by a bunch of boy scouts, but the Blue territories are a different story. They have security professionals, ex-military guys, ex-FBI. There is no sneaking into Blue areas. That's for sure."

"So, what's your plan? You said you can help me. Where's the help?"

"A lot has changed since Andre gave you that note in Battle Mountain. For one, our divide-and-conquer strategy failed. We had three other offices in addition to Paoli, and they were all compromised. To be honest, we were a lot more confident just a couple months ago. Now we're trying to build a strong foundation here in Paoli before we go out again."

"And how long is that going to take?"

Ryan brings his hands up to his face. "I don't know, Leo."

I exhale, visibility annoyed. I'm exhausted. I'm defeated. I need time. Time to think. I've been building Ryan up in my head like he's a prophet. He's nothing. He's a guy who got us into this mess and is now making a half-assed attempt to atone for his sins. That's all.

I force myself to stand up, maintaining my poker face as my vision clouds. I sit back down before passing out. "So, I can't rely on you. That's what I've learned here. That's what I've learned after traveling the country through Red territory after Red territory, being shot at daily, narrowly escaping death every day. I thought—back when I got that note—I thought, *finally*, this is it. My first decent lead in six months of wandering. And now what? You're telling me she could be at one of these Blue camps, while at the same time telling me that we can't go there. It's too dangerous. Like that's gonna stop me? Something being *too dangerous?* Do you know anything about me, Ryan?"

"Not really, honestly," he says, staring at the ground. "And that's my own fault."

"What do—"

Ryan stands up and faces the stained-glass window at the front of the room. He breathes deep for a minute, his breath beginning to tremble.

Cherry stares at the ground.

"I've made a lot of mistakes, Leo. I realize that. I left Megan. I left Nova. On my own. I was a coward. I told myself I couldn't do it anymore. I have no excuses. Then Nova met you and got married. Then had a baby. I was a grandpa. By the time I realized that I'd made a horrible mistake, it was too late."

My heart sinks in a way I didn't know was possible. I can feel my heart beat through my skin. My mouth gapes open involuntarily.

Broncos 24.

He looks up at me. "I'm the real reason Nova and Megan were killed."

I stand up again and immediately feel the blood rush to the back of my head. I imagine myself leaping toward him, punching him square in the face, getting my hands around his throat—*something*. Instead, I sit back down. My hands and feet go numb. I don't feel rage, I feel pure defeat.

"Ray knew I had a daughter. He knew I cared about her, even though I wasn't in contact with her. He knew she was married to you and had a daughter. He knew that you lived in Raton. Leo, you were being watched by Ray's people. Of course, I didn't know this at the time. I didn't think anything like this would have ever happened. Now it seems obvious, but back then, no way. When you and Nova took the trip into the Wild, he jumped on the opportunity. He knew that he could do whatever he wanted in the Wild without raising questions from the Feds. You know what I'm talking about?"

I stare at the ground, purposely ignoring his question. "It was supposed to be me. They were there to kill me."

"From what I've gathered, yes. They were there to kill you and kidnap Nova. Instead they—well, you know what they did."

"Bullet hole straight through her forehead," I say. "I didn't get to say goodbye, I didn't get any last anything. She took a bullet for me. She took a—" I bow my head, the pressure behind my eyes becoming unbearable.

"Once Nova was no longer an option to use as leverage, Xandra was the next best bet. Killing Megan was just the cherry on top. We were divorced, you know. They knew they had to beat you to Raton. So, they did and—"

"You are like a—like a demon, you know that? What good have you done for anyone? You screwed Megan. You screwed Nova. You screwed Xandra. You screwed me. You screwed the country. All those innocent people out there in the Wild who were cleansed? That's on you. All of this is on you."

"I'm—I'm really sorry, Leo," Ryan says.

I dart a mean look back at Ryan. "*How* are we going to fix this?"

"I've made several missteps. That much is clear. I personally screwed up your life and for that, I'm incredibly sorry. You have to know something though—I'm a terrible, putrid, sorry excuse for a person for leaving Megan and Nova. I fully acknowledge that. My decision to leave will haunt me forever. It will be the last thought that flashes through my brain as I lay dying—*that* I'm sure of. But Xandra is my blood, she's Megan's blood, she's Nova's blood, and if there's anything I can do to even partially make up for my mistakes, I will do it. Saving Xandra, to me, is my one chance at some smidgen of redemption."

I can tell he's sincere, but I'd rather continue stewing in hatred. It feels good, almost healing.

"You have lost a lot of blood. You need to recover. This was probably too soon to talk about all of this. I don't expect you to forgive me, ever, honestly. I just hope that you see that I *can* help you. I want to work together to find Xandra. Get some rest, then when you're ready, come back here. I can show you everything we've been working on."

Even though I'm mad as hell, I can't help but feel a comradery with him. I have no one left. He's the closest blood relative to my daughter besides me.

And that's something.

28

The first half of the walk back to the hospital was done in silence.

My head is spinning trying to recall anything Nova may have said about her absent dad, but don't come up with anything. I mean, I knew her dad left them when she was young but that was it. I tried diving deeper earlier on in our relationship when we were still getting to know each other, but she never gave more than the basics—*my dad left us when I was young, I don't remember much about him.*

Megan never said anything either. Not that I remember, anyway.

Now more than ever, I'm at a critical junction. Do I rely on Ryan, or do I take what I've learned and go it alone? I've learned where the Blue camps are. Certainly, that's valuable. But Ryan and his team are not equipped to get into a Blue camp.

Cherry and I navigate down a curb, across a street, and back onto the sidewalk.

"Tell me about these Blue camps," I say, breaking the silence.

A young couple jogs by us. "Cherry, what's up girl?" the woman says.

Cherry waves.

"We know there are six of them. They are fully functioning towns, similar to what we have here in Paoli, only populated almost exclusively by women and children. The women are there for childbearing and nurturing the children, and that's about it. And there are schools. Rigorous schools where the ways of the Unicorn are taught."

"The ways of the Unicorn—that's kinda catchy."

"Came up with it myself."

"Has anyone tried going in undercover?"

"We did early on and it was a big mistake, couldn't get them back out. I know we have a nice little town here, but we're a small operation. We can mess with Red camps cause they're disorganized as hell, but Blue camps—those are a different breed."

"What about going undercover as a Red?"

"That's difficult. Because there's so much secrecy around the recruitment process—all these secret passwords and handshakes—it's easy for them to spot a fake."

"Have any of you gotten slash tattoos?"

"Yeah, you'll see a couple around town. They were some of our early attempts at implants. The ones who are still living, that is."

We make it to the front of the hospital. I want to feel proud of Paoli—of the X. I want to feel excited, fired up, but I don't. I don't feel like I'm part of a rebellion or a revolution, I feel empty, cheated, like I was given a new car only to open up the hood and find that the engine is missing.

We take the elevator to floor 2.

—

I didn't sleep well.

I had hoped that in the moments I did sleep, my dreams would offer some sort of inspiration. That didn't happen either.

The light comes through the window, painting the stale off-white walls of my hospital room a soft pink. I pick up a pad of paper and pen on my nightstand and write *BLUE*. Xandra's favorite color was blue. She wanted everything blue. She pointed out blue cars. She painted her nails blue. I wonder if Xandra knows she's at a 'blue' camp—do they talk about themselves like that?

A nurse named Sami brings me a stack of books, one of which is Siddhartha—the novel that always turns up. Between breakfast and lunch, I spend a couple of hours reading it, mostly thumbing through random sections.

Nurse Sami delivers a grilled cheese and another bag of Lay's potato chips. I eat in silence, reflecting on my conversation with Ryan the day before. I try anyway. My brain seems to pursue several trains of thoughts at once, so following one coherent string isn't happening.

He's simply a bad man. He can't be trusted.

Shouldn't an anti-authoritarian utopia prize personal freedom above anything else? Why cleanse?

That man is Nova's dad. Nova's dad. He's Xan's grandpa. He's Xan's only living grandparent. Let that sink in.

I realize that I haven't heard from Cherry or Ryan or Joseph or anyone today. In fact, the only people I've seen so far is Nurse Sami and Dr. Adler one time in the morning. Ryan did say they would give me space. I guess I am recovering too. I do need space. I won't be able to think through things rationally until I'm off these meds anyway.

Sami comes in to replenish my IV. "Feeling okay?"

"Sore still. Head hurts. I suppose not as bad as yesterday."

"We'll just phase the pain meds out as you feel better, K?"

"Great."

She finishes the IV and steps into my direct view. "How would you like to go for a walk, hun?"

"Please," I say, sitting up.

Sami is in her mid-40s—older than me, but still too young

to be calling me 'hun'. Her straight, dyed black hair runs down her dark blue scrubs. Her thin face is worn like she's spent too much time in the sun, intentionally. Regardless, she's warm and helpful like everyone else I've encountered in Paoli.

The hospital is more active today. Nurses and doctors hustle in and out of rooms. Patients roll up and down the hallways on hospital beds and in wheelchairs.

"A lot busier today, huh? Yesterday, this place was like a ghost town," I say.

"That's how small towns work, I've learned. Everyone needs the hospital one day, no one needs it the next. Something in this farm air, I guess," Sami says.

We take the elevator to the ground floor.

"You were a nurse pre-Move?"

"Yeah. Newark, New Jersey. You ever been?"

"I've passed through."

"On the way to the Big Apple?"

"Yep."

"You actually lived in the Belt for a while, didn't you?" she asks.

"Yeah, almost a year. Raton, New Mexico. A border town. You ever been?"

She laughs.

"It seems like everyone here has been personally touched by the Reds. Same for you?"

"Yeah. That's sort of what brings people together here. We see the injustice of the Reds and Unicorn and we want to do something about it. Everyone pitches in where they can."

"Sounds… Utopian."

She smiles. "It kind of is, I guess."

We walk through a half-planted garden as she tells me about her life in Newark. Her two kids and her regret for always calling them 'little brats' when they were young. I hear all about her cheating ex-husband who was a cop in Newark. *He called his trips to the red-light district 'sting operations' that sonofa—*

We finish the garden walk and continue, following a creekside path. As Sami goes on and on about her family, friends, and her friends' families Pre-Move, the hospital drifts further and further behind us. Not that I mind—I don't have anything better to do.

Ya know everyone thought that smoking wouldn't be "a thing" anymore once all the health effects were known. I mean, who saw a resurgence coming?

The path turns into the thick woods and leads to a wooden bridge. Something dangles beneath it.

I'm a fifth-generation smoker so I didn't have a chance.

Is that a noose?

Just then, my fingers and toes start to tingle. The sensation moves up my arms and legs. My vision gets foggy. "Samiiiiiii," I mumble, my head bobbing up and down as I try to maintain consciousness.

My car smelled like smoke, my clothes smelled like smoke, my bread smelled like smoke, my coffee, everything. You don't notice it after a while.

Is she not seeing what's going on?

We stop on the bridge and she kneels down to my level. The outline of her face sways up and down, the background slowly fading to black.

"You know, Leo. It's a real shame that you couldn't take this anymore. That you realized that Unicorn was a force much too powerful to disrupt," she says, pulling the rope up.

"Newest X member, Leo Kline, committed suicide when he realized that Dr. Ryan Urban's prized creation—the X— was nothing but an embarrassing attempt to undermine mankind's greatest social experiment of all time. What. A.

Tragedy."

She wheels me closer to the edge and places the noose around my neck. She slowly tips me backward. "And to think, now your daughter really is an orphan."

My limp head falls backward, hanging off the back of the wheelchair. I can still hear everything, but my vision has been reduced to random orbs of light.

"Sami stop!" A deep voice booms in the distance.

"Dammit," Sami says and slams my wheelchair against the metal rail guard.

My limp body bounces off the back of the chair and falls forward, spilling onto the concrete bridge. The noose slips awkwardly over my face.

Sami drags my body to the edge and attempts to lift me above the rail—a task that proves difficult given her tiny stature and my uncooperative lifeless body.

"Sami, stop now and I won't shoot," the voice says, much closer now. I recognize it as Dr. Adler. I can hear his panting.

Sami continues gripping my upper body from behind, but stops trying to lift me. She's breathing heavy.

"We're gonna need back up," Dr. Adler says, I assume into a walkie-talkie.

The voices grow muffled, my vision is nearly completely gone.

"Listen Sami. This doesn't have to be the end of the road for you. Put him down, come with me."

Sami continues breathing heavy above me. "No," she finally says.

"Others are coming, Sami. You know that," Dr. Adler says.

Sami slips the noose off my neck.

"That's good Sami. Take the rope off, set Leo down. We'll be ok here."

I hear struggling above me and my body falls back against the railing.

"No Sami! Stop—" Dr. Adler yells, running toward me.

I hear the sound of a stout branch breaking.

Then I hear the creaking of the rope tightening against the metal guardrail.

That wasn't a branch breaking. That was a neck.

"Gosh, Sami," Dr. Adler says, sighing with a finality that can only mean death.

The gentle flow of the creek sounds in the background.

29

"Ryan Urban has been notified. He and Cherry will be here soon," Dr. Adler says.

"Thanks, Doc. You saved my life."

"I think we got a bit lucky there. I realistically couldn't have made that shot. If you didn't tumble out of that wheelchair, we'd have a much different ending."

It hasn't been more than three days since the first time I woke up in this hospital bed without feeling in my limbs.

"Dr. Adler?"

"Yessir."

"How do you know there aren't others? I mean, clearly there are defectors in here. There could be more in the hospital."

"The staff is aware. We have security posted outside your doors."

"That doesn't mean much."

Dr. Adler exhales and looks across the room to the window. "Let me talk to Cherry." He leaves the room, closing the door behind him. A security guard stands outside my room.

Well, at least I felt safe for a few minutes there. Although, realistically I'm still safer in here than I am out in Red country. Sure, there'll be a few defectors, why not?

Nice blind optimism there, Leo.

I pick Siddhartha back up and turn to a random page, realizing that Cherry's copy of Siddhartha is somewhere among my things—assuming it was recovered from the ambush. I spend a minute reading before realizing my mind is elsewhere. I set the book down and take a deep breath. Aside from the bruising on the left side of my face and a few scrapes here and there, I ended up ok from the Sami incident. Here I am narrowly escaping death again. I can't keep doing this. The odds can't keep going in my favor. I can't just keep letting crap happen like this, I need to take control. I *need* to be in control of this story.

Rise to the occasion.

You can't rise if you're dead.

Ask Jesus.

My frenzied mind eventually calms down enough for me to fall asleep.

—

A knock at the door jolts me awake. The familiar orange hue of a late afternoon fading to evening casts shadows on the walls. The door cracks open and the security guard, a portly man with a sandy brown comb-over and a padded jawline, leans in. "I have a Zara here to see you. That okay?"

I sit up suddenly. "Of course."

The door opens and Zara rolls in, pushed by a nurse. "I hope you have insurance," she says, a smile stretched across her thinned, wrinkly face.

"Zara!" I swing my legs around as if I will try standing up on my own again.

"No, no, no, you stay sitting," she says, wheeling to the side of my bed. "Look at us bags of bones!"

The nurse leaves and closes the door behind her.

"How are you feeling?" I ask.

"Oh Lord, I am healed, I tell you. I didn't think I was going to make it out alive. After the bomb and everything."

"You remember it all?"

"Like it was played in slow motion."

"Huh. I've seemed to block the whole thing from my mind."

"Probably shock. I mean, it was traumatic," she says.

"Forget that. You're really okay? You were unconscious for a couple of days there."

"Yes, swelling on the brain. It went down though. I'm a bit sore, as I'm sure you are. I'm also about quadruple your age, so these things take a while."

"You have no idea how good it is to see you."

Zara grabs my hand and squeezes. "How are you, Leo?"

I tell her about being drugged and nearly hung by a rogue nurse just a few hours earlier.

"People really want you dead, Leo."

"I don't know how much longer I'll last out here. How many brushes with death can one man have before it wins?"

Zara's face turns stern. "You can't think that way, dear. Your life is being preserved for a reason. You need to find your girl. You have guardian angels watching over you. I *know* that, Leo. How else do you explain it?"

I look down at my hands and arms. What new bruises am I going to have tomorrow after being thrown around like a ragdoll by Sami?

"I can't trust anyone, Zara," I say.

She nods.

Over the next half hour, I spill the rest of it to Zara. I tell her about Jame being kidnapped—something she already knew. I talk about my meeting with Ryan, my father-in-law, the architect of the X and de facto architect of Unicorn. I explain the Red, Whites, and Blues and Ray Ward's grand Utopian experiment. I express, through shaking sobs, that Ryan is a major let down, in more ways than one, and that I'm struggling to see the benefit of working with him.

"Leo, have you ever heard the parable of the poisoned arrow? It's Buddhist," Zara says.

"No," I say, my hands covering my face.

"I know that it might seem out of character to quote Buddhism, that was Jazz's thing, but there are some good nuggets in there."

I look up and smile, hot tears running down my face.

"The parable tells a story of a man who is shot by a poisoned arrow. His friends rush to his side, bringing with them a doctor and all the needed medical equipment. The man, however, refuses service until he knows *everything* about the attack—who shot the arrow, what he looked like, whether he was tall or short, where he was from, his familial status, what style of bow and arrow he used, etc. His list of questions was so long and clearly unrealistic that he died awaiting answers. Now, the parable was meant to help Buddhist monks when faced with existential, metaphysical questions about the nature of existence—things that they simply did not have answers to, and that frankly did not matter as much to the immediate matters at hand. Now let me ask you this, if you were shot by a poisoned arrow and you had a doctor at your side, would you allow the doctor to operate without knowing all the minutiae?"

"Of course."

"Of course you would. You wouldn't care about all the details. You would know two things: that you were shot, and that you need to fix it. The rest is irrelevant."

"I see."

"What I'm saying to you, Leo, is that there are clearly a lot of unanswered questions here. A big mess that you—that we—have been thrown into. But we don't need to know *everything*, we just need to get our girls back. It's that simple. Whether the Unicorn has twelve million members or twelve members.

Whether Ryan is a decent guy or a crappy guy, the material facts are the same. Our girls are missing, and we need to find them. Let's learn what we can—things that will help us with our simple task of getting the girls back—and use it. We don't need to get involved with the rest."

I nod slowly, taking Zara's words in. I thought a fundamental requirement of Christianity was to speculate on the unknowable. Oh well, Zara marches to the beat of her own drum and that's what makes her who she is.

Zara exhales deeply and releases my hand, smiling.

Let's learn what we can… and use it…

"I'll let you get some rest, which is my way of saying that *I* need rest," she says.

We say our goodbyes and she rolls through the door. Long after she's gone, I'm still smiling. Zara is the one bright spot in this whole damn town.

—

Exhaustion is the only reason people ever sleep in hospitals. Between the beeping monitors, nurses coming in and out, and fluorescent hallway lights, it's not exactly a sleep oasis. Every time I nod off, the image of Nurse Sami slipping the noose over my head appears. That and the sound of her neck snapping.

My last security guard has been replaced by Nick, a younger black guy with short hair and a scar above his right eye. Aside from introducing himself when he first arrived, he hasn't moved from his chair outside my room. From the hospital bed, I can see the top of this head.

Have other people in Paoli heard about what happened? Rogue nurse attempts to stage a suicide. I'd think that would keep people looking over their shoulders. As I reflect on my isolation, I drift to sleep.

—

I wake up to a food tray clanking on my side table. Morning light has crept into the room. My new nurse, Nurse Dias, apologizes for waking me and helps me to the facilities. "Listen, Mr. Kline, I am so sorry about what happened with Sami," she says as I return to the bed.

"Did you know Sami?"

She bows her head and quietly sobs. "I did—"

"It's okay. All's well that ends well," I say, realizing the situation definitely did not end well for Sami.

She looks at me directly, terror on her face. "It's Unicorn. They get into people's heads. They get them to feel like they're on this divine mission, I don't know. They lose all sense of being a rational, decent human being, and—oh God." She looks up toward the window, her breath quivering. "And then she just kills herself. Just like that. These people are not on a divine mission. They are pawns."

She sits on the stool next to the monitor and continues.

"I knew Sami pretty well. All us nurses know each other pretty well. Yesterday we were all the best of friends, now no one is talking to each other. Not to mention, Sami is *dead*. Even though she's not who we thought she was, we're still grieving."

I nod.

"We're not all like that, Leo. I mean, *I'm* not like that. I'm not Unicorn. I don't think the other nurses are. But, oh God, I'm not one to say, obviously. I—I'm really sorry, Leo." She scoots closer and leans in. "News has spread fast about Sami. People are freaked out. I don't know what this does to us now—for the X."

A knock on the door announces Ryan's arrival.

"I'll excuse you guys," Dias says, nodding at Ryan.

He nods back and turns to me. "How you feeling?"

"Not bad, considering."

Ryan pulls up a chair and sits, looking me up and down. He leans forward, opening his mouth a moment before speaking. "This is my fault. Unicorn is trying to send me a message. You're still alive—thank God—but I got the message, loud and clear."

"I don't get it, what do they want from you? Don't they have your roadmap—your blueprint of Unicorn?"

"They have it, but they've botched the execution. They've tried to conquer too much territory too quickly. The men are spread out and isolated from one another. You know what happens when you have hundreds of small groups of rejects isolated from each other? They get ideas. Unicorn is trying to run a tight ship, but it simply can't in this environment."

"How do they fix it?"

"I don't know that they can at this point. Rebellion factions have risen up all over the country. Particularly in Zone 1. The biggest and most organized is the Lions."

I think back to the sign in Monon.

Belters not welcome, Lions not welcome, X not welcome.

"Why all the rebellion?"

"Oh, who knows. It's all about power for them. Reds think Ray is a weak and/or incompetent leader and that they can do better. Unicorn is centralized in theory, but extremely decentralized in practice."

"Where do you come in?"

"Ray thinks that I can come up with a plan to correct course."

"Can you?"

"Probably not, realistically."

"So, what's the purpose of the X if Unicorn is going to self-destruct?"

"Well, they may be disorganized, but there's enough cohesion to do something meaningful. That is, finish the Cleanse, build a society in the Wild, spark a civil war with the Belt."

"Huh," I say and pick up my coffee mug.

"Xandra is the leverage, Leo. They know I won't do anything significant with the X until Xandra is safe. But I don't know how much time is left."

"Until what?"

"Until they decide I'm not worth it—I'm not needed."

"And then Xandra—"

"Then they wouldn't need Xandra as leverage anymore."

"So, killing me is a message to you that you're running out of time?"

"Probably. They also know that you are dangerous to them. You are motivated to get Xandra back."

"I *am* her father. That's what I'm supposed to do."

"Point taken," he says, pursing his lips.

"So, let's say you have Xandra back, what would you do?"

"Well, the nice thing about being one of Unicorn's architects is that I know how to create chaos. I know where training facilities are. I know where weapons are stored. I have ideas on how to disenfranchise Reds. There's enough in our arsenal to disrupt them, we just can't do anything until Xandra is back. I know I can't make up for leaving my family, but I can at least right this one wrong."

Righting wrongs. I think about Nova. I think about Megan. I think about Xandra. I think about Zara's church. God's Army.

Cherry's parents. Jame's boyfriend. There are a lot of wrongs to be righted.

———

Cherry knocks on the door and steps in.

"I've asked Cherry to hang out with you today. Just for extra protection. Is that okay?" Ryan says, standing up.

My eyes move from Ryan to Cherry to the window. "Sure."

"Leo, I'm sorry again about all this. About Sami. About Jame. We'll get Xandra back, okay?"

I purse my lips and nod.

"We'll talk tomorrow."

Tomorrow's a long way away.

My head throbs on cue with the door closing behind Ryan. Cherry stands up and walks to the window. She looks outside for a moment, closes the blinds, then sits down. She pulls a tablet out of her bag, runs her finger back and forth across the screen then starts tapping away.

Dias enters the room, nods at Cherry, then changes my IV. "How's your pain?"

"Ok. My head kills."

She turns the dial on what I assume are my pain meds. "Can I get you anything?"

"A way to get out of here," I say.

Cherry looks at me briefly, then returns to her screen.

Dias smiles, not sure if I'm talking about the hospital or Paoli and if I'm sarcastic or not. I don't really know either.

"Alright. Well, I'll check on you in a few, okay?"

"Thanks." I exhale and turn my attention back to the outline of the TV on the wall.

"You want out of here, huh?" Cherry says, not breaking

her gaze from the screen.

"You know what I mean," I say.

She diverts her gaze from the blue glow of the tablet to me, lowering her glasses. "No offense, Leo, but what else are you gonna do? You think you're better off without us, don't you?"

"What exactly is the path forward? I haven't seen one yet. All I've heard is Ryan say that you guys have tried a few things that haven't panned out. Learning the back story to the X and the Reds is interesting, but it doesn't change my situation at all. No offense to *you*, but I don't care about being a part of the X. I just want Xandra back. That's all."

"I don't know what to tell you, Leo."

I expected as much.

I pick up Siddhartha and try reading a passage again. By the time I finish one sentence, I can't remember what I had read the sentence before. I set the book down and feel a wave of fatigue pass over me. I close my eyes. The thump thump thump of Cherry's fingers dancing on the screen lulls me into a nap.

I dream that I've been handed the keys to a single engine Bonanza propeller airplane. I step into the plane and take off with ease, the controls mimicking a kid's airplane ride at a carnival—pull the lever back to go up, forward to go down. I'm alone in the cockpit. Once I'm in the sky, an overwhelming feeling of freedom washes over me. I fly over a waterfall running down a lush green mountain. I fly over beaches. I fly over snowy peaks. I see elephants migrating through the brush. I see panda bears lounging in the tops of bamboo trees. I approach an unidentifiable city in the middle of plains. As I get closer, I see the city is on fire. I see mini mushroom clouds. I see buildings toppling. I see the peppering of gunfire. The cabin heats up. Wiping the sweat from my brow, I look for a place to land. Not only are there no runways in sight, but I realize I don't even know how to land a plane. I circle the city repeatedly, eventually leaving for the plains. Aiming for a spot in the flat wheat fields, I lower the plane, close my eyes, and clench the sides of my seat in anticipation of a crash landing.

I jolt awake and gasp for air, shooting forward in my hospital bed.

Cherry jumps. "Jesus, Leo!"

"Oh gosh—I'm sorry." I take a moment to catch my breath.

"You have bad dreams a lot?"

"Yeah, I don't know—mostly weird dreams," I say, cracking my knuckles. "They all seem to follow a similar storyline, though."

Cherry rests her chin on her closed fist and stares at me. "What's that?"

I take a sip from my water. "They start out normal— sometimes great—but as they progress, they take on dark twists. Like my family decaying in front of my eyes or flying an airplane above a city on fire."

"Yikes."

"I think they are all metaphors." I bring a hand up to my face and fix my gaze on the TV outline. "I worry that everything I'm doing is in vain. That I'm gonna end up dead. Or Xandra's gonna end up dead. Or maybe Xandra is already dead."

"Listen, I get why you're frustrated," she says, her voice hushed. "I'm a bit frustrated too, to be honest. Ryan has all these big ideas all the time—and I get that he's a big thinker— but as soon as we implement things, he changes his mind. We change course every two days. I can't keep up with it. And at the center of it all is—" She pauses and looks at the ground.

"Is what?"

"Xandra," she says.

I furrow my brow in confusion.

She exhales slowly, the air filling her cheeks. "I don't have anyone. Not anymore. My parents are gone. My friends are all in the Belt. My siblings don't talk. And Christian and Adam—" She sniffles. "I finally had something to be excited about—the three of us in Empire. We'd take long walks through the desert at sunset. Take our guns and hunt coyotes." A smile flashes across her face then disappears. "We were careless. That's why we were attacked. We thought we were isolated." She shakes her head slowly. "They were killed right before we found you, but before Andre got word. Finding you meant that we were a step closer to getting Xandra back, which meant we were a step closer to facing Unicorn. But without having anyone left, personally, it feels pointless."

"Y'all good in here?" Dias pops her head in the door and glances at us. Her smile turns serious upon sensing the mood.

Cherry looks at me.

"We're good," I say.

—

Nurse Dias brings dinner for us; grilled ham and cheese sandwiches, Lay's potato chips, and Cokes. Cherry and I talk about music, the weather, our lives before the Move. I ask questions about Paoli—how it's powered (solar and wind), where the food comes from (farms and a Belt 'runner'), and what people do for fun (same things people did before TV was invented; ride bikes, go on walks, read books, gossip).

"What do the scouts do?"

"We have a team of fifty scouts, they explore the Wild and

map anything that might be useful—broken bridges and roads, stocked grocery stores, gas stations, etc. They also map Red, White and Blue territories."

"Can't they do that by drone? It seems a bit dangerous to do that in person."

"They do a lot by drone. Or they try to anyway. The Reds shoot them down pretty quickly, though. Reds don't have drones, so if they see one, they know it's ours."

"Didn't you use drones to find us?"

"Yes—but only cause we had to. We figured there was a good chance you'd be intercepted before making it down here. Especially traveling through Zone 1."

"I traveled across the entire country through Red territory after Red territory, almost dying about a thousand times. How do the scouts do it? They must have some killer hacks."

"That they do," she says, and glances over her shoulder. "Can I show you something?"

—

Paoli's main street is dark and empty. Besides one street light in front of city hall, nothing lights the sidewalks. Cherry pushes me in my wheelchair, navigating the obstacles the best she can in the moonlight.

"It's right up here."

"What exactly are we seeing?"

"You'll see."

The smooth buzz of a saxophone flows down the streets.

"What's that?"

"That's Clive, he plays about three nights a week out here."

"I haven't heard live music like that for a long time. In fact, the last time I heard saxophone was—"

Clive stops playing as we approach. "Cherry my dear," he says. "Beautiful night, eh?"

Outside The Move Blues.

"Hey Clive, meet Leo."

"Leo, Leo, great to meet you my man. Thanks for joining us in God's country," he says and extends his hand.

"Wow, thank you Clive," I say and shake his hand. "Please continue, it's beautiful."

He nods and resumes his crooning as we continue into the sleepy town.

"What's the deal with *Broncos 24*? Those were Megan's last words to me."

"Really? Wow," she says. "Ryan and Megan got engaged on Super Bowl Sunday, a game that the Denver Broncos won 24 to 10 against the Carolina Panthers. They weren't football fans, ironically enough, but it was an easy way to remember their engagement date. When Ryan and Megan were married, they used 'Broncos 24' as kind of a password. Like when a new babysitter went to pick up Nova, if the babysitter said, 'Broncos 24' Nova would know that he or she was sent by Ryan or Megan—they were safe. Ryan figured that Megan would have passed the message along before dying, knowing that Ryan would eventually get in touch."

We get to a blue brick storefront with decorative lighting and maroon framed windows. Its sign reads *Mocha Joe's.*

"Coffee?"

Cherry smiles and lifts up a keypad cover next to the front door. She enters a four-digit code on the keypad. I can't quite see what numbers she inputs, but I try to follow her finger movements.

Right mid – right mid – left bottom – right top.

The keypad beeps and the door unlocks with a metallic

snap. I stand up and follow her in a moderately controlled hobble. She hits the lights. From the looks of it, we're indeed in a coffee shop. An espresso machine, blender, and drip coffee machine sit behind the counter, funky hippie art covers the faux brick walls, colorful leather seating is spread throughout.

"Back here," she says, leading us to the rear of the store and down a well-worn hallway past the restrooms. We stop at the door at the end of the hall and Cherry removes a hanging canvas from the wall, revealing another keypad. This time I do see the combination.

3357

The keypad beeps and the door's bolt retracts. Cherry opens the door, leading us to a descending staircase lit by sleek blue lights. Overhead lights click on as they sense our motion. I stop halfway down to catch my breath. After descending another twenty feet, the landing opens up into an underground lab.

"*This* is how the scouts do what they do," Cherry says.

"Not bad."

The basement holds a collection of uniformed mannequins, guns, knives, motorcycles, and camping—or wilderness survival—equipment. Every item is covered with a grey, digital camo with specks of what looks like TV static.

Cherry points to the mannequins. "These outfits are weather-resistant and are nearly invisible to drones and motion-activated cameras."

"I thought the Reds didn't have drones."

"Reds don't, but Blues and Whites do. If one of our scouts ventures too close to a Blue or White territory, they will most definitely be picked up. If the drones don't catch them, one of their motion-activated trail cams—like what people used to use for tracking animals—certainly will. If they wear these suits and are careful, they can evade detection."

"Huh."

She points to the tents. "Same deal here, invisible tents. Then we have classic equipment, guns, ammo, everything you need to scout."

"Is this for the XD too?"

"No no no. I mean, this stuff is great for scouts. We have a whole separate lair—so to speak—for XD. That's up closer to the mountain. That'd be a trip to get to. Rain check?"

"Yeah, no problem. I appreciate you showing me this place."

More than you know.

Cherry pushes me all the way back to the hospital, our path lighted by the moon. I tried to stay conversational, but my mind was elsewhere.

…At the time she was kidnapped—probably Salem, Indiana. About twenty miles east of here.

—

I wake up at 3:00 AM and slowly sit up. Cherry is asleep on the pull away bed by the window, the security guard sways in his chair fighting sleep. I walk to the door, feeling surprisingly sprightly on my feet. No nurses in the nurses station. I watch the security guard's swaying until it stops and slumps to the right.

I only need a couple of seconds.

I carefully open the door and slip out, walking as briskly as I can toward the staircase next to the elevator bank. I look one more time behind me just in time to see the security guard's magazine slip from his hand onto the floor. I ascend the stairs to the third floor and push the door open. A nurse enters a room down the hall and exits a few seconds later. She stops at the nurses station for a minute then continues to another room. I slide into the hallway and gently close the stairwell door behind me. The nurse enters the hallway again and I freeze. She goes back to the nurses station, picks up a clipboard and continues down the hall, turning a corner and disappearing. I move as fast as I can to Room 3114.

I walk around to the back side of Zara's hospital bed and crouch down.

"Zara," I whisper, lightly nudging her. "Hey, Zara."

She shifts and opens her eyes staring up at the ceiling.

"Over here," I say.

She turns her head sluggishly toward me. Her eyes narrow as she realizes a human is trying to communicate with her. "Leo?"

"Yes, it's me. Zara, I have an idea for you."

—

I return to my room, security guard and Cherry both still asleep. I join them in the world of slumber and have the best night of sleep I've had in months.

30

"Care to join us? Stretch your legs a bit?" Dr. Marcus says, poking his head into the room.

I look up from my coffee. Cherry sets her book down. Zara is standing next to Dr. Marcus, smiling in her blue hospital gown.

"I'll stay here. You go, Leo," Cherry says.

"Sweet!" I say and ease my legs off the bed, my bare toes grazing the cold tile floor.

Zara, Dr. Marcus, and I do five laps around the third floor. Zara and I are both slow, but stable. We make small talk with Dr. Marcus—asking about his wife and kids (whole family lives here in Paoli), his life before the Move (orthopedic surgeon in Cleveland), and what he does in his spare time (fishing in the Lost River).

Zara and I flash glances at each other during the walk, sizing each other up. We have some decent mileage ahead of us tonight. We part ways at the elevator bank.

Cherry's in the same position I left her in when I return—reading in the chair pulled close to the window. She stands up upon my return and offers to help me get back to bed. I respectfully decline.

Right mid – right mid – left bottom – right top.

I prop myself up on the edge of the hospital bed and take a sip of my cold coffee. "So why Paoli?" I ask.

"Like why did we end up here?" Cherry says.

"Yeah."

"The idea was the proximity to the National Forest. We're sort of nestled in here. It was easier for defense purposes."

"You like it?"

"Yeah, although I don't get much opportunity to get out." She checks her watch and stands up suddenly. "I gotta run. Meeting with the Scouts."

"No worries."

"I'll be back in a bit," she says, scurrying out the door.

A new nurse slips in just before the door closes. She is tall and thin, with blonde hair tied in a bun. Her eyes squint with her big smile as she enters the room with a tray of food. "Lunch time!" She announces.

"You're not gonna try to hang me too are you?"

The smile on the nurse dampens, turning the mood extremely awkward. She puts the tray down and turns around to leave.

"I'm sorry, bad joke," I say.

She turns back around. "I'm really sorry about Sami. We are just—we are heartbroken as a nursing staff. We just feel so betrayed."

"I bet," I say, severely regretting my poor attempt at humor. "And really it's okay. All's well that ends well," I say, a phrase I use often these days.

"Indeed," she says and turns to leave.

"Oh, hey nurse—"

"Perkins."

"Nurse Perkins, do you have a roadmap? Maps are kind of my thing."

—

The rest of the day passes by very, *very* slowly. Ryan stopped by asking if I was free tomorrow and well enough to go on a walk through the woods. I said yes.

Right mid – right mid – left bottom – right top.

As afternoon fades to evening, the butterflies in my gut intensify. I run my finger along our route for the hundredth time. Not that it really matters—roadmaps offer little insight to foraging through the raw forest.

An intense pressure flashes through the back of my head, like a balloon reaching its capacity. I look at the clock. 6:50. Ten more minutes until I can take another round of Percocet. The rest of my body is sore, now more from my ragdoll of a tumble out of my wheelchair than from the ambush.

Zara's not in great shape either. She was virtually unconscious for two days. Not to mention she's 70 years old. Seven miles a day. Can she do seven miles a day? Can *I* do seven miles a day? That would put us in Salem in three days. And then there's Cherry and Ryan. What will they do when they discover us missing? Can I tell them my plan? No—no way. If the scout's special camo truly evades drone surveillance, then they won't be able to find us. Unless there's GPS tracking in the suits. Guess it's worth the risk.

Cherry returns at around 8:30 PM. I try to tell her I feel safe enough to stay on my own, but she says she'd feel better if she stayed one more night and then I'll be discharged in the morning. She said they have a house for me on the east end of town, on Juniper Street. I think about that house—a house I've never seen before—with a preemptive pang of regret, like I'm *never* going to see it. If our mission is successful, will I still come back to Paoli? If so, will I still be welcomed here? If the mission is unsuccessful, then—well, then it doesn't matter.

While Cherry sets her things down, I pull my wallet-sized family picture out. Xandra with bangs sprawled across her forehead, her blue and white striped spaghetti strap dress dangling just high enough above the knee to reveal scabs and bumps—the knees of a three-year-old. Her smile is big, but her eyes are slightly off camera. Her natural smile lit up her whole face, but if she knew she was posing for a picture, her smile became forced and her gaze went slightly to the left of the camera. Unless there was something more interesting to stare at behind the camera.

Nova is wearing a short white dress covered by a denim jacket. She wore red lipstick that day. Something she didn't usually do and didn't particularly enjoy doing. A feeling of guilt washes over me, just like I knew it would, and I put the picture down.

Cherry sets up her tablet in the chair next to the window.

I pick the picture back up and force myself to confront it.

I'm coming for you, Xandra.

Cherry drifts to sleep at around 11:30, and I fall asleep shortly after that, the roadmap sprawled across my lap. Cherry had asked about it, but it wasn't difficult to sell it as a harmless curiosity. I'm awoken shortly after midnight to Nurse Perkins checking my monitor. Zara's nurse should be checking in at 12:30. Our next check-ins are at 2:00 and 2:30 AM respectively. Then it's go time. I try to clear my head and fall back asleep before I get too riled up.

I sleep well for the next two hours. When Nurse Perkins comes in at 2:00, I shoot awake with drunken optimism, like waking up to start a road trip to Disneyland as a kid.

"So sorry to startle you," she says.

"I—" I look around the room, orienting myself. "It's okay."

I close my eyes, pretending to be asleep, as the nurse finishes her check-in and leaves. Cherry stirs in her sleep. I look at her for a moment then pull the pad of paper off the nightstand.

Cherry,
Thank you.

I study the words for a minute, then wad the paper up and toss it into the garbage bin. I get dressed and step into the hallway. Nurse Perkins appears to be one of two nurses tending the floor. She's out of sight and the other nurse is nodding off at the nurses station. The security guard's chair outside my room is empty. I can't remember if there's supposed to be someone there or if they discontinued my security detail. Once clear, I move swiftly to the elevator at the end of the hallway and press the up button. On the third floor, I walk carefully down the hallway toward Zara's room. On two occasions, I jump into an empty room to hide from a nurse. I turn the corner of Room 3114 and see Zara sitting on her bed, still sporting the hospital gown.

"Are you ready?" I ask, speaking barely above a whisper.

She turns her hospital gown so I can see her clothes on underneath.

"Alright, let's move," I say, peeking my head into the hallway. Two nurses move in and out of rooms. I watch them for a minute.

"I'm going to the bathroom," one says to the other.

"Ok, you want any coffee?"

"Please."

One heads down the hall to the bathroom, the other disappears into the break room behind the nurses station.

We move down the hall to the elevator and take it to the ground level. We walk through the dark, deserted hospital lobby and into the crisp Paoli night.

"Now what?"

"A little shopping trip on Main Street."

—

Right mid – right mid – left bottom – right top.

The bolt lock to Mocha Joe's front door clicks open and we walk inside and straight to the back of the store, past the hippie art on the wall, the restrooms, and janitor closet.

Three… three… five… seven…

The second door unlocks and we step onto the stairwell from the future. The stairs illuminate with pale blue light. A clean, metallic smell wafts up from the chamber.

"Cherry just up and showed you all this?"

"Yep."

"It's like NASA."

We reach the bottom of the stairs and the automatic lights come on revealing the contents of the Scouts' lair.

"Oooooh," Zara says, hand over her mouth.

I grab a tent, an ax, flashlights, and a bundle of food packs and stuff them into an oversized backpack. Both of us fumble awkwardly through the metal crate of camo suits to find our right sizes. A medium for me shows up much sooner than the XL for Zara. We pick out hats, sunglasses, and shoes then put the room back in order the best we can.

Main Street is unoccupied and, besides that one street light outside City Hall, dark. We follow a nondescript residential street to the edge of town, the occasional lamp post illuminating the worn asphalt and cracked concrete. I find myself assuming I'm walking through another abandoned town, but no, these houses are occupied. Nearly all of them are. The world is just asleep, that's all.

Unless…

Unless what?

I push the thought out of my mind and remind myself of the parable of the poisoned arrow. No conspiracy theories, I need only work with material facts. Material facts and a smattering of assumptions. The assumption that Ryan is who he says he is, the assumption that Salem really is a Blue camp, the assumption that Xandra is there. And alive.

On the outskirts of town, we pass the Eastview Baptist Church, prompting a quiet outburst of gospel music from Zara.

Jesus loves me! This I know; for the Bible tells me so.

We walk in the middle of the two-lane county road, lit only by moonlight. Zara walks in front, setting our pace. Our suits and shoes allow us to move inaudibly through the night. Except for two ten-minute breaks for water and food, we walk consistently until about 5:30 AM when the morning twilight begins. According to my map, we've covered close to five miles. Not bad for a couple of hospital patients—one of which is 70 years old no less.

Even though we feel like we can keep going, we decide to play it safe and hide during daylight. We forage into the brush about two hundred feet from the highway and find a small clearing amidst the trees to set up camp. Zara sits on a log, stretching her legs and breathing heavy. I pitch the gray, digital camo tent and set up sleeping bags inside.

We climb in, bringing all our gear with us, and slide into our sleeping bags. We both lay in silence for a minute, but I can tell Zara is still awake.

"Tell me about Rose," I say.

She adjusts in her sleeping bag. "That girl gave me new life," she says. "I hear all the time that it's good to have kids when you're young cause you have oodles more energy to chase around toddlers than when you're older. You can't exactly climb up the playground and do the slides when you're 65 years old like you can when you're 25, obviously. When Jazz passed away, leaving me with this little girl, I had no choice but to become young again. I was climbing on the playgrounds. I was kicking around a soccer ball. I was getting down on my hands and knees and pretending to be a dinosaur. I was going to do everything in my power to give that girl a normal childhood. It was exhausting, but I loved every minute of it.

"My mother used to hate how women, especially older women, were always treated so gingerly. When they were moving furniture around the house, she refused to let people take her place carrying her end of the couch or bookshelf. Just because she was an old woman did not mean that she couldn't do hard things. She would tell me she never wanted to give up lifting heavy items or doing hard things in general *because of her age* because then she'd lose the strength. I thought a lot about my mother while raising Rose. I had to stop treating myself the way the rest of the world treated me—like an old frail woman that needed everything to be done *for* her. Granted, there are legitimate limits to that. My body is not the same that it used to be, but *I am* stronger than I think I am. I believe that."

She takes a moment to catch her breath. "I'm sorry—I got off track again, like I always do."

The whir of a drone passes slowly overhead. We lay in silence until it passes.

"Did that come from Paoli or Salem?" I ask.

"Can't tell."

"Do you think Rose and Xandra are friends?" I ask.

"I bet they are. I guess we don't know how many boys and girls are gonna be at this Blue camp, but I bet they're all friends. They have to rely on each other—being away from their parents at such a young age."

Would Xan even remember me?

"You know, Xan is probably the most social little girl I've ever seen. She was just like her mom, making friends wherever she went. But it was more than that. There was something with Xan that would draw people to her. Kids *and* adults. She's adorable and everything, but she has this presence about her. She feels for people. It's a kind of emotional intelligence that can't be taught," I say.

"She sounds amazing."

"I was—I *am* so excited to see her develop as a person."

"We'll get our girls back. We will," Zara says, finishing her sentence with a drawn-out yawn.

"We will," I say and turn to my side.

Zara's breathing turns heavy. I hear the trees rustle in the wind, scratching gently against the roof of our tent. I hear another drone whir past. This time I listen alone. Eventually, I drift to sleep.

—

We sleep through most of the day. I wake up midafternoon with a sinking feeling. The feeling when Nova and I saw the first snowmobile parked below us at Chrystal Peak. The feeling when I turned the corner to our house in Raton to a sea of police lights. The feeling of pulling up to the second bridge in Lafayette. The feeling that somehow, something horrible is about to happen.

I breathe in deep and close my eyes. The smell of summer morning brings me back to sophomore year in high school, waking up early for practice for a short-lived high school football career. How much simpler times were then. My parents were still alive, Salt Lake City was still intact, there was no Belt or Upper States or Reds or Unicorn. Nova was alive. I didn't know her, but she was alive.

If only you never even met Nova.

But I *did* meet Nova. And we had a kid. And that kid is my own flesh and blood. I will fight to the end of the earth to protect her.

"What time is it?" A groggy Zara asks, rolling over in her sleeping bag.

I check my watch. "Just after 4:00."

"Can we walk?"

"I guess we'll find out if these camo suits work sooner or later."

We share a couple of granola bars and take down our pain meds with cold water before packing up camp. We hike through the trees about a hundred feet parallel to the highway. We move a lot slower than we did on the road but still cover three miles before dinner.

We eat PB&J and sit on the ground debating the nature of God—a dialogue that's entertaining but not particularly enlightening with Zara. The conversation runs its course and we lay down at around 8:00 PM. What was meant to be a catnap turns into half a night of sleep. I stir awake at about 11:00 PM and nudge Zara awake. We hit the road again, trudging through the trees in the dark until 2:00 AM when we finally move back to the highway. The terrain is consistent the entire trip—flat, thick trees, patches of farmland. We cover ground much faster than anticipated. Zara's gospel music helps. The closer to Salem we get, the more frequent we see drones flying overhead. When they get close, we hold still to avoid motion detection.

At around 5:00 AM we cut back into the trees, now less

than a mile from Salem. Being caught on the road would be a death warrant assuming everything we've heard about Blue camps is true, that is. We slog around the forest, cutting through thick brush and unforgiving tree branches. We forage relentlessly, sweat pouring down our faces, until we finally see it about a quarter mile in the distance.

Salem.

As far as we can see, the entire city is bordered by a tall, prison-caliber fence topped with spiral barbed wire. *For keeping people in or out?*

We wander the forest for another thirty minutes until we find a lookout point on a small knoll facing the northeastern part of town. The confines of the fence include a collection of nondescript two- and three-story buildings clustered with narrow streets and sidewalks running through them. The town is neat, well-kept. There are no people out, but I do see evidence of people—bikes with inflated tires, fresh flowers hanging outside a store.

I continue panning the town with my binoculars until I come across what appears to be a kid's area in the back of a public square. My heart skips a beat. A playground, basketball court, and small grassy field. "Here we go, we have a kid's area—and fresh chalk drawings," I announce, my eyes still glued to the rings of the binoculars.

"Praise God. Oh Lord," Zara says. "What else? What else do you see?"

"Playground, with ladders and slides."

"Yes!"

"Basketball hoops."

"With nets?"

"Ummm… yep."

"Oh God, that's a good sign." Zara flails her arms in the air. "They can only be intact if kids use them, right?"

"I think you're right."

"Can I take a look?"

I hand the binoculars over to her and set up camp. I try to

stay composed while snapping the lines of the tent and feeding them through the narrow polyester passages, but I begin to break.

Xandra could be *right there.*

She'd be five now. Kindergarten age. She'd be able to speak fluently, assuming people talk to her. But they have to be. The people here are taking care of the kids. Xandra has been taken care of. No matter what cause the Blues are a part of, my baby has been taken care of.

Once again, your optimism is inspiring, Leo.

—

As Salem stirs awake, Zara and I patiently wait, taking turns with the binoculars. When I don't have them, I pace the camp, checking my watch twice a minute. We watch as mostly women, wearing gray or white clothes, wander throughout the town. Some ride bikes, most walk. Some are holding young children and babies. Some appear to have destinations, a lot don't.

"I mean, they're probably here, right?"

"That's what you told me," Zara says.

"Well, Rose has got to be here. She was only taken a couple hundred miles from here. Xandra was taken on the other side of the country."

"But this was the closest camp to you at the time she was taken. That's what you said."

"That's what Ryan told me."

"You worry too much, Leo."

"I know," I say and sit down on a tree stump. My legs bounce uncontrollably.

"Here," Zara says and extends the binoculars toward me. I

get up and take them. "Try and relax, sweetheart."

"I can't. You know that."

I take position in a small clearing of trees and scan the town. I see a little girl in tears sitting on the curb by herself outside of an old movie theater. She covers her eyes with her little rolled up fists. A pit grows in my stomach and my heart pounds. She has a long, shiny light brown braided ponytail running down her back. She's wearing royal blue shorts and a gray t-shirt. *Could it be*—

An older woman crouches down next to her and puts her arm around her. The girl puts her hands down for a minute, revealing a face that is *not* Xandra's.

"Oh gosh," I say.

"What?"

"I thought I saw—"

Just then, a group of girls skips out into the play yard with a red dodgeball bouncing between them. My breathing picks up and my heart pounds again, although it hasn't recovered from the last time.

"Look out for a little black girl, okay? She has long—"

"Dreadlocks!"

"Oh my God," Zara says, and paces toward me.

I hand the binoculars to her, my hands shaking. Zara looks through the binoculars and freezes for almost thirty seconds.

"Is it her? Is it Rose?"

A tear falls down her cheek from behind the binoculars. "Oh my—my God. Praise the Lord and everything holy. It's my—" She puts the binoculars down and covers her mouth with the back of her hand. She shakes. "It's my baby!" She puts the binoculars back up to her face. "Leo, it's my baby!"

"Oh Zar—" I start before getting cut off by the lump in my throat. Zara wraps her arms around me and squeezes tight.

She returns to her post. "She's playing foursquare with some other girls. She's smiling! She's happy! Oh Leo, do you think she even wants me to come back?"

I clear my throat and wipe the tears from my eyes. "Of course she does. A kid needs her family," I say, mostly reassuring myself.

"You're right, Leo, you're right." She shoves the binoculars in my chest and her eyes start frantically bounding around the camp. "Leo, I gotta go. I gotta get my girl."

"I know, I know. You get ready. I'll keep watching."

She pauses. "Leo, yes you keep watching. Your little Xandra is there. She has to be."

—

An hour later, I'm still watching, and I still haven't found Xandra. Kids have come and gone in small pockets, usually supervised by older women. Occasionally a man passes through with the pace and alertness of a security guard. The sky is cloudy, bringing an added mugginess to the humid Midwest air. I wipe the sweat from my brow and set the binoculars down to find Zara standing on my side with a paper cup extended.

"Sweet tea, hun?"

"I'd love some." The sweetness of the tea dances around my tongue. It's the first time I realize I have had nothing to drink all day. "You know, even if Xandra isn't here. I still want you to go in there. Rose needs you. And you need Rose."

"She'll turn up," Zara says, and takes the binoculars from me. "Let me see that family picture again."

I take it out of my pocket and hand it to her. I sit on a rock and close my eyes.

For a moment, I'm standing at the bottom of a playground slide—the metal kind that circles around—waiting for Xandra to come down. I have a blue M&M in my hand. 'Here I come' she says, and scoots down the slide, giggling. She gets to the bottom and throws her head back with her mouth wide open and her eyes closed. 'Good job, Super Xan,' I say and pop the M&M in her mouth. She hops off the slide and runs around to the ladder again.

I open my eyes and see Zara scanning the town. I exhale and close my eyes again.

This time I'm on the balcony of our home in Breckenridge. Nova and I are sitting watching the stars when Xandra comes out. 'Can I snuggle you?' she says. Her round eyes gleaming. Nova and I look at each other. Sleep training is no easy task with such a cute kid. 'Of course you can,' I say and set her on my knee. She rests her head against my shoulder and looks up into the stars. I turn my head just enough to see the reflection of the stars in her eyes. So much wonder, so much innocence behind those blue—

"Leo."

I open my eyes, Zara glances at the family picture in her hand then goes back to the binoculars.

"Leo, get over here."

I stand up too quickly, a feeling of lightheadedness washing over me.

"Here," she says, handing me the binoculars. "I don't know for sure, but in the window of the second floor of that building—the one with the sort of yellow stucco—"

I find the spot with my naked eyes then use the binoculars. Just outside of the playground is a small two-story corner market. There is a group of kids in gray and white uniforms on the second floor in what appears to be a classroom. There is a small redheaded boy closest to the window standing in front of a girl.

My heart thuds, my skin feels hot. I try to say something, but my mouth is bone dry. The world around me spins.

It's not *a* girl.

It's *my* girl.

She looks about five years old. She has two braided pigtails resting on her shoulders.

She has Nova's nose. She has my eyes. Those eyes that I've stared into a thousand times before now looking attentively to the front of the classroom. She's taller than I remember. And thinner.

My view gets clouded by the tears filling up the eyepiece of the binoculars. I put them down and jump into Zara's outstretched arms.

"It's really her," I say through sobs.

"We did it," Zara says.

"We did it."

I fall onto my knees, unable to support myself. I try putting the binoculars up to my eyes, but I'm shaking too hard. *She's okay.* I lay down face first in the dirt and let the tears flow. *My baby is okay.*

After a minute, I put the binoculars back up to my eyes. Xandra maintains focus on the front of the room, occasionally looking down at her desk or out the window. At one point she smiles. At another point, she giggles along with her classmates.

My joy quickly turns to envy—a pain that I can't be there with her, that all these other adults in Salem get to be there with Xandra. Envy then transitions to a deep, dark, unsettling guilt. *I did this to you. I got your mother killed and you taken away.* For a brief moment, I feel unworthy to even show my face in front of her. *Will she still love me? How can she?*

"Let me walk you to the road at least."

"No no, I'm fine. We've been through the route, and I have my map."

"The front gates are likely here," I say, pointing to the south end of town on Main street. "You need to sort of wander in, like you've been told to find Salem. And remember, you are there because you want to join—"

"Unicorn. Yes, Leo. I know."

"Why?"

"Because socialism is poison."

"Yes—hopefully that will do it."

"And I want to raise up the next generation of Unicorn for a free and prosperous Wild."

"Good."

"You don't need to worry about me, Leo. I'm as charming as they come."

I smile.

I pick Zara's pack up off the ground and place it on her back. "We dumped all the gear from Paoli, right?" I ask.

"I think so."

"And you'll dump the jacket right before you get to Main Street."

"Yep."

"Ok. You'll be there by sundown?"

"Shouldn't be a problem."

"And Rose—"

"I don't know Rose," Zara says.

"At least at first, until you have a good sense for the

situation."

She nods.

"I'll be looking for you," I say.

Zara purses her lips and nods; a tear falls down her cheek. I lean in and we squeeze each other.

"This isn't goodbye, Zara. We will get you guys back. I promise you."

"I know you will, Leo. I just—I need to thank you," she says, fanning her eyes. "I had given up. I had accepted defeat. I had no reason to keep going until I met you and Jame. You renewed that old fightin' spirit in me. Now look where we are." She glances down at her feet and back up to me.

"Thank you for sticking with me. I couldn't have done this without you. I mean it."

We both turn and look out over Salem.

"You tell Xandra her daddy loves her."

—

I scan the town, snacking on granola and sipping on cold instant coffee. I check my watch anxiously. Zara left for Salem about an hour ago, which means she should be arriving at the south gate any second, if she hasn't already.

Xandra left the classroom shortly after Zara departed, and I haven't seen her since. I briefly consider moving lookout spots, then realize that Zara wouldn't know where to find me if things go haywire. As afternoon turns to evening, town activity quiets down. I still see no sign of Zara. She knows where to go once she's inside, I remind myself, I just need to be patient.

I surveil the town until activity comes to a complete stop right around 10:00 PM, which is also about the time that total darkness takes over the summer sky. I return to my tent and stare at the family picture under my flashlight.

One step closer, Super Xan.

———

I wake up as morning twilight begins and drink another cold instant coffee. The smell of the morning dew makes me think of renewal. Someday, a hundred years from now, two hundred years from now, new growth will come from that burnt-down house in Empire. Someday, the wood holding Chrystal Peak Lodge together will rot, and the chemicals in the drywall, the glass of the floor-to-ceiling windows, the canvas paintings will dissolve into the soil. Along with Nova's bones. And out of that, new life will be born.

I resume my post in the clearing and look over the town. The morning starts the same as yesterday, with women slowly wandering onto the scene, popping in and out of shops, riding bikes, holding hands of children.

An hour later, groups of kids in school uniforms enter the scene, skipping, bouncing balls.

Still no sign of Zara. No sightings of Rose or Xandra.

I spread peanut butter on bread I swiped from the hospital for a late breakfast.

Zara has a fighting spirit, that's what's kept her alive so far.

As the sun positions itself directly overhead, my optimism fades. Zara is too old, too weak. I shouldn't have sent her by herself. I should've at least walked her to the road. Did she really know the route? What if she was picked off by someone? What if she told someone she was with the X? What if—

Let. Go.

I walk back to the lookout spot and bring the binoculars to

my eyes. I chew the dry bread and peanut butter, realizing how desperately thirsty I am. A group of young girls comes into view crossing the grass field and I adjust the focus of my lenses to get a better view. Rose comes into view, a bright smile stretched across her face. She is skipping eagerly with the red dodgeball under her left arm, holding the hand of an old, jovial black woman in a gray uniform.

Zara is officially a Blue.

Rose brings Zara over to the corner of the playground and they face each other. Rose's arms flail in all directions as she appears to tell Zara all about the last few months. Zara looks overjoyed, her wrinkles framing her eyes more pronounced than I've ever seen. After a couple minutes, Rose jumps into Zara's arms and Zara squeezes tight. Then Zara sets Rose back in front of her trying to contain her excitement.

My cheeks hurt from smiling.

Another minute passes and a different group of young girls enters the square. From the back, they all look the same, but when they organize themselves to play, I recognize one of them as Xandra. My heart races again.

She *is* taller than I remember. She's not a baby anymore. That's for sure. She's a full-on kid now.

I pan back to Rose and Zara on the other side of the playground. Zara notices Xandra, points to her, and whispers in Rose's ear. Rose nods and Zara stands up. Rose leads Zara to the playground and calls for Xandra.

Xandra signals to her friends that the game is paused and takes the biggest slide to the ground. She's brave—something she's had to develop in the Blue camp, no doubt.

Xandra runs over to Rose and Zara. *She runs like a big kid.* Zara gets down on one knee and extends her hand to Xandra, which she shakes enthusiastically. Zara says something to

Xandra and gets choked up. She covers her mouth with the back side of her hand and tears stream down her face. She finishes saying something to Xandra and Xandra looks at the ground.

Zara continues talking then pauses, looking over at Rose. Xandra looks up at Zara, studying her for a few seconds, then jumps into her arms. Zara's eyes are closed, holding Xandra tight, tears running down her cheeks.

While still gripping each other intensely, Zara looks in my direction and smiles.

THE LONELY WILD: JAME FOLKE'S STORY

ATLANTA—Earlier this year, Jame Folke got an itch; "I don't know what it was exactly. I guess I've always been a curious person."

Folke packed his belongings and drove across the border in Raton, NM, leaving behind family, friends, and a stable job as a police officer.

"It seemed like a fun idea at the time. I thought I'd be able to see the house I grew up in. I thought the deserted landmarks would be cool," he said.

What was intended to be an adventure quickly proved to be anything but.

"It's not that anything bad happened necessarily, it was just dull out there. Lonely, boring, empty. I didn't see a single soul the whole time. Getting anywhere was nearly impossible with the roadblocks and downed bridges. Not having access to cell phone or internet was nice at first, but honestly, after a while, I couldn't take it. What if I broke my leg? What if I needed medicine? What if a family member died at home?"

Folke, who has a history of mental illness, said that his lonely trip into the Wild brought his depression out "stronger than ever," taking him to the brink of suicide on at least one occasion.

"Overall, the whole experience taught me that we need to be in the presence of other humans. It's just how we're programmed."

Would Folke ever take a trip to the Wild again? "Absolutely not," he said⋯

ABOUT THE AUTHOR

Derek Walker's stories have been featured on the NoSleep Podcast, Otis Jiry's Scary Stories to Tell in the Dark and Creepypasta. This is his first novel. He lives in Salt Lake City with his wife and two daughters. Follow his work at phantomfevers.com